Red Rock Canyon

Willow Gate Justice

A Tyrell Sloan western adventure

Written by Brian T. Seifrit

Email: **briantseifrit@gmail.com**

Web site: www.booksbybriant.ca

Cover art by: Getty Creations, Burnaby, British Columbia

Published by

Edition 1

ISBN: 978-1-9992595-0-1 Paperback
ISBN: 978-1-990215-12-4 Hardcover
ISBN: 978-1-9992595-1-8 eBook

Willow Gate Justice
A Tyrell Sloan western adventure

Chapter 1

Days came and days went. For three weeks, Matt Crawford travelled great distances to find work, and Tyrell under the name of Travis Sweet shadowed Gabe Roy. He had learned a few things about Gabe and had gathered more evidence into Gabe's shoddy business deals. Things were coming together concerning that investigation. As for the investigation into Heath's death, there was nothing more known about that than what Gabe already assumed, or so that is how Tyrell was playing it for now.

The ranches and farms that Matt applied to, for work, showed little interest in hiring anyone who hadn't worked cattle before or farmed. It became clear to him as the weeks came and went, that he only had one option left, and that was to return to law enforcement. He headed back to the Fort and on November 17, 1891, through early winter snowstorms and sleet, the Fort finally came into view. He slowed his horse to a stop, as he pulled the collar of his felt jacket up, and around his neck. A cold November wind seemed to have picked up. He looked around. The streets were silent and the Fort was like a ghost town.

He made his way down the street to McCoy's office. Tethering his horse, he walked inside. Brady, Ed, and Riley greeted him.

"I'll be damned. Hello Matt!"

Matt nodded. "Hello, Ed, Brady, Riley," he said as he approached the front counter.

"Wasn't expecting to see you, how have you been?"

"Pretty good Ed, I'm alive at least. The Fort seems quiet, not many folks are out and about."

"It's that time of year when folks are staying home near their fires. It has been damn cold around here," Brady mentioned as he leaned up on the counter.

"It has been cold I can attest to that, I've travelled through most of it. I went east then north, stopped off at every ranch or farm I came across. Folks in this area I have learned would rather not hire less experienced hands. I decided to see if perhaps you folks are looking for help. I can work the stable, keep your horses fed, and stable clean." Matt looked at Ed who had a big grin on his face.

"Nope, don't need anyone to work the stables, but we could use a fellow with your credentials to work investigations. Are you interested in something like that?"

Matt tilted his head and nodded, "I certainly would be interested."

"We're all pleased about that," Brady said as he smiled.

"Damn right," Riley added, "You missed, Ed by an hour the day you left. Shit, he had everything ready for you to sign."

Surprised by that, for a brief moment Matt felt like an ass for not sticking around and at least saying 'Bye' to Ed and Riley, all those weeks ago when he left.

"It is true. I was going to offer you a position on that day. I've kept the documentation, hoping one day you would return, and by God here you are."

"I have had a lot of time to think about it, I know Brady was trying to convince me to stick around, to work law again. Only thing was, back then, all I wanted was some space to clear my head. Since then I have concluded law is what I'm accustomed to. I don't know what all the legalities are to work under McCoy's, but whatever they are I will abide."

"There no legalities that stops you from working for McCoy's. Lieutenant Cannon and the Police Commissioner, both assured me that you would be free to work for us if you were inclined," Ed pointed out and made clear.

"I thank you for that. I'm ready and willing to start anytime."

"We'll have to swing by the Mounted Police station. Bash will get you to read an oath and you will be finger printed, then we can go over our contract. First things first, though. Let's all go have a sit down and a coffee."

Ed gestured to Matt, Brady, and Riley.

Making their way into the backroom kitchen, Ed poured coffees as the men sat down. He handed the coffee out then sat down himself. To have a man such as Matt Crawford, an ex-US Ranger working for McCoy's was a big deal. There was no doubt about that. The vast training he had received as a United States Ranger from survival to shooting ability would only improve McCoy's Private Investigations and Security. There was no downside having Matt on McCoy's payroll.

"I am glad to have you with us Matt," Ed said, as he looked him in the eye.

Brady nodded his approval, "You ain't the only one, old man, I'm happy too," he said as he took a swallow of coffee.

Riley nodded in agreement, "I feel the same way as they. You are a welcome addition to this crew, Matt."

Matt listened to what each had to say, and he thanked them for the kind words.

"My turn to speak now I guess, I am honoured to work with, and be among men like you. Thank you for the opportunity to redeem myself."

There were a few short minutes of awkward silence as the men reminisced what each had said. Brady finally broke the silence.

"C'mon old man, let's get Matt signed up, and get him on the payroll."

Brady stood up and shook Matt's hand.

"Welcome aboard. I look forward to working with you," he said as he made his way back to his desk, and to a stack of paperwork, he had been working on. Riley, too, shook his hand and welcomed him, then went about doing whatever it was he had been doing before Matt showed up.

Ed and Matt headed over to the Mounted Police station, where Matt read back the oath that Constable Rick Bash read to him. After signing, the documents and giving up his thumb and trigger fingerprints he became a full-fledged Private Investigator under Canadian law. Bash gave him the documents and badge that came with the induction. From there, it was back to the McCoy's office and the signing of a few more documents. As of that day, November 17, 1891, he began working for McCoy's Private Investigations and Security.

Ed gave him a key to the backdoor of McCoy's office, and to start him off, offered him the backroom cot and kitchen to use for as long as he needed, or until Tanner McBride returned, whichever came first. The upstairs apartment was, and would always remain assigned to Travis. Ed could tell by the gravel in Matt's voice, that, he was grateful, for what Ed had offered.

"I don't know how to thank you, Ed. I will tell you this though, I will never let McCoy's down. I will do my job as well as I possibly can. Thank you."

Ed waved his hand through the air, "No worries, I know you'll do your job. We should be thanking you for signing up with us. You're a blessed addition, if you ask me."

The two men grew silent for a moment and then Ed smiled.

"The first case I want to throw at you isn't anything special, but it is needed to get done and I think you are quite suited for it."

"Whatever it is, throw it at me."

"That, five hundred dollars in gold nuggets, that Brady got from that Vanfell fellow, when you two were making your way back here. Needs to be delivered by hand to Whisky Tooth George, and he's a helluva codger to catch up to."

Matt chuckled, "I know old Whisky Tooth, and I know where to find him too at this time of year."

Ed was surprised, "How do you know old George? And how come you never mentioned that to Brady?"

"I didn't have a reason to mention it then, anyway, I ran across Whisky Tooth a few times. I have even drunk some of that putrid whisky that he brews in that still of his. I am quite familiar with Whisky Tooth," Matt assured.

"Ain't that something? Well, there you go. You know where to find him and already know he's a cagey son-of-a-bitch," Ed chuckled, "You are the perfect one to see he gets that gold then," he smiled.

"I'll pack up and head out right now," Matt began to stand up.

"Hold on, no need for you to do that yet. Rest up some and get familiar with the way we do things first. Maybe head out at the beginning of next week. You've been on the trail for more than a month already, I can't justify sending you off today."

Matt nodded in agreement, "I am a bit weary from all the miles I've put on. I could probably use a cleanup too. You know Whisky Tooth has a five hundred dollar bounty on his head. Should I bring him in too?" Matt questioned.

Ed shook his head.

"Nope, no need for that. We only want to see that he gets the nuggets."

"All right, that is how it'll be then," Matt confirmed.

The rest of the day went quickly after that. As the tradition had always been with McCoy's, Ed bought everyone a steak at the Snakebite as a way to welcome

Matt into the ranks. They stayed away from the whisky this time, though.

Chapter 2

Monday came quickly and Matt loaded up his gear, signed off on a few dollars cash, saddled his horse, and got ready to head into uncharted territory. He knew where to look for old Whisky Tooth, but chose not to use any of the main trails or wagon roads. He could find Whisky Tooth a lot sooner he knew if he went cross-country and so that is what he decided to do. He told Ed, as he was about to leave, that he'd send a wire back to McCoy's once he got into the Athabasca territory, in about ten days he had guessed.

Ed looked at him, "Ten days?" he asked confusedly. "Does your horse have wings, or what? You can't make it into the Athabasca in ten days, Matt."

"I ain't going to be using the common trails. Nope. I know another way and it is a lot quicker, I'm going cross-country, directly northwest over the Rocky Mountains, through the Indian territories," Matt looked in the direction and inhaled deeply. "The snow might be up high, but I'll be staying down low."

"Not sure that is the best idea. Would hate like hell if something went wrong. Why not stick to the main routes?" Ed asked with concern.

"I have my reasons. One is the fact that although I may be on McCoy's payroll and be an officer of law in a sense, I know that, my name ain't been cleared yet. That'll take time. There are those still looking for Matt Crawford and until such time that those looking for me have stopped looking, I feel safer staying away from public eye as much as possible. Not to worry, I know where I'm going," Matt made clear.

"All right then, I ain't going to try and convince you otherwise." Ed leaned on the horse rail and looked northwesterly himself.

"The Athabasca can be brutal they don't always like white men passing through their territory. Are you aware of that?"

"As sure as I know that the sun rises in the east and settles in the west. Besides the Athabasca and I have a kinship of sorts. They know me and I know them," Matt cracked a smile as he turned his horse. "Expect a wire from me in the days to come," he said as he heeled his horse and headed north.

Ed watched as Matt disappeared into the fog and dawn's early light.

"I sure hope you ain't going to get blindsided, Mr. Crawford," he said quietly to himself as he made his way inside. It was cooler than he liked and he added wood to the backroom stove, sat down, and poured a coffee. He looked at the clock on the wall. It was near 7:00 a.m. He had another hour to wait before Riley and Brady showed up.

With coffee in hand, he stood up and headed to his own office where he thumbed through paperwork and whatnot. His mind was racing with all the events that had led up to Matt Crawford's apprehension and his release from all and any wrongdoing in Canada. He was grateful that Matt was now working for him. He had made up his mind during the past week that come January he was going to retire. He had yet to tell his wife, Beth, or anyone for that matter. He had decided to keep it to himself, until the right time to announce it.

He was unsure how Riley or the others would take the news. As for Brady, he knew that he would likely tell him that it was about time, and Beth, well, she'd simply be ecstatic. She had wanted him to retire for a while. The job, as far as she was concerned, was getting a bit too dangerous for him. In fact, if she could have it her way, their son Brady would also give up the job. That, though, would never happen, not until Brady himself grew old like Ed.

The front bell that hung over the door rang as someone stepped into the foyer. Ed stood up and made his way to the front counter to meet and greet whoever it was, that had entered. To his surprise, it was a United States Ranger.

"You Ed McCoy?" the ranger asked as he stepped forward.

"What brings a Ranger up here into Canada?" Ed asked a bit uneasy.

"I'm looking to talk with an Ed McCoy?"

"I am he. Now who are you?" Ed was frowning.

"I'm Lee Griffith a United States Ranger. I understand that Matt Crawford ex- US Ranger was apprehended by McCoy's, am I right in that understanding?" the Ranger asked as he leaned up on the counter.

"What does it matter to you?"

"Come on Mr. McCoy, you know as well as I that he's a wanted felon in the US. I'm here to gather him and bring him back to face the justice that awaits him," Ranger Lee Griffith said with arrogance.

"The Matt Crawford that you're asking about works for us now, and is a law-abiding officer of Canadian justice."

"You are saying he works for you?" Ranger Griffith questioned with apprehension.

"That is what I said."

"I only want to be clear in the understanding."

"He does work for us, has been for a while," Ed responded, there was nothing more he needed to say.

"What time are you expecting him today then, Mr. McCoy?"

"I ain't expecting him today. He's on assignment."

Lee Griffith looked sternly at Ed. "Assignment?" he questioned with a southern drawl.

"That is what I said and as you know the law doesn't require me to say where."

"I know. Prolonging his detainment though, doesn't make him any less of a felon."

"That ain't my concern now, is it? He, like I said, is a law-abiding officer of the Canadian Justice system," Ed pointed out. "He has committed no legally binding crimes here in Canada. Now, if you would excuse me, Lee, I have work to do. You can see your own way out," Ed invited as he gestured toward the front door.

US Ranger Lee Griffith smiled and tilted his hat.

"If you change your mind, Mr. McCoy, I'll be around."

With that, the Ranger turned heel and exited into the early morning sun. His first order of business was to start poking around and asking questions about the McCoy's and Matt Crawford. Most folk, though, said nothing about Ed McCoy or Matt Crawford. They knew that the man asking the questions was a US Ranger and so they buttoned up their lips. It was obvious that tracking down Matt was going to be a headache at best.

He had been Matt's superior back in the day when Matt walked the line. He knew the training Matt had received and that he was one of the most adept US Rangers to wear the badge. He certainly did not embrace the fact that he had to take Matt in, but that was his job. He held no jurisdiction in Canada, but he could arrest Matt and begin the extradition process, which would not be any easier than tracking him down. Ranger Griffith sighed as he thought about that and made his way to the telegraph office.

Sending a wire to the Head of Public Safety, he wrote- *In Canada. McCoy's claim Matt working for them. On assignment. It is unknown by me where. More details to follow.* Paying the fee, he thanked the telegrapher and exited into the street. Making his way back to his hotel room, he slumped onto the bed and stretched out. It had been a long few days since he had fully rested and he took the time now to do exactly that.

By now Ed McCoy, Riley Scott, and Brady were conversing about the Ranger in town looking for Matt.

"Even if this Ranger fellow, arrests him, he'd still have to be detained in Canada until the extradition papers are in order and that, we know, could take months," Riley pointed out.

"True as that might be, it is still a hurdle I wasn't expecting so soon."

"Does he know where Matt is heading?" Brady asked.

"Hell no, I know my rights better than to spew that information. There are no laws that say I have to say where he is. I did admit though, that he works for us and I made sure he was clear that Matt is a law-abiding officer of the Canadian Justice system. That is the only information I'll ever share with him." Ed took a sip from the coffee in his hand, "Once I get a wire from him in the next couple of weeks, I'll reply and let him know that US Ranger Lee Griffith is looking for him. Maybe send him further north. Maybe he could sit on the side lines up in Hazelton with Tanner." Ed sighed, "I don't know, but I'll be damned if I'm going to make his apprehension easier for that Ranger."

"You know what, old man maybe we're looking at this at the wrong angle. Matt needs to stay clear of the US and any Rangers snooping around. Could we not send him into the Yukon, Buck Ainsworth's territory, he stays clear of the Rangers for two years he's as Canadian as any of us sitting in this room."

"Shit, that might be one of the best ideas you've had in a long time. We could send a wire to Buck. See if he could put Matt to work up there. He could do hotel security for Buck's family hotel up that way. His family does own a hotel, don't they?" Ed asked. It had been some time since Buck sat with him and he was unsure.

Riley nodded his head, "Damn right they do. I remember him clearly pointing it out. His brother runs it, from what I recall. I remember Buck himself saying that he was going to take his rightful place in the business. That is our answer it keeps Matt busy and the Rangers wondering where he is. As long as he is on assignment, McCoy's are not required to reveal that information to anyone including a lawman from the States."

"I'll send Buck a wire, right now," Brady said as he stood up. "Not much point in putting off something we can get a handle on right now."

"You go ahead and do that. Keep clear of that Ranger. Don't let him know a damn thing about anything."

"Come on, old man, I know better than that. I ain't in grade school anymore," he sighed. "I know what I'm doing, and you need to snap out of it," Brady said with confidence, as he looked at Ed. "I know this business old man." Brady slid his chair in and shook his head as he exited into the street.

"He's right, Ed," Riley began when the front door closed. "Brady ain't a kid anymore. You got to start letting the slack off the leash."

Ed lowered his head and nodded. "Yeah, I suppose you are right, to me though he's just a kid. You know what I mean?"

"Of course I do, but he ain't wearing nappies anymore. He is a man and a damn fine one too. Like I have always told you, he has a lot of you in him."

Ed raised his head and looked at Riley. "I suppose you are right. I guess I have been holding him back some, ain't I been?"

"A lil' bit I'd say, but, that is okay. He's grown up now and it is time to let the fledgling soar," Riley finished his last swallow of coffee, "with that aside, what are our plans for today?"

"Paperwork, I guess, and we hope like hell that some work comes our way soon."

"What if I don't have any paperwork?" Riley asked. "I'm getting bored sitting around."

"It is the nature of this business, ain't it? If we ain't chasing after bad guys, then we sit and wait for some action to come our way," Ed said as he too now finished his coffee.

"Late fall and winter in this business does seem to always taper off, don't it?" Riley pointed out.

Ed agreed as he stood up and put his coffee cup in the sink. It was around this time that Brady returned from the telegraph office.

"That is taken care of. Got a wire off to Buck, now we wait for his reply." He sat down and tossed his hat onto the table.

He looked at Riley and Ed who were leaning on the counter.

"You old folk look like you came from a funeral. What is a matter?"

"Boredom," Riley replied.

"Boredom, shit, there ain't nothing at all boring about sitting behind a desk and thumbing through paperwork." Brady said with sarcasm, he too was bored.

Chapter 3

Tyrell Sloan, under his alias Travis Sweet was sitting at a table with Gabe Roy as he had done many times. They were eating eggs and bacon, discussing business.

"I have a meeting with an old business associate of mine come tomorrow, owes me a lot of money. I don't want him leaving here without paying up."

Gabe took a bite from the eggs on his plate.

"What are you saying?" Tyrell asked as he sipped his coffee.

"You've been working for me for how long? A month or longer, I think you know what I mean."

"Honestly, I don't."

Tyrell leaned back in his chair. He knew exactly what Gabe was asking him and that was to commit murder. In the time that he worked for Gabe, he had been able to come up with a plethora of information that would, if proven in a court of law, see Gabe hang or spend the rest of his life in prison. Tyrell knew he needed to play his cards right.

"You are an enforcer, Travis. I want you to enforce payment. I want all the money my old associate owes me and I want it all by tomorrow evening."

"If he ain't got the money, how do you expect him to pay?"

"Beat it out of him or bury him in the woods. I don't care how you get him to pay."

Tyrell looked into Gabe's eyes.

"I ain't going to do anything of the sort. No sir."

"You like the money I have been paying you, don't you?"

"This has nothing to do with money, and I'll have you know I get only a percentage of the coins you throw at McCoy's for the service you have hired us to do. You're asking me to do something that isn't within the laws that I uphold. I can't help you there, and you know that."

"What if this said fellow was to pull a pistol on me? Would you not do the job I hired McCoy's to do, which is to protect me and my assets," Gabe questioned snidely.

Tyrell inhaled deeply, "If an unprovoked man pulls a pistol on you, Gabe, you know damn well I'd do my job. It don't mean I'd kill him," Tyrell made clear.

He was beginning to see the picture that Gabe was painting for him. In all actuality in such a case, it would be legal for him to act accordingly. There were better options however than simply killing a man.

"What makes you think this fellow would pull a pistol on you?"

"I ain't sure he would or wouldn't, but if he did would you be there to stop him?"

"It is what you hired McCoy's to do, isn't it? To protect you and your assets, like you mentioned earlier," Tyrell responded as if it were a questioned that Gabe needed to ask.

Gabe wiped his mouth with a napkin and tossed it onto his empty plate.

"That is all I wanted to hear. Come on Travis," Gabe began as he stood up and slid his chair in. "I want you to meet somebody."

Tyrell donned his hat that was hanging on the back of his chair and stood up to follow Gabe.

"Who is this you want me to meet?" he questioned as he and Gabe exited the big house and made their way over to the horse stable.

"He goes by the name of Pete Cross," Gabe began as he gestured for the stable hand to bring them their horses.

A northern wind came and went in gusts and a few snowflakes fluttered to the ground, as the two men saddled up their horses.

"It is a bit of a ride but it is a nice jaunt," Gabe continued, "he owns a piece of land north of here, at one time ran cattle on it. I have been looking to buy that land for quite some time. It came to my attention recently that he might be up for selling it. I want to be the first to make an offer," added Gabe, as the two of them finished saddling up their horses, "We'll be joined by four other men down the road some, so don't be startled when they pull up beside us."

"What's with the four other men? Why do we need four more men to go and make an offer on land?" Tyrell asked with curiosity as he whistled for Black Dog and they headed north along the road.

He had a clear idea. They were likely a crew of Gabe's henchmen. The ones that helped Gabe bully homesteaders. This would be the first time since he started working for Gabe, that he might witness the bullies at work. He would make damn sure to document anything he found to be unjust, cruel or otherwise.

After all, that was the real reason he was working for Gabe in the first place to bring Gabe Roy to justice for the crimes he committed. From illegal land deals, hired kills and so on, right up to and including the accusations made by Crying Wolf, of the atrocities Gabe and his men had put the Athabasca people through, which included rape and murder. Tyrell's job was to gather all these facts, while at the same time working for him. Gabe he knew grew his fortune by cheating hard working, God fearing, men and women who he had lied to, cheated, and in some cases killed.

"One is a lawyer, one is a banker, and two are land surveyors. They're business partners Travis that is all they are." Gabe tried to convince, but Tyrell was not stupid. Still, he would leave it at that as to not miss a chance at meeting the four men.

"You are hoping on buying that land today, then?"

"If old man Cross decides to sell it to me today, I'll be ready to buy it."

"Yeah, I suppose so. With a banker, a lawyer and land surveyors meeting up with us, I guess you would be ready to buy. I must admit though I never heard of business being done like that. I guess it is better to be ready to buy than to be sorry you weren't."

"If you have the means, why would any man want to wait?" Gabe threw at him.

"I can't argue that point," Tyrell responded as they carried on in silence for a few minutes.

Finally, four riders came into view and pulled their horses to a halt as they waited for Gabe to approach. Gabe slowed his horse down and gestured to Tyrell.

"There they are now."

"I see them," Tyrell said as they approached the riders.

Two were dressed in suits, two wore work clothes and their horses, were geared up with surveying equipment. Perhaps it was as Gabe had said.

"Morning, Gabe," the first man spoke.

"Morning, men," Gabe began as he turned toward Tyrell and gestured. "This here is Travis he's the man I was telling you about. He works for McCoy's out of the Fort. Travis, this here is Archie Hauser, a banker from Coastline Bank and Trust, down west."

Tyrell tilted his hat in acknowledgement.

"And that there," Gabe began as he pointed at the second man in a suit. "That is my personal lawyer, Ted Applegate from Applegate and Associates, also from down west. These other two men are from near here. That is Neil and Rodger Kormac. They're surveyors."

"Nice to meet you all," Tyrell said as he looked at each of them and nodded.

"Now that we're all cozy with one another, Cross's homestead is up yonder a couple of miles," Gabe said as the riders turned their horses and continued.

Not long afterward, the homestead came into view. The land, it seemed, rolled on for quite the distance.

"How much land does Pete Cross own?" Tyrell asked as they rode onward to the farmhouse.

"He owns a full section of six hundred and sixty acres. All prime land, too. I hope to pick it up for less than a dollar an acre." Gabe replied as he lowered himself from the saddle and tied his horse to the horse pole outside.

"That is likely less than he paid for it. You sure he'll settle for that?"

"Only Cross knows the answer to that, but I can be pretty persuasive."

Gabe walked up to the front door and knocked. Getting no response, he knocked again. This time the door opened a crack and a man looked out and as quickly closed the door.

"I told you before Mr. Roy my land ain't up for grabs. You're wasting your time coming here," the voice on the other side of the door said.

"You're not going to survive another winter out here. You know that, Mr. Cross. I have cash on hand. I'm willing to pay you a fair price."

"What you figure to be a fair price, Mr. Roy, isn't enough, I assure you. I will survive the winter. Don't ever fool yourself."

"You're alone out here, Mr. Cross, other than that Indian squaw, Renatta. How is an old man like yourself and squaw going to get along when the snow flies and the cold makes your bones ache? You could be down south by then sitting in the sun, if you take my offer."

"Nope, I don't want your offer nor are Renatta and I alone out here."

"What do you mean the two of you ain't alone? You know it and I know it, the two of you is alone."

It was then they heard the cocking of three guns and saw the barrels sticking out the windows. Gabe stepped back and looked on.

"By you sticking those guns out the windows, Mr. Cross, doesn't convince me, that you aren't alone," Gabe responded as he tried to look through one of the windows.

"Any closer, Mr. Roy, and I'll clean blow your head off," an unfamiliar voice replied.

"And who the hell might you be?" Gabe questioned as he stepped out of view.

"It matters not who we is." Another voice came. "You've been asked to move along. Mr. Cross's land isn't for sale, now go on, get."

It was then Tyrell spoke up. "Come on, Gabe. We best do as they say."

"Yep, you best do that Travis." A familiar voice responded from the other window.

Tyrell looked inquisitively at the window, "Alex? Alex Brubaker?" he questioned with trepidation.

The door swung open and out stepped Alex, Cape, and Brett Brubaker.

"Hello Travis, it's been a while, I couldn't help noticing, but it looks to me, like you're sitting on Colby's horse. Now how did you manage that, since it was a band of Indians that stole him?" Alex asked as he pointed his pistol at Gabe Roy, while at the same time keeping his eyes on Tyrell.

At that moment, it all became clear to Tyrell. Obviously, Crying Wolf was that *band* of Indians. He felt like laughing aloud, but he held back.

"It is a long story on how I got this horse, Alex. I had no idea it was Colby's horse."

"A long story you say," Brett started, "I'd suggest that you swing off that red dun and remove the saddle. The law would say you are a horse thief and in these parts you could hang."

"I reckon you'd be wrong in that assumption. You must be one of the cousins?"

"He is indeed. That is Brett and this here is Cape." Alex said as he pointed at each of them.

"That is what I thought," Tyrell responded as he slowly slid off the red dun.

"How did you know they might be cousins?" Alex asked.

"I was informed in a wire sent from Ed that you, Colby and three of your cousin's was headed this way, in hopes of gathering Matt Crawford and the ten thousand dollar reward on his head," he was humored by the fact that Alex and the others assumed Matt Crawford was still running loose.

"That's right, and as soon as Colby and Martin make the distance here, we'll be looking for him again. For the time being though, we work for Mr. Cross. Protecting what is his from the likes of Mr. Roy."

No one knew that Colby and Martin were only a day's ride east but were snowbound. The snow had forced them to stop riding and seek shelter. They built a crude shelter, and were now huddling over a fire. The snow squalls were intense at times. Cold as they were, they were certainly glad they had geared up before leaving the Fort for the second time.

"I knew the snow was coming, but did expect it to be this damn cold," Martin said as he warmed his hands above the flickering flames of their fire.

"We might be stuck here for a while too, 'less the snow breaks off," Colby added as he too warmed his hands above the flames.

Looking west he squinted as the snowflakes battered his face and the cold wind made his eyes water. He wrapped the collar of his thick felt coat over his face and turned back to look into the flames of the fire. Martin sat on the other side, his bedroll like a cocoon draping over his back and shoulders. They sat in self thought shivering at times uncontrollably, as the wind and snow continued to swirl in whirlwinds of unpleasant coldness.

Back at Cross's place Alex looked at Gabe and gestured for him to get up on his horse.

"Go on, Mr. Roy, get up on that horse of yours and be gone or we'll bury you out back along with the other riders you got with you. You, on the other hand, Travis, stay put. I want an explanation from you on why you have Colby's horse, and if it satisfies me you might live another day. If it not, then maybe today might be the day Travis Sweet dies."

At that moment, Tyrell wanted nothing more than to pull his pistol and make short work of the Brubaker 3. For now though, he would abide and play it the way Alex wanted.

"The rest of you got to the count of three to turn your horses around or reap the consequences that we will lay upon you. Now go on, get," Alex fired a shot in the air, as Gabe and the other four riders turned their horses and headed back the way they came.

"All right they is gone, Brett, get over there and take his guns." Alex gestured for Tyrell to put his hands up. "So, how is it, Travis, that you are riding Colby's horse?" Alex asked as he kept his pistol pointed.

Tyrell explained in detail, but it only made the Brubaker 3 laugh in disbelief.

"What you're saying is that one bloody redskin took the five of us on alone, stole our horses and ran them off, but kept Colby's red dun. Then later on stole your horse which was Brady's and left you Colby's."

Tyrell was nodding his head as Alex said all that. He could understand how unbelievable it all seemed.

"That is what I'm saying."

"Jesus, I don't know if I should simply shoot you or buy you a whisky for telling such a tale."

"I'm telling you, Alex. That is exactly how I ended up with this red dun. You can go ahead and shoot me if that is what you want. I honestly don't think you will though, you know I wouldn't feed you a line of crap like that if it weren't true."

Alex could tell that Tyrell was sincere by the look in his eye. Letting the hammer back on his pistol, he holstered the weapon.

"All right, I'll give you the benefit of doubt this time. My next question is what in the hell are you doing in presence of Gabe Roy? He's worse than most of the folk you hunt down and put behind bars."

"It is business Alex. I am up here in Willow Gate on business. That is really all you need to know, isn't it?"

"Fair enough, you keep your business away from this land, Cross isn't selling, and that friend Gabe of yours, has been told that a time or three, by Mr. Cross himself. Keep him away from here. The next time you and he and whoever else you bring along to try and weasel Mr. Cross's land, are going to be in for one helluva gunfight."

Tyrell looked at Alex and then Brett and Cape. "I know all about Gabe Roy's shady land deals, and other illegal activities, that brought him his fortune, and arrogance, and from that I'll leave it up to you to decide, on what my business with Gabe is. Alex, you know how much I hate being threatened, I will however stay clear of whatever your business is here with Mr. Cross, and you stay clear of my business with Gabe Roy, or you and I are headed for destination hell. Now, would you be so kind, as to hand back my pistols, and I'll be on my way."

Alex gestured to Brett, "Go ahead, Brett, give him back his side arms. I think we have come to an understanding. I ain't allowing you to take that red dun back though. That is Colby's horse. You have a five-mile walk ahead of you. But, before you go, take off your boots."

"My boots," Tyrell repeated with disdain.

"Go on take them off and toss them here."

Tyrell shook his head as he complied, "I ain't sure what your purpose in all this is, but I can assure you, I'll want these back and I'll get them, too." Tyrell tossed his boots over to where Alex stood.

"I suggest you start off," Alex looked to the sky. "There is a storm coming. You might make it half way back before it hits. I figure you took a couple of my fingers some time ago, a fair trade I reckon, would be a couple of your toes. They say the onset of frostbite is more painful than a bullet to the gut. I'm sure the next time we speak, you'll tell me all about it."

Tyrell looked again at Alex and shook his head, then, simply turned and walked away. By the time he made the distance to the main road, his feet were icy cold. He was grateful for the thick woollen socks he wore. The wind blew as it did before, coming in gusts and bringing with it each time more snow, until finally the darkening clouds completely shrouded the mid afternoon sun. Tyrell's feet began to throb with each step he took as the temperature continued to drop. Three hours later he finally made the distance back to his shack on the outskirts of Willow Gate.

At home, he waited patiently for his thick socks to thaw, then slowly peeled them off and examined his feet. He was surprised that they showed no sign of frostbite, but damn did his feet hurt as they gradually thawed. It was hard to stand and he had to crawl when adding wood to his fire. The warmer the place got the more pain he felt, until finally all he could feel of his feet were pins and needles.

"That son-of-a-bitch Alex, really pulled one on me, eh Black Dog?" Inhaling deeply he shook his head. "I don't even have a second pair of boots. Damn."

To the east, still huddled around their fire sat Colby and Martin. Neither one was saying much. The cold wind that blew made any words they did say to one another hard to hear. Instead, they sat in silence, waiting for the blizzard to pass. It was some time later when finally there was a break in the snowstorm. Colby added a few more sticks to the flames and poured another hot coffee for himself and Martin.

"How close do you figure we is to Willow Gate?" Martin asked as he looked into his cup of black coffee.

Colby shook his head, "I ain't sure. We've been riding steady for a few days already, got lost a couple different times and if the damn storm hadn't blown in, we'd be a day closer."

Colby brought the coffee up to his lips and took a swallow. He looked westerly again to the mountains that lie ahead. "What lies over the horizon might be Willow Gate, for all I know. I ain't ever been there so I can't even guess how much further. Being slowed down today means we is a day late already."

"Yeah, a day late," Martin looked into the flames of the fire. "What do you suppose my brothers and Alex have been up to? Think they've made Willow Gate by now?"

"I can only make an assumption, but I'd assume that they made it before the weather turned rough. What they might be doing while in Willow Gate is beyond me. Likely sitting back and wondering, where the hell we are, and why, we ain't there already."

Colby half chuckled. "We'll get there, Martin, you don't need to worry about that none. Once we get down lower, the weather likely ain't going to be as it is up here. We get through the night and by noon tomorrow I reckon we'll be doing okay."

"Getting through the night is another story though, ain't it? We could end up froze." Martin shivered as he wrapped his bedroll tighter around his shoulders.

"Nah, we ain't going to end up froze. We got a fire blazing and the storm I think has passed. We'll get through." Colby said with hope.

He really wasn't sure, but he wasn't about to give up now, nor was he going to let Martin. Sitting once more in silence and as near to the fire as possible, the two cousins spoke sporadically as the dark cold evening slowly approached. Adding bigger pieces of wood to their fire, they made themselves comfortable and closed their eyes. Tomorrow would be another day. Tomorrow they would be that much closer to Willow Gate.

Chapter 4

Tyrell woke the following morning to a pounding on his door. He slowly stood up and answered.

"Who is it?" he questioned as he made the distance.

"It's me Gabe. Open up Travis."

"Yeah, yeah," Tyrell responded as he opened the door. "Morning, Gabe," he said as he gestured for him to come in. "What do I owe this visit to?" he asked as he and Gabe sat down.

"I wanted to make sure those folks at Cross's place didn't fill you with lead. Who was that bunch anyway, it seemed you knew them," Gabe wanted an answer.

"I do in a round-about-way. That was Alex Brubaker and his cousins. There ain't much I know about them to be honest. I had a run in with Alex, who is Earl's younger brother, by the way. He drew a pistol on me trying to avenge Earl's death. I took off a couple of his fingers. It didn't take long though for the bastard to learn to shoot with his left. That is about all I know of him. I have never once met his cousins, except for Colby Christian, another Brubaker who was running with the Rebel Rangers some months ago. You ever hear of the Rebel Rangers?" Tyrell asked as he stood up and added a piece of wood to the stove and set his coffee pot up to brew.

"The Rebel Rangers," Gabe repeated, "yeah, I've heard of them. That fellow Matt Crawford was once one of them."

"That is true. He ain't run with them though for a while, years even." Tyrell sat back down, "I have a question for you. Any chance you can pick me up a pair of boots? Alex took mine, and the horse I was riding, the prick even made me walk home. I'll need another horse too."

"Jesus Christ, you walked from Cross's place in that storm we had yesterday with no boots on?"

"I had no choice, really, but yep, I walked."

"You're lucky you didn't end up with frostbite. I'll pick you up a set. What are your sizes?"

"Size eleven, wide," Tyrell answered.

"All right, I'll get them to you. I guess you won't be going anywhere, until you have boots, and a horse. I have plenty of those. I'll get one to you. I was going to get you to tag along with me today. I have some more business to look into. One of my men has told me that there has been an Athabasca brave snooping around Willow Gate and asking questions about me. He told me this Athabasca fella has been camping out northwest of here some. Don't know what any Athabasca might be doing in these parts or, for that matter, trying to find me." Gabe lied. He knew exactly why and so did Tyrell.

"An Athabasca brave, you say?" Tyrell wanted to be clear.

"That is what one of my men has told me. I figured you and I might make an appearance where he is held up. I got questions for him."

"I don't know, Gabe. An Athabasca brave ain't likely going to be alone."

Tyrell knew already who the brave was. It was undoubtedly Crying Wolf.

"You might be wiser to stay away from him for now. Let me do some looking into, before you go off half-cocked." Tyrell stood up and offered Gabe a coffee.

"What do you mean stay away from him? To hell with that, I don't fear no single Athabasca brave," Gabe pointed out as he accepted the coffee.

"Like I said, he likely ain't alone. You might be making a mistake in going to look for him. Let me look into it. If he is looking for you, there has to be a reason. Have you done anything to the Athabasca?"

"What the hell kind of question is that? No, I haven't done a damn thing to those bloody redskins." Gabe once more lied.

Tyrell took a swig from his coffee. "What I know about the Athabasca is that they don't go looking for white men, without reason. You must've done something, even if you don't know what it is or was."

Gabe took a swallow from his own coffee as he contemplated. "Nope, I can't think of a damn thing I have done."

"Until I can clarify that Gabe, you best keep your eyes peeled. One Athabasca is as dangerous as a pack of wolves."

"What are you saying?" Gabe questioned with a frown as he looked at Tyrell.

"Once I have boots and a horse, I'll go on alone and find out what I can. I would think you'd be a lot more concerned than what you are."

"I ain't concerned 'cause I ain't afraid of no bloody redskin. I've put a few into the ground. One more ain't going to make a difference," Gabe let out.

"Maybe you have done something after all to the Athabasca, you just don't know it. If you killed one of his own, you might want to re-evaluate what it is you might be up against."

Gabe inhaled deeply, "I have ten men counting you that got my back. Why would I fear a single Athabasca?"

Tyrell took a slurp from his coffee. "One Athabasca can easily take out ten men and we wouldn't even know what hit us. I say you bring me a horse and pair of boots and I'll do what I can to find out what it is this brave might want from you."

Gabe shook his head. "All right Travis, we'll do it your way." Finishing his coffee, he stood up. "I'll get those boots and a fresh horse sent to you. Give me about an hour."

Tyrell nodded and walked Gabe to the door. "You said your man told you this brave is west of here?"

"That is what he told me. Near Gold Creek, he said."

"Gold Creek and where is that?" Tyrell needed to know.

"It's about three miles northwesterly. You can't miss it there is a sign and all that says *'Gold Creek'.*"

"Easy enough, I suppose. Once I get the horse and boots, I'll head that way. Until then, though, keep your head down."

Gabe waved his hand through the air. "Ah, I ain't so worried about it that I need to keep my head down. I will wait until I hear back from you, before I decide on what next to do." Gabe swung up onto his horse, "I'll have boots and a horse sent to you within the hour, Travis."

"Good enough. I'll stop by your place sometime today and let you know what I find out."

Gabe turned his horse and headed back to Willow Gate. Tyrell closed the door and sat down to his second coffee of the day as he waited for his new boots and a fresh horse.

Chapter 5

Colby and Martin by now had made their way off the mountain and were now only a few miles east of Willow Gate. The winter storm from the night before dumped enough snow on the trail making it hard to discern, but they trudged on as best they could.

"See Martin, I told you we were going be okay. The trail is a bit snow covered, but I know that we are on it. Folks have passed by since yesterday. I reckon Willow Gate ain't much further. We can smile now. It ain't even as cold as it were up top."

"I ain't sure I'm well. My lungs ache with every step this horse takes. We're going to have to stop soon and light a fire. I need to warm up."

Martin began to cough uncontrollably. He could hear his own lungs rattle and it hurt like hell. He spit to the ground a gob of green goo and blood, and then fell from his horse. Colby stopped and swung off his own horse and helped Martin up.

"Jesus, you're burning up." There was concern in his voice. The last thing they needed was one of them becoming sick. Martin, though, was certainly that.

"It don't feel like I'm burning up, feels like my lungs is freezing," Martin wheezed as he tried to catch his breath.

"Here, c'mon sit down here," Colby helped him over to a snow-covered log. He kicked the snow off and got Martin to sit. "I'll get us a fire going," he handed Martin a woolen blanket. "Wrap yourself up."

It took a few minutes to get a small fire going and during this time all Martin did was cough, wheeze, and spit up phlegm. "There is blood in that shit I'm spitting up. I think I'm frigging dying," Martin grabbed his chest as he coughed again. "Goddamn it, I can't..." he began before he fell over.

Colby ran to his side and pulled him out of the snow. He propped him up against a tree making sure he was still breathing, and thanking God that he was. He put his hand on Martin's forehead. He was burning up and beads of sweat trickled down his face.

"Shit, you have one hell of a high fever, Martin."

Martin didn't hear him he had passed out by then.

"Jesus Christ," Colby said as he hastily made hot coffee. He needed to get some warm liquids into Martin and he had to do it quickly. Once the pot was set on the fire, he wrapped Martin up with the woollen blanket and one of his own bedrolls. He'd go without if they had to stay put for another evening, keeping Martin warm and breathing was more important than worrying about a chilly evening under the stars. It wasn't noon yet and maybe in a couple of hours they could once more continue onward. If not, then he'd keep the fire going and the flames as high as possible to chase away any cold the evening might bring. For now, his only concern was Martin.

By 11:00 a.m., the sun was warm. Even the snow-covered trees and branches began to drip as the snow melted under the rays of its yellow glow. Martin was finally awake and was somewhat coherent. He spoke in mumbles and slurs, but he was talking and this alone helped put Colby's mind at ease, even if half the time he didn't understand a word he spoke. An hour later, they were again on their way although at a slower pace. Nonetheless, they were making ground and inching their way closer to Willow Gate.

It was around this time that Gabe had Tyrell's boots and horse delivered. Tyrell thanked the kid that brought them to him and he tossed him a quarter.

"Thank you, Mister," the kid said with half a smile. A quarter really wasn't that much to make a fuss over and so he didn't.

"And I thank you for bringing these to me."

Tyrell nodded his appreciation as the kid turned his own horse and headed back the way he had come. Tyrell looked at the boots in his hand and slipped them on. Surprisingly they fit well, a little too clean and proper but in time they would wear in, and in time, he would get his old boots back too. He gathered his saddle, strapped it onto the horse and with Black Dog at his side he headed northwest. It didn't take long even in the snow to find Gold Creek. He slowed his horse down and looked around.

There were no telltale signs that anyone was near. Any evidence of a horse and rider was lost due to the snowfall the night before, but in the distance, a mile, or so off the trail, he spotted smoke rising. He turned his steed in that direction and trudged through the forest. Finally, he could see through the wall of pine and cedar a small fire flickering and one man huddled next to it. As he had suspected, it was Crying Wolf. Tyrell shook his head. Now that he knew what he knew, he carried on. He didn't take Crying Wolf by surprise, Crying Wolf had already heard him approach, and when he was able to see, he knew who it was. He rose up and looked at him.

"Hello, my friend. You are here on Gabe Roy's behalf?"

"Damn it, Crying Wolf, why are you here?" Tyrell swung off his horse and walked over to where Crying Wolf stood.

"You already have this answer. I gave it to you many weeks ago along the trail."

"You mean when you stole my horse and left me with another stolen one. I'm glad at least to see you're still riding him." Tyrell looked at the horse, shook his head, and smiled.

"I borrowed him. The one I left was getting trail tired. I needed a fresh one," Crying Wolf replied with a smile of his own.

"You also killed some men along that trail," Tyrell knelt next to the fire and warmed his hands as he looked into the flames.

"Yes. Carl, Smitty, and their 2 friends, it was me or them, I had no choice."

Tyrell looked up from the flames and into Crying Wolf's eyes. "Carl and Smitty?" he questioned. "You knew their names?"

"Only by what they called each other, I did not know them," Crying Wolf made clear. "Do you condemn me for killing them?"

"Nope, I don't condone it either, but it matters little. I put them into the ground for you. I reckon they did deserve what they got. That ain't why I'm here, though."

"I know. You want answers on why I sit here. I told you this once already."

"Yeah, I know. I have to tell you, Crying Wolf, Gabe was going to saddle up a bunch of men and come looking for you. I convinced him I'd go alone and see what I could find, although I already knew it was you I'd find."

Crying Wolf now squatted and warmed his hands above the flames. He was solemn and content. "I travelled many miles closer to my home. Then I had a vision. The vision convinced me that Gabe Roy's justice should come in the form of death." Crying Wolf inhaled deeply, "the white man's justice will only see his freedoms being taken away. The winter snows will come and go and once more, he will again have his freedom. That isn't justice." Crying Wolf pointed out.

"I've been able to come up with a lot of evidence against him for the crimes he has committed, Crying

Wolf. Gabe Roy will be an old man when he finally gets his freedom back. He may even die in prison. That won't happen though if you interfere with my investigation. Killing him only makes his killer nothing less than what Gabe Roy is. You understand that?"

"It may make a white man that, but it makes an Athabasca a coward, if he does not kill him. Especially one that knows about his doings and one that is within striking distance. Do you understand that?" Crying Wolf questioned.

"You're answering questions with questions, Crying Wolf. To answer your question though, I will say this, I understand how you and others must feel about Gabe, and if I wasn't involved I would care less if you put an arrow in his heart. However, I am involved and I am required to follow the laws of the land. Us white men do things a lot differently I know than the indigenous folk. I have to ask you though as a friend, don't kill Gabe Roy, you will be a wanted man and you will hang a lot quicker than any white man."

"Would it be you that hunts me down?" Crying Wolf wanted to know, where Tyrell stood on their friendship.

Tyrell shook his head unsure either way. What he did know is that somebody within the law would. "I would hope not. But I can't say," he sucked on an eyetooth as he contemplated the possibility.

Crying Wolf still crouching crossed his arms, "Your honesty is enlightening. You are a good man. You uphold laws and bring the lawless to justice. The Athabasca, we have laws too, but our laws as you have said are different. It is only because you are my friend that, I will wait for the prevalence of the white man's justice, to be, served, upon Gabe Roy. I will do that because once the news reaches my people, I will then know that you are no longer involved. If, by chance, somewhere in time I or any other Athabasca meets up with Gabe Roy his crimes against us will be justified at the end of an arrow. For now, we wait."

Tyrell nodded his head in appreciation. If after it was all said and done, and Gabe's fate was death at the hands of the Athabasca, then so be it. He could live with that. Between now and then, though, there was no way he could let anything happen that would otherwise see Gabe dead.

"I am relieved to hear you say those words. Let the white man's laws deal with him."

Tyrell looked again into the flames of the fire, his mind racing as he wondered if that is how it would end up. It mattered little. Gabe, he knew, was nothing more than a bully with a lot of money, most of which he took from those he conned. There were other things too that made him a lesser man then most.

His raping and killing always came to mind. The thing was to him it was nothing more than daily business or a little bit of fun and it sickened Tyrell. Even being in Gabe's presence sickened him, but he had a job to do and so he let all the other stuff he hated about the man sit in the pit of his stomach. That was the hardest part, letting all that other stuff ferment, while at the same time investigating Gabe's past.

The evidence he had on him regarding all the crimes, he had committed were often covered up by those required to uphold the laws of the land. There was a chance he knew that the corrupt law would do all it could to kibosh his findings. It was no secret that the Mounted Police of Willow Gate were corrupted by, Gabe Roy's money. The good thing was he was getting close to exposing that too. Things could always go wrong though they often did, in which case, it might be he himself, who ended Gabe Roy's life.

"I sense apprehension. You cannot be sure that Gabe Roy will face any justice, can you?" Crying Wolf questioned when he noted that Tyrell was in deep thought.

"Bringing any man to justice can never be guaranteed," Tyrell said as he looked across the fire to Crying Wolf. "We can only hope that what is set before a judge is enough to prove guilt. If it isn't then most will walk free, yep."

"And this is what the white man calls justice? You must know how pitiful that sounds. Gabe Roy deserves death or life behind iron bars. I am not so sure now that I can walk away," Crying Wolf stood up and gestured for Tyrell to get on his horse and leave. "You go. I will think about what it is we have talked about."

Standing Tyrell looked one more time at Crying Wolf then swung up onto his horse. Looking back, he nodded. "I understand your words my friend. I will tell Gabe that I never saw you." Turning, he headed back the way he came. He knew as he travelled that Gabe was likely going to find his throat slit or an arrow between his shoulders. His job in protecting him now became complicated.

Chapter 6

On the trail east of Willow Gate, Colby Christian and Martin Brubaker were slowly gaining ground and were closer to Willow Gate than either one could know.

Colby looked over his shoulder at Martin, who was only a few steps behind, was a bit wobbly on his horse and he noted this. He slowed his horse to a stop and swung off.

"Hey Martin, I think we need to take a rest here, you ain't looking so well on that steed." He made his way over to Martin and helped him down from his horse and over to a boulder on the side of the trail. "You sit tight here. I'll get a fire going."

"You think we is getting close, Colby... you know to Willow Gate?" Martin asked as he looked west down the trail. His head ached, and his lungs, felt like they were coated in ice. It hurt with every breath he took.

By now, Colby had an arm full of dry broken branches that he busted off a few nearby pine trees. He swept away some snow with his boot heel and stacked the branches in a teepee so he could set them to flame. Kneeling he looked over to Martin as he struck a match.

"I reckon we are. Not sure how far or close, but we're making progress."

It took a few minutes for the flames to dance, and when they did, he added bigger pieces of wood.

"There, that should give us some heat," Colby sat next to the fire and warmed his hands. "How are you feeling?"

"Same as earlier; lungs hurt and my head is all clogged up. I ain't sure I'm going to make it. I feel like I'm dying," Martin replied.

"Hell, you ain't even close to that. You got a cold, maybe the flu, or a lil' bit of hypothermia, but you are a far way from dying. We'll rest here for a bit and I'll get some coffee brewing. In a couple hours, we'll set off again." Colby stood up and fetched the fixings he needed to make coffee. He added snow to the pot, grinds to the basket, and set the pot onto the flames.

"A few more minutes, and nice cup of hot coffee is going to give you some strength and warm up your insides."

Martin looked at Colby and smiled weakly. "I sure hope you is right. We got to get to Willow Gate and the sooner the better."

"We'll get there. I ain't worried about that none," he, poured Martin a coffee and handed it to him. Then took his own cup into his hands and brought the cup up to his lips. He blew gently on it and took a swallow. How he wanted a hot cooked meal and a bed to sleep in.

They had been on the trail for too long already and neither one had a clue on how much longer it be. They had no idea if Willow Gate was a long way off or if it were around the next corner. All they knew is that was their destination and the sooner they made the distance the better. Warming up and resting for a while, they finished their coffees then once more headed west.

When Tyrell made his way back to Willow Gate after his meet up with Crying Wolf, he meandered over to Gabe's place. It was near 2:00 p.m., he knew he would find him sitting in his office, likely drinking brandy. Tethering his horse to the horse pole outside, he walked up the steps to the front door and knocked. Neeada answered the door.

"Afternoon, Neeada. Is Gabe home?" Tyrell asked as he stepped inside.

"Yes, in his office." Neeada closed the door and gestured for him to go on ahead to Gabe's office upstairs.

"Thank you, Neeada." He nodded with a smile and made his way up the stairs to Gabe's office. He gently knocked on the door. "Mr. Roy it's, Travis," he said as he waited for a response.

"C'mon in Travis," he heard Gabe reply.

Entering, he made his way over to the big oak desk that Gabe sat behind and pulled up a chair.

"Did you meet our Indian friend?" Gabe asked as he sat down.

"Nope, never saw him. No signs of anyone near Gold Creek at all," Tyrell lied.

"That doesn't make any sense. That is where I was told he'd be," Gabe rubbed his whiskered chin. "You saw no signs of anyone?"

"Not a soul, Gabe. Nothing," Tyrell answered.

Gabe leaned back in his chair and put his hands behind his head, "If you didn't see anyone, I wonder where the hell that redskin might be."

Tyrell shrugged. "I haven't a clue. Could be he's left the area or I was looking in all the wrong places."

Gabe leaned forward again and put his hands on his desk. "I guess for now we ain't got to worry then about a bloody redskin. I will have to speak with Donavan again. He is the one that brought it to my attention. He usually knows what he's talking about, if he says there was an Athabasca 'round here asking about me, I don't have any reason to not believe him."

"I'm not saying Donavan don't know what he's talking about. I'm saying I never saw no-one over at Gold Creek, not a bloody soul," Tyrell convinced.

"I ain't about to second guess, you. We still have to meet up with that old business partner of mine that owes me a handful of money," Gabe stood up from his desk as Tyrell followed suit. "He's meeting me over at the Willow Gate Nugget Hotel, should be there about now. C'mon, Travis let's go meet him," Gabe said as he led the way.

Outside they swung up onto their horses and headed to the Nugget Hotel. Sure enough, Gabe's old acquaintance was sitting at a table with a pitcher of draft. He saw Gabe come in and he waved him over.

"Hello Gabe," the man said as Gabe and Tyrell made their way over to the man's table.

"Hello Will," Gabe said solemnly as he now introduced Tyrell. "This here is Travis Sweet."

The man nodded and reached out his hand to shake Tyrell's, "Nice to meet you Travis."

Gabe interjected. "Travis, this is Will Novall, an old friend and business partner of mine."

Tyrell nodded acknowledgement, "Nice to meet you too, Mr. Novall," he said as he and Gabe sat down.

"You got my money or not, Will?" Gabe asked right off the bat.

"C'mon, Gabe, we're old friends, have a draft." Will poured both Tyrell and Gabe a draft from the pitcher.

"I haven't got time for idle chit-chat. Do you have my money or not?" Gabe asked again as he took a swallow from his glass.

"I need a couple more days, three or four tops?" Will, tried to plea.

"I've already given you enough time. I ain't going to wait three or four more days. I want all twelve thousand by this time tomorrow or you'll be paying the piper," Gabe slammed his glass down and stood up. "This time tomorrow, Will. Come on Travis, let's leave this deadbeat to come up with the damn money he owes me," Gabe said as he turned and walked away, Tyrell close behind.

"Jesus, shouldn't you have at least listened to what he might have had to say?" Tyrell asked as they stepped out onto the street. He was hoping more would have been said so that, he could jot it down. Anything he could dig up on Gabe only improved the case he was making against him. He had no idea why Will owed Gabe twelve thousand dollars.

"I've listened long enough to what he has to say and it would've been no different from what he would've said now."

The two of them swung up onto their horses.

"If he doesn't have my money by tomorrow, he's going to wish that he never owed it to me. Goddamn, I wish Carl and Smitty's crew would get here."

Tyrell, startled by the names Gabe mentioned, looked over to him. "Carl and Smitty, who are they?" he questioned already knowing who they likely were. His meeting with Crying Wolf had revealed the names of those he had killed along the trail as he made his way to Willow Gate. Carl and Smitty were never going to show up. Only Tyrell knew where they were and that was deep in the hole he had dug for them.

Gabe waved his hand through the air as though it mattered little who the men were, "They're crew of cattle wranglers. They have worked most every ranch south of the Rocky Mountains. I hired them some time ago to head my cattle operation once I get Cross's land. They also like to brawl, and I could use a brawler right now to muscle Will Novall. He'd pay that twelve thousand he owes me right quick once Smitty smacked him around some."

There was nothing more Tyrell needed to know. He did however want to know why Will Novall owed him money.

"If you don't mind me asking, why the hell does he owe you that money anyway?" he asked directly, as the two carried on back toward Gabe's house.

"It doesn't matter, why he owes it to me. The only thing that matters is that he does."

That was all Gabe said about it and so Tyrell would leave it at that. They were about to turn down the street that led back to Gabe's house when the first shot rang out. The bullet ripped into the dirt in front of them and the two riders turned their horses to see who it was that had fired the shot.

Of course, it was Will, and he was reloading! Tyrell pulled his pistol as Gabe jumped from his horse and headed for cover behind some sacks of grain and wooden barrels. A second shot rang out this time hitting one of the barrels. Willow Gate residents began darting this way and that. In the confusion, Will managed to get up onto his own horse and high-tailed it out of town.

"Gabe, you all right," Tyrell hollered as he looked in the direction he last saw Will.

"I knew that son-of-a-bitch was going to do that," Gabe yelled back. "Is he still there?"

"Nope, he headed east. It was Will, though, as sure as the sun shines."

Gabe came out from cover and dusted himself off. "Why the hell didn't you shoot him?"

"Had no clear shot, too many folks were in the way," Tyrell swung off his horse and met up with Gabe on the boardwalk. "I know which way he went. If you're all right, I can likely catch up to him."

"Go then, get after that bastard, he's going to have an attempted murder charge for that fiasco, let me tell you," Gabe said with anger.

Tyrell swung back onto his horse and headed in the direction he saw Will go.

Gabe hollered after him as he rode away. "Kill him for all I care, or bring him back alive. Makes no never mind to me!"

He watched as Tyrell headed east and out of sight. By now, the one Mounted Police constable stationed in town that week approached.

"You all right, Mr. Roy?" the constable asked as he made the distance to where Gabe stood.

"That son-of-a-bitch Novall just tried to kill me and you're asking if I'm all right. What the hell do you think?" Gabe questioned with a sneer.

"You sure it was Novall?" the constable questioned.

"I know damn well that it was. Travis is heading after him right now. You might want to gather up some redcoats and do the same."

"I'm the only one at the station, Mr. Roy. I'll get a posse together though," the constable said as he darted off. It took only a few minutes to raise a posse of six men and soon they too were heading east.

Gabe had made his way back to the Nugget Hotel and was sitting at a table with a bottle of whisky. He was downing the shots left, right, and center. The more he thought about how close he came to dying that day the more whisky he drank. Drunk now, he stumbled up the stairs to his private hotel room and passed out on the bed.

Will Novall had been running hard and fast for almost an hour when he and his horse passed Colby and Martin, he never look back. Colby and Martin watched as the horse and rider carried on at a gallop.

"Jesus, wonder what that fellow might be running from?" Colby questioned as he heard yet another horse and rider approach also at a gallop.

He recognised Tyrell, and Tyrell recognised Colby. He simply nodded at the two of them as he passed. With no time to spare, he never bothered to say 'hello'.

"That there was Travis Sweet, Martin. We must be damn close to Willow Gate. I guess we know now why that other fellow was running," Colby chuckled, "he's being chased by Travis. C'mon Martin, let's forget about that for now and get going in the right direction, Willow Gate ain't too much further I reckon," Colby said as he and Martin turned their horses and continued onward.

A few minutes later another rumble of horse hooves echoed in the wood as six more horses and riders came around the bend. Taken by surprise Colby and Martin's horses reared up almost knocking the two of them to the ground, but they managed to gain control and got their horses to settle down as the six riders darted by.

"What the hell... Holy shit, Jesus Christ, I reckon we're witnessing something going down," Colby said with excitement.

"I wouldn't argue. What do you suppose is going on?" Martin asked in a weak voice.

Colby shook his head. "I ain't rightly sure. We can assume, though, that first fellow being chased, ain't having a very good day. He has Travis Sweet on his ass and six other riders coming on fast. That can't be good for him."

They watched as the last horse and rider vanished from their sight then, turning west, they continued onward.

Daylight was fading when they finally made the distance to Willow Gate. They rode into town and pulled up to the first hotel they came to. Colby swung off his horse and tethered him to the horse pole, then helped Martin off his.

"Here we are, Martin, the town of Willow Gate. I'll get us a room and get our horses settled while you rest up."

They entered the hotel and booked a double room.

The clerk handed them a key. "Room sixteen at the end of the hall on the second floor." He looked at Colby and Martin, "Is your friend all right? He looks a bit sick," the clerk asked.

"We've been on the trail since early October, mister. Lost our way a few different times and had to stay put for a couple of days due to some damn nasty weather. I reckon he has a bit of trail weariness, maybe a bit of a cold. He'll be all right," Colby replied as he and Martin climbed the stairs to the second floor and made their way to the end of the hall and room sixteen.

Inside were two single beds. A washbasin sat on a dresser and next to that were two chairs.

"Here is home 'til we find Alex and your brothers," Colby said as he looked around and tossed their gear onto one of the beds. Martin made his way over to the next, kicked off his boots, and sprawled out.

"Are you going to be okay, whilst I take care of our horses?" Colby asked.

"I'll be fine. Feels good to lie down on a bed," Martin responded.

"All right, I'll get our horses stabled and see if I can find the others."

Colby looked again at Martin who had already fallen asleep. Tossing a blanket over him, he stepped out of the room. Making his way outside, he asked a passerby where the stables were.

The man pointed, "At the end of the street, you'll find it."

"Thank you, mister," Colby said as he swung onto his horse, and leading Martin's horse, he made his way to the end of the street where the stables were. After paying the stable fee, he trudged back to the hotel. He stuck his head into the saloon and looked around hoping to see Alex or one of the others, but saw neither. Looking around he noted there were two other hotels in town. However, tired as he was he had no desire to visit each. Instead, he decided to head up to the room and join Martin in some well-deserved shuteye.

Chapter 7

It was early morning, when Tyrell gave up trying to catch up to Will. He had followed him all through the night only to be disappointed when, he found Will's trail heading off into the Rocky Mountains. The horse Tyrell was riding, one of Gabe's, didn't have the strength or stamina to trudge after him, nor did he have any gear to continue.

Swinging off the horse, he marked the trail where Will headed northwest. He would tell the Willow Gate, Mounted Police where to find the trail once he made it back to the Gate. For now, his concerns were getting back to town as soon as possible to protect Gabe from possible further attempts on his life. Crying Wolf was a particular concern.

He had only been travelling for a short while when he came upon the six-man posse. He slowed his horse down, a couple of the men he knew off hand and he questioned them.

"Are you folks looking for Will, Ben?"

"Yep, the redcoat sent us after him. You ran after him too huh, no luck though I see."

"Nope he darted northwest into the Rocky Mountains. I marked the spot. It is down the trail some, you can't miss it."

"Damn. We ain't geared up for a trip into the mountains." Ben looked back at the others, "You men want to carry on?"

"Personally, I don't give a shit one way or the other. I kind of wish Will got a good shot off on that bastard Gabe," one of the riders pointed out.

"What about the rest of you?" Ben asked.

"I say we carry on. Will ain't going to make much distance up in the hills. We'll likely catch up to him before sunset, if we get going now," another rider suggested.

Ben nodded in agreement. "All right fellows, let's get. Thanks for pointing us in the right direction Travis."

"Good luck to you Ben."

Tyrell watched as the six-man posse led by Ben headed east along the trail. Turning his steed, he continued westerly toward Willow Gate. He was tired, a bit saddle sore, and anxious to get back. It took the better part of the morning to make the distance. He made his way to Gabe's place and knocked on the door. Neeada answered.

"Good morning Travis. Gabe is not here, he didn't return last night," Neeada said with concern.

"Damn it. You have any idea where he might be Neeada?"

"He sometimes stays at the Willow Gate Nugget when he drinks, maybe he is there?"

Tyrell nodded. "Yeah, that is right. I bet he did drink some yesterday. Thank you, Neeada, I will go and check. If he shows up here, will you let him know that I'm back? I'll swing by later if I don't find him."

Tyrell put his hat back on, swung up onto his horse, and headed into town and to the Nugget Hotel. He found Gabe sprawled out in his private room.

"Tied one on last night Mr. Roy?" he questioned as he stepped inside Gabe's private room.

Gabe rolled over and looked at him all groggy. "I guess I must've. You put lead into Will?" he rubbed his eyes and sat up.

"That I did not. He slipped into the Rockies and I ain't geared up for anything like that, not to mention the horse ain't very submissive to my commands. Likely he was as tired as I. Ben and the others, though, have carried on."

"Shit. Well, give me a hand here in standing. I'm still a bit off center."

Tyrell helped Gabe stand up.

"There, that's better. I need coffee, and lots of it." Gabe stretched and slipped into his boots. "C'mon, let's go get some."

The two men headed to the saloon and sat down at Gabe's table.

"So, that bastard, Will slipped away?"

"I don't reckon he's going to get far. Ben and the others are on his tail," said Tyrell as he pulled himself into the table more.

Gabe raised his hand in the air and signaled that, he wanted service.

"A round of strong black coffee." he requested when the young woman approached.

"Yes sir, Mr. Roy. I'll get it for you right away," she said as she turned and made her way back to the kitchen.

She returned a short while later with a pot of strong black coffee and set the pot and two cups down on the table. "Do you want any breakfast?" she asked.

Gabe looked over to Tyrell, "You want any food Travis?"

"Sure would settle for some eggs," he replied.

"There you have it. Bring him some eggs. Myself, I ain't in need of anything right now but coffee." Gabe poured his first cup of the day, and took a long slurp.

"Okay, let me know if you need anything else. I'll get Travis his breakfast," the young woman said as she once more turned and made her way back to the kitchen.

"You were saying earlier that Ben and the others carried on after meeting up with you?" Gabe questioned as he slurped again from his coffee.

"They were a bit better prepared than I was. B'sides my job is keeping you safe, can't do that if I ain't here," Tyrell pointed out as his breakfast of eggs arrived. He looked at the young woman and smiled. "Thank you very much."

"You're welcome Travis. I'll ask again while I'm here, Mr. Roy, do you want anything else?"

"Looking at them eggs does make me want to have a serving. Yeah, bring me a serving. I want ham though, not sausage."

"You bet, so the usual?"

"That's right. Now go on and get it for me."

"Coming right up," the she answered as she pranced away.

Tyrell looked up from his plate. "Some food will smarten you right up, Gabe. It's damn good fixings."

He continued to eat and slurp his own coffee, as they grew silent. Sometime later finished with their breakfast, they drank another coffee and headed back to Gabe's place. Tyrell followed Gabe up to his office and pulled up the chair he always sat in.

"What is on the agenda today, Mr. Roy?"

"I really want to grab that land from Pete. That is what I really want. Those fellows he has working for him though, the Brubakers, I think they're going be trouble. We need to get them out of there so I can strong hand Cross into signing the land deal."

Tyrell shook his head. "They're going to be a lot more than trouble, Mr. Roy. I passed Colby Christian and I'm assuming the younger Brubaker, who Alex called Martin, yesterday. They was heading this way. Chances are they're going to be meeting up with the others soon."

Gabe looked at Tyrell not amused. "Big deal, two more bullets we'll need to waste. Are you afraid of them?"

"Never once did I say that, no sir, I ain't afraid of them, but messing with them ain't something I'd recommend. They is a force to reckon with Gabe, that is all there is to it. The five of them, I was informed by Ed took down the Montana Ridgeback Gang not long ago. Slaughtered a dozen of them together and Alex and Colby took down two more in the Fort. That is something one doesn't want to dismiss if one knows about it."

Gabe showed little concern as he waved his hand through the air as though swatting at a fly. "They'll be nothing more than horseshit on the soles of my boots when I get done with them. I can get twenty men, hell I could get thirty men, to dance with them, if they want to play. No problem."

"Ask yourself, Gabe, is slaughtering five young men to get Cross's land worth it?" Tyrell questioned as though, he weren't sure that is what Gabe was alluding to, even though he knew Gabe Roy was willing to do whatever it took. Once Gabe admitted it for a second time, he would certainly add it to the collection of quoted evidence he already had on him.

"I wouldn't send the men in shooting up a storm. I would have them ride back to Cross's place with us. The minute them boys tried anything, they would be slaughtered, damn right," Gabe, blurted with malevolence.

It wasn't exactly what Tyrell wanted to hear. It did prove however, that Gabe was willing to kill to build up his capital as he stole from the less fortunate.

Tyrell inhaled deeply, "I don't know. For a piece of land, it seems a bit off center."

One thing was for certain, if there were a gunfight, he would be shooting from the other side.

"You might see it that way, Travis. To me it is business," Gabe said with conviction.

"You can call it whatever you want. Either way, it'll be a damn blood bath and I ain't so sure we'd be the ones walking away."

"You're saying that six unseasoned men could wipe out twenty to thirty seasoned gunmen?"

Tyrell removed his hat and fiddled with the brim as he contemplated. "Those fellows will bear down on you the second you give your men the command to fire. You will be dead, Gabe, it is that simple. Those boys ain't stupid, they know if you cut off the snake's head it'll die."

"What are you saying that I'm a snake?" Gabe was clearly perturbed.

"I didn't say that, but I know that is what they think of you. They'll do whatever it is to keep you from bullying Mr. Cross, I can assure you of that, 'cause that is exactly what Alex said to me when they chased you and the others off the day that son-of-a-bitch took my boots."

Tyrell grew silent for a moment as he thought about that. "I'm telling you we won't be dealing with unseasoned men. They are young, fearless, and each of them can shoot as good as any man you can hire. The only difference would be the numbers. Numbers though mean little when a man has had the time to barricade himself, against what he knows, is coming. Trust me, they know that you aren't going to stop trying to muscle Cross out of his land. I would suggest against that, leave it alone," Tyrell said with sincerity.

"Leave it alone, no bloody way!" Gabe was seeing black, he was that irate, "I want that land and I'm going to get it, one way, or the other. If you aren't going to help me attain it, then I guess your services are no longer needed."

"Are you firing me Gabe?" Tyrell wanted to be clear.

How he hoped that was the case, it would give him the freedom to pursue the case against him through judicial proceedings. Perhaps he could bring him to justice for the crimes he had committed sooner rather than later.

Gabe stood up and poured himself a brandy, "I have no reason to keep you. You haven't been much help in satisfying our contract," he pulled back the curtains and looked out across his land. "I say, pack up your gear and leave Willow Gate. You don't get to keep that horse either. You can find your own damn steed."

"All right, Mr. Roy. But I ain't leaving Willow Gate," Tyrell assured as he stood up.

"I'll have my men run you out of town then. I don't want you 'round here. Now go on, get the hell out of here. This town belongs to me, and I don't want any man that defies me getting comfortable," Gabe pointed toward the door in anger. "Go on, get!"

Tyrell smiled, nodded, donned his hat, and exited Gabe's office. He was going to stick it to Gabe good. First things first, though, and that was to gather up his gear and settle into the Owl's Nest Hotel. Then he would track down a horse and pay a visit to Pete Cross.

Walking the distance to the house he had been using on Gabe's land, he gathered his gear and whistled for Black Dog who came scampering out of the woodshed.

"Well, old friend looks like we are without reason to stay here, we are moving to the Owl's Nest for now. Gabe no longer wants McCoy's services, which suits me fine, I would rather look out for the law-abiding than an ass like him. C'mon Black Dog, let's get."

With Black Dog at his side, his saddle over his shoulder and gear in a gunnysack, Tyrell and Black Dog turned and headed for the hotel. Paying for a week in advance, he walked up the stairs to his room, tossed his gear on the bed, and looked around. The room would do.

Chapter 8

Colby Christian watched Tyrell enter the hotel on the other side of the street and he waited a few minutes before ambling over and finding out what room he was in. He wanted to say 'hello' if nothing else. He was also curious to know if by chance he had seen or spoke to Alex. He knew Alex and the others had made the distance to Willow Gate, but since his and Martin's arrival, he hadn't seen hide or hair of the other three. Knocking on Tyrell's room door, Colby waited for a response.

Tyrell hesitantly asked who it was, a bit reluctant on why anyone would be knocking on his door.

"Hey, Travis, it's me, Colby Christian."

"Colby," Tyrell responded somewhat shocked.

"That's right, you going to let me in, or what?"

Colby waited a few seconds and the door opened.

"God damn, hello, Colby," Tyrell said as he looked at him. "Jesus, I only now got settled. How did you know I was here?" he asked as he motioned for him to come in and have a seat.

"Me, and Martin is over at the other hotel. I saw you coming this way. Thought I'd stop by and see how you're doing."

"Nice of you to check up, but we ain't what one might call friends," Tyrell said as he sat down at the foot of the bed.

"Martin and I is looking for Alex and the others. You ain't by chance seen them, have ya?" Colby asked. "I know you've been here I'd guess as long as they. Thought maybe you would've seen them about?"

Tyrell nodded. "I've seen them. They work for a rancher goes by the name of Cross. Five or so miles down the road northerly. You're here to meet up with them and go looking for Matt Crawford?" Tyrell asked, not knowing that Colby already knew Matt was or had been in the custody of McCoy's for the last while.

Colby chuckled, "Shit, c'mon, Travis, Matt has been picked up already and you were one of ones that helped bring him in. I've already learned that from Ed and Riley. I ain't here to go traipsing for a wanted man that no longer runs free. I only want to catch up with Alex and the others. You say five miles north I could find them?"

"If they are still there, that is where you'll find them, at Cross's ranch. If you want to wait a while, whilst I get myself a horse I could take you there."

"What happened to that horse you were riding the other day when you passed me and Martin?" Colby asked out of curiosity.

Tyrell told the story.

"Gabe fired you 'cause you weren't going to play his game no more, and that is how you stumbled into Alex and the others, they are protecting the land of Pete Cross, from sticky fingers Gabe. And to top all that off Gabe has threatened to run your ass out of town?" Colby wanted to be clear as he half chuckled.

"Yes sir that is how all this has come about. He ain't going to run me out of town though, and since I ain't working for him anymore, I thought I'd fill old Cross in on what it is Gabe Roy might very well be planning," Tyrell responded with clarity.

"If Alex and the others have been hired to protect that fellow Cross, there ain't no way Gabe will take it as easily as he thinks. Add me and Martin to the equation and Gabe won't stand a chance." Colby smiled, "It has been a while since any of us have seen any action."

"I can tell you, Colby, he is talking about twenty or thirty men accompanying him when he makes up his mind to try and get Cross out of the way. That is a small army you folks might be up against."

"The numbers don't matter much though, once a man gets wind of what might be coming," Colby said as he looked into Tyrell's eyes.

Tyrell smiled and nodded. It was funny how only a few hours earlier that is what he told Gabe, himself.

"You want to hear something else, which I'm sure you'll get a kick out of?" Tyrell asked.

"What might that be?" Colby asked, curious to know.

Tyrell told him the story about his red dun, how he ended up with it. And how Alex took it away along with his boots.

Colby listened with half intrigue and half confusion.

"That is one helluva tale. I'm surprised Alex didn't shoot you on the principal that he thought you stole that horse of mine. I find it hard to believe that one damn redskin could pull something like that off. I'm glad to know leastwise that Alex has that old red dun though. He's a fine damn horse. Once I get him back, I'll sell you the one I'm riding if you want. I picked him up at the Fort. Bash sold him to me."

"I thought that buckskinned looked familiar. I guess that then takes care of my need to go looking for a horse. Sure, I'll take him off your hands once you get that red dun of yours. I guess we could head over to Cross's place now. I'll double behind you if that is okay?"

"Better than that, you could use Martin's horse. Martin is a bit under the weather, picked up a sickness along the trail. Likely the flu, I think. He was feeling better this morn. Said he needed a few more hours of sleep is all. Wasn't throwing up and he weren't sweating from fever. I think he'll snap out of it."

"All right, let's head over to Cross's place and I'll get my boots back, you'll get your horse, and I'll buy the one you've been riding." Tyrell said as he stood up. Colby followed suit. They talked between themselves as they walked the distance to the stable where Colby and

Martin's horses were. They saddled up and started heading out of town toward Cross's place when they were confronted by two heavily armed, well-dressed men. It was easy to tell that they were gunslingers.

"Hold up there, Mister. You fit the description of someone, we is lookin' for. Are you Travis Sweet?" the first rider asked as the second rider circled around both he and Colby and sat on his horse behind both of them. Colby turned his steed to face the rider. What none of the four men knew was that not far away coming towards them was Alex Brubaker and his cousin Cape. They were simply on their way to pick up supplies and spend some time in the big town of Willow Gate. They had as much of an idea that ahead of them was Colby and Tyrell, as Colby and Tyrell had that Alex and Cape were near.

"What exactly is this about? And who wants to know if I'm Travis Sweet?" Tyrell asked, somewhat uneasy. He knew Colby was facing the other rider and if the two men asking the questions were going to cause trouble, his back was covered.

The first rider leaned forward on his saddle as he locked eyes with Tyrell, while the second rider stirred uncomfortably in his saddle, as Colby stared him down.

"The question was Mister, are you Travis Sweet?" the first rider asked again as he tried to intimidate Tyrell.

"That was your question all right. And mine was who wants to know?" Tyrell questioned back.

The first rider began to chuckle.

Tyrell tilted his head. "I ain't so sure I see or said anything funny," he paused as he looked at the man. "I am indeed Travis Sweet and if you're going to pull that six-shooter, you best make peace with God almighty, before you do so."

Tyrell waited his eyes never leaving the rider who sat in front of him.

It was then they heard the approach of a couple more riders. Tyrell looked beyond the man in front of him. He could see two more riders approach. The man sat back up in his saddle, his gun battle with Travis Sweet, although long in coming would have to wait for another day.

"I don't think t'day is the day, Mister Sweet. We'll meet again though rest assured," the man said as he signaled to his partner and the two of them continued onward toward Willow Gate.

"What the hell do you suppose that was all 'bout, Travis?" Colby asked as he and Tyrell watched the men galloping off.

"I reckon it means only one thing, I best keep my eyes open."

That is all Tyrell wanted to say about the confrontation.

"Hey, Colby take a look," he said as he pointed toward the horizon. "Two more riders approaching, and I'll be goddamned if it ain't Alex and another."

"Holy shit, yes it is and looks like Cape is with 'em," Colby chuckled. "Hey, Alex," he hollered as he and Tyrell rode toward them.

"Jesus! Is that you, Colby?" Alex hollered back with excitement and relief to know that Colby had finally made it to Willow Gate.

"Is too!" Colby yelled back as they made the distance.

"Sure good to see you, Colby. Ain't sure why you brought along Travis, but whatever... I'm damn glad to see you made it. Where is Martin?" Alex asked with genuine concern.

"Back at the hotel, he picked up the flu or something along the way, but we're both here and we're ready to ride. How the hell have you all been?"

"We is working for that fellow Cross, which I'm sure Travis here has already informed you of; which brings me to another thought. Why the hell are you here, Travis?" Alex wanted to know.

"It's only by coincidence on why I'm here with Colby, but I was coming this way today anyhow. I wanted to let you folks know, Gabe is going to be doing whatever he can to take over Cross's place. You all might want to think about that."

"Why would a fellow that works for Gabe want to tell us that?" Cape Brubaker asked.

"No, he don't work for Gabe no more, Cape. Gabe canned his ass," Colby made clear. "What he says about the coincidence and whatnot is true. I'm the one that found Travis. I wanted to know if he had seen any of you. He told me where to find you and was coming this way. I think he wants his boots back," Colby said with a chuckle. "He also told me about my horse, a tale of which I still can't wrap my head around. Nonetheless, I'm glad to know my horse is fine."

"Shit, as Brett would say, 'sounds like a goddamn dime novel'. Yeah, we have your red dun and I guess Travis can get his boots back, if he wants them. I tossed them into the horse corral."

Alex smiled.

"Goddamn it, Alex why would you do that?" Tyrell questioned not seeing the humor at all.

"They didn't fit none of us and they was yours. What else would you have expected?"

"I don't know. If you don't mind I'm going to carry on to Cross's place and get them boots. Is that all right with you?"

Alex shrugged his shoulders.

"You might get 'em if Brett don't kill you first."

"Well then, why don't you come along with me? Maybe he'll live to see another day." Tyrell teased, as he turned his horse and began to trot away.

"Hold up, Travis. You still want this buckskin. We could do the trade off now. That way I can bring back Martin's horse back to him. He'll be pissed if I don't."

Tyrell slowed the horse down and turned back.

"How much you want for him anyway? We didn't get that far."

"Same as I paid for him."

Colby reached into his saddlebag to find the receipt Bash had given him.

"Here it is. One hundred bucks and he's yours." Colby said as Tyrell approached and swung off the horse he was riding.

He took the receipt from Colby and looked at it. Satisfied, he reached into his vest pocket a paid fifty dollars up front, told Colby once he retrieved his boots, and made his way back to Willow Gate, to come by his room at the Owl's Nest and he'd pay him the balance.

"How about when you make your way back you also bring along my red dun?" Colby asked with a smile.

"Nope, don't think Brett would allow that, Colby." Alex responded. "He might let Travis get his boots, but he won't for certain let him bring along that red dun. You'll have to double back with Martin, or one of us."

Colby sighed with disappointment. "Yeah I suppose you is right. Never mind. I'll double back with someone."

Tyrell shrugged and nodded.

"I'll tell ya what, I'll let Brett know you and Martin are in Willow Gate with Alex and Cape. He decides to come this way he can lead your red dun."

All Tyrell really wanted were his boots.

That settled and out of the way, Alex, Colby and Cape headed into Willow Gate to gather Martin, spend some money and drink some whisky, not necessarily in that order. In the meantime, Tyrell carried onward to gather his boots.

The two riders that Tyrell and Colby had run into before meeting up with Alex and Cape, were tethering up their horses when Martin, whom was feeling a lot better stepped out onto the street looking for Colby.

"Look at that, if it ain't little Martin Brubaker," Scott Tellman said as he recognised Martin. "All alone without his brothers, what do you make of that, Steve?"

The Brubakers and Tellmans had a history and it wasn't pretty. Martin stopped and looked at the two brothers.

"What makes you think I ain't here without Brett and Cape, you pieces of shit?" Martin responded. He didn't fear them but being alone he was certainly at their mercy.

"Any other time we've come across you Brubakers, it is like you're holding hands with each other and since I don't see no hand holding, I guess that means you is all alone."

"I guess I shouldn't expect you to be smarter than that, since the two of you don't have but two school years between you. Are the two of you going to keep talking shit or are you going to try and start something?" Martin asked as he stepped closer.

"Lighten up Martin, we ain't here looking for trouble from you or your brothers. I'm funning with you. B'sides we have bigger fish to fry then a bottom feeder such as yourself." Steve Tellman said as he and his brother Scott chuckled.

"Uh huh, I thought as much. Chicken shit as usual." Martin said as the two Tellman brothers laughed louder and entered the hotel saloon. Martin watched as the two of them sat down at a table inside. *That was close, damn, bad news seeing those two,* he thought to himself as he now continued looking for Colby.

He made his way down to the livery stable and was informed that Colby and Travis had headed north an hour or so earlier.

"They didn't say where they was going and you're sure he was with that Travis fellow?" Martin asked the stable hand.

"I know he was with Travis. Nope, they didn't say much that I heard. They saddled up the horses and headed northwesterly out of town," the stable hand replied as he continued cleaning horse stalls.

"Hmm, all right. I guess I'll wait and see what comes of that."

It seemed odd to Martin that Colby would leave him behind without saying one thing or the other. It was even odder to be told that Colby left with Travis. A bit confused and unimpressed, Martin turned heel and began to walk to back to the hotel where he and Colby had been staying.

Colby spotted Martin as he stepped up onto the boardwalk. He slowed his horse down and pointed.

"Look at that Alex, Cape, there is Martin. He must be feeling better. Hey Martin!" Colby shouted as the three riders drew close.

Martin turned and looked. "Cape, Alex, goddamn, good to see you guys!" Martin said with excitement as he waited for them to pull up beside him. "And Colby, what was the big idea leaving me here, and taking off with that, Travis, fellow?" he questioned with annoyance as the three of them swung off their horses.

"Travis happened to know where these sons-of-bitches were, so I rode with him down the road some. They was already on their way here when we bumped into them. So, get your under-shorts unknotted, Martin. I guess you is feeling better?" Colby replied as Martin came closer.

"I reckon I'm back to life. I got some bad news for you, Cape. The Tellman brothers are here."

"Who the hell are they?" Colby asked.

"You ain't never met them, I don't think, Alex though has. They are a couple assholes who grew up near where we did back in the day. Said they was here to fry a big fish. I think they was playing chicken-shit games though. I don't know," Martin shrugged, "but they is here, in the flesh, Cape."

Cape nodded and inhaled deeply.

"Damn, wouldn't have ever thought we'd see those two here. They didn't try to rough you up none, did they?"

"Hell, no. I think they was contemplating it, though. I was ready."

Martin smiled.

"I say we forget about them. They ain't stupid enough to try anything against us. Where is Brett by the way?"

"He's back at Pete Cross's place. He hired the three of us to keep that Gabe Roy fellow from snooping around and trying to strong-arm him into selling his land. Brett is back there, keeping an eye on things. It sure took the two of you long enough to get here. Shit, Matt Crawford, might by now be in the U.S.A.," Cape commented.

"About that, Matt has already been taking in. Brady McCoy and Travis managed to grab him, some time ago. Ed, Riley, and Matt was with Brady actually, when he came across us stranded without our horses. I guess they, along with Matt, circled around us, making us believe that Brady was alone and Matt was still at large."

Colby could see the disappointment in Alex and Cape's eyes.

"There are other ways we can make money, though, and other bounties still kicking it somewhere."

"Yeah, but they ain't worth no ten thousand cash dollars, like Matt was. That really put a dump of shit on my day," Alex said as he looked around. "I wondered about that when we saw Brady. The bastard convinced us though, son-of-a-bitch. I guess that is it then. We still got work with Cross, I s'ppose, and now with you two finally here we can pretty much stand up against Gabe, and the twenty or thirty men, Travis said was gonna accompany

Gabe on his next visit to try and convince Cross to sell. So, there is that I guess."

Alex shrugged, *it was what it was.*

The four of them continued to catch up with each other as they made their way back to the hotel where Colby and Martin had been staying. They walked into the saloon and sat down at table.

"How long have the two of you been here?" Alex asked as the barmaid came by and took their order of a round of draft beer.

"We rode into town yesterday. It seemed to take forever and a day to make our way here. We were caught up in crappy weather, turned back to the Fort to buy gear. That is when we found out about Matt being in McCoy's custody. I guess if we hadn't found that out, we'd be looking like fools trying to track him down, so as you'd say, Alex, there is that."

Colby took a long swallow from his draft, and the others followed suit. The cousins were certainly happy to all be together again.

By now Tyrell was making his way down the road that led to Cross's place. He could see that Brett and Cross himself were sitting on the front stoop. Brett stood up, walked down the few steps, and waited for the oncoming single rider to get close.

"Hold up a minute there, mister, this is private land." Brett said before he noticed who it was.

"It's only me, Brett."

"Yeah, I see that now. What is it you want?"

"I met up with Alex and Cape as they headed into town, Alex said I could grab my boots. That is all I want, Brett," Tyrell said as he approached. "I don't work for Gabe no more. I'm here on my own to gather my boots and to let you know that Colby and Martin is in Willow Gate."

"Colby and Martin, you say?"

"Yep, they rode into town yesterday, I guess. I was bringing Colby here when we came across Alex and Cape. They headed back into town to gather Martin, I reckon. Now, about my boots, Alex said he tossed them into the horse corral. Is it all right if I go gather them?"

"I might have a few more questions for you. Why ain't you working for Gabe no more? And why should I believe you?"

Tyrell told the tale.

"Gabe is going gather up some men and try and raise some more shit, eh?" Brett chuckled. "That'd be damn stupid of him, 'specially since Colby and Martin are here. Our crew just got ten-fold better. I say let him and his henchmen come along. We'll kill everyone of 'em, Gabe first."

Tyrell now chuckled.

"That is pretty much what I told him when he fired me. There ain't no law that says you can't protect this land. Feel free to kill him all you want. No one would blame you, but if I get him sent to jail before then, you might be out of luck."

"Tell me, would you rather see him dead or in prison?" Brett was curious to know.

"I think you know my answer to that, Brett. I work within the law." Tyrell pointed out.

"You'd rather see him go to prison for a couple of years than buried in dirt?"

"It really don't matter what I'd rather see. I know he's crooked as a slithering snake. I know he's done things that he'll never be accused of or found guilty of, but he will see some sort of justice one way or the other. Death or prison. Who knows? Maybe he'll see both."

"You think a man like him would hang? There is a lot of doubt to that." Brett remarked.

Tyrell gestured that he couldn't be sure, and he shrugged his shoulders.

Pete Cross interrupted the conversation. "What is that he said, Brett?"

Brett looked back toward Pete. "Says he don't work for Gabe no more."

"Ahh, I see. Sorry, I can't hear so well, I'm deaf in one ear you know," Pete replied as Brett and Tyrell continued to converse.

"About my boots, Brett, you gonna let me liberate them or what?"

"I reckon we ain't got no use for them, go ahead." Brett pointed toward the horse corral. "They is likely ruined."

"I guess I'll know soon enough." Tyrell said as he and his horse traipsed by Brett.

Swinging off, he tethered the horse to the top rail and stepped inside. It took only a couple of seconds to find his boots. He wiped them off and looked at them. They were in as good shape as they were the day Alex made him take them off. Satisfied, he climbed back onto his horse and began to ride back to the hotel. Brett stopped him though as he passed by the porch.

"You found them I take it?"

"I did." Tyrell said as he stopped the horse.

Brett looked at him oddly then back to Pete Cross.

"Mr. Cross would like to know, if you is looking for work?"

Surprised by the question asked, Tyrell raised his eyebrows and leaned forward on the saddle.

"Come again? Did you say Cross wants to know if I'm looking for work?"

"Are you interested or not?" Brett asked.

"I ain't no hired gunman, Brett. You know that. I work for McCoy's."

"I told old man Cross that. He'd like to hire McCoy's to keep his land safe or at least safer then he assumes the five of us can do. I told him we'd do fine without you, but he's persistent. You interested in working for Cross or not. A simple yes or no is all you need to say."

"Shit, I dunno. He'll have to pay a hefty price for McCoy's services. I'd have to run it by Ed himself to find out if it is something we'd be interested in."

"What I understand about McCoy's is that you folks are paid Private Security and Investigations or something like that, ain't ya?" Brett pointed out.

"We are, but I don't know what it is Cross would want me to do?"

"Security, you know, protect his assets; the same shit you were supposed to be doing for Gabe Roy. Since you ain't working for him no more, Cross will pay you the same I'm sure."

"I need a couple days to think on it Brett. I ain't saying no and I ain't saying yes at this time. You let Cross know, I'll swing by in a day or so. I'll have decided by then."

Tyrell nodded as he turned his horse and continued up to the main road. Brett watched as he headed back toward Willow Gate. Turning heel, he made his way to the porch where Pete and he had been sitting.

"What did he say?" Pete asked, "You were too far away for me to hear much."

"He's gonna think about it Pete. He says he'll swing back in a day or so."

"I see. It would be good if he decided to take my offer. Having a man like him around here, could never hurt."

"What about us? We ain't chicken scratch," Brett pointed out, somewhat upset.

"No, no, you, Alex, and Cape, are good to have around too."

"If we're so good to have around, why the hell would you want Travis here? Do you even know anything about him?"

"I might be old and partially deaf, but I know and have heard enough about Travis Sweet to not take the opportunity to ask for his services. I would be a stupid man if I didn't, Brett. Just as I would have be a stupid man, if I had not hired the three of you. And there is room here to for your brother Martin and your cousin Colby too." Pete made clear, and he meant every word of it.

Indeed, he was old, perhaps a bit fragile, but he was far from stupid. He knew how dirty Gabe Roy could get. Many of his neighbors gave into Gabe's constant bullying, took his offer of money, and left the area completely. He, on the other hand, wasn't so easily convinced to give up all he had worked for. Slowly he was building up his own army and if things went his way, then Travis Sweet would be his General.

Chapter 9

Making his way back from Cross's place, Tyrell rode over to the telegraph office and sent a wire back to Ed, telling him that he had been fired by Gabe and had been offered another job, which entailed Security work for a rancher named Pete Cross who Gabe Roy was trying to strong-arm into selling his land. He added at the end more details to follow. Paying the fee he headed back to the Owl's Nest Hotel and his room.

Sitting on the foot of the bed, he looked through the information he had been scribbling down as he investigated Gabe. It was he knew enough information to obtain an arrest warrant. The only thing was he knew he couldn't expect the Willow Gate law, to write up the appropriate writ. He'd likely have to seal all the information he had in an envelope, and have it sent back to the Fort and McCoy's.

He couldn't trust the information he had to be kept private if he sent it in a wire to Ed. His best bet was to find a Pony Express outfit and send it that way. The time he spent in Willow Gate, though, he hadn't seen such an outfit. He'd have to find out if there was one. If not, then he'd have to send it by rail. There was a railroad in the next town over, some fifty miles away, but he wasn't sure it would be running through the Rockies at that time of year. The mountain passes were likely snow covered. Still he needed to get the information to Ed one way or the other. For now, he would wait for the return telegram from Ed regarding the new job opportunity, which, still pertained to Gabe Roy.

It was early evening, that Wednesday, when Cape spotted the Tellman brothers. The two brothers sat down at an unlit table in the corner of the saloon, where the Brubakers and Colby had been drinking. Cape nudged Alex and gestured in the direction the two brothers sat.

"Check it out. There they is, Scott and Steve, the Tellman brothers. I don't think they have spotted us yet."

Alex looked in the direction.

"I see them. I ain't saw them in a long time. They still look like the asses they are," Alex chuckled.

"Is that the two brothers you was telling me about, Martin?" Colby asked.

"Yep, that is them," Martin replied as he took a swig from his draft beer.

"They is the ones Travis and I ran across as we headed toward Cross's place. I think they is here to try their hand at Travis. They was taunting him before Alex and Cape showed up."

"Now that is god awful funny," Alex responded. "I say we tell them that Travis Sweet is washed up, can't handle a gun no-more. If they is here to kill him for whatever reason, that might give them the incentive to try. Hell, we could rid the earth of them or Travis and not even raise a finger ourselves."

"Jesus Christ, Alex, that is one helluva cowardly way to see a couple folks killed and why the hell would you want Travis dead?" Colby asked.

"You can't be serious, Colby. He killed Earl, took off a couple of my fingers. I don't care one bit what happens to that son-of-a-bitch," Alex replied coldly.

You really need to let that stuff go. Shit, it's been a long while, since all that happened Travis ain't so bad. And we all know how likely it is what went on b'tween Earl and Travis, is quite simple. Earl drew his gun and Travis beat him to the kill. As for your fingers, that right there is your own damn fault," Colby pointed out.

As the two of them bantered back and forth, Cape and Martin sat idly in their chairs and continued drinking, listening to the idiotic argument. That was the thing about

Alex and Colby, they always found one thing or another to argue about, and both sides were usually half-right. Finally, Cape spoke up.

"All right you two, cut the bullshit arguing. It don't matter either way. We're here together right now and we have a couple of problems that need our attention. We have a possible confrontation coming from Gabe Roy and right now in Willow Gate; we have the Tellman brothers snooping around possibly gunning for Travis. I like actually what Alex says 'bout feeding them Tellmans a line of horse shit 'bout Travis being washed up. We all know he ain't, but they don't."

Cape stopped there and looked at the others.

"The Tellman brothers are more of a menace than what Travis ever will be. We could kill them ourselves, but it ain't likely they'll even try anything against us 'cause they is out numbered. Now, I would like to be the one that shoots at least one of 'em, but like I said, they ain't 'bout to try anything stupid against us. Against one man, 'specially one man that they may be looking for, that is more to their liking."

Cape took a long swallow from his glass and emptied it. "You see where I'm going with that?"

"Yeah, it is the same thing Alex was trying to explain. We give them a line of shit, point them in the direction of where Travis can be found and hope Travis puts lead in both of them."

Martin smiled. "That is correct, Martin," Cape smiled back.

"I don't know," Colby began, as he too now emptied his glass. "I think it is a chicken shit way to get revenge or whatever. I'd still put my money on Travis, though."

Colby honestly didn't feel good about what he was hearing or for that matter what was being planned. He didn't know the Tellman brothers, but he knew his cousins well enough that if they said the Tellmans were menaces, then they probably were.

Whatever it was that went on between the Brubakers and the Tellmans meant nothing to him. He didn't like what it was his cousins were trying to do. They could ignore them all together. If they found Travis on their own, then, whatever the fate was during that meeting would be the outcome.

Trying to set Travis up, though, really wasn't how he would have dealt with the situation. He would have chosen the later and ignored the Tellmans. He was part of the Brubaker crew though, hell, they were family. Whatever it was they decided to do, would be something he would have to accept. He was confident, that if the Tellmans were there gunning for Travis, there would be only one outcome and the town of Willow Gate would need two wooden boxes.

Colby looked again at the table in the corner and to the two Tellman brothers. It was then one of them noticed him. Cape and Alex's backs were toward them, so they didn't know who the other two were sitting at the table. Scott, though, recognised Martin and Colby.

"Hey, Steve look over yonder; ain't that Martin? And that other cowboy looks like that fellow that was with Travis Sweet earlier t'day."

Steve Tellman looked on.

"That is Martin and the other does look like that fellow we passed earlier. Could be Travis is sitting at that table with them. It don't matter, though. There is four of 'em. We best keep our eyes on 'em for now. We ain't here looking for trouble from the Brubakers. If we see Travis sitting with them, we'll wait 'til we can get him alone, b'fore we confront him. From what we know, he alone is damn quick on the draw. Don't need no other quick drawing cowboys getting involved. We'll deal with the Brubakers another time," Steve responded.

"You want us to go over there and have friendly conversation. We'd know then who is with Martin," Scott said, "it's always been fun getting their feathers in a ruffle."

"Right now ain't time for friendly conversation with that lot. We'll keep our eye on them for now."

"Ahh, all right, we'll do it your way," Scott said as he looked toward the bar and signalled the barmaid to bring them another round.

"The Tellmans recognised you Martin. They was looking right at ya," Colby made him and the others aware.

"Is that right? I bet they is shitting themselves. They is probably wondering who is sitting with us. Hey, Alex, Cape why don't the two of you turn your heads, let them get a good look at you," Martin chuckled.

Alex and Cape looked over their shoulders. Scott and Steve were looking back and they all locked eyes. The Brubakers nodded and smiled, then turned back to the table.

"Well, they've seen us. Now let's see what they do about it," Cape said, as they continued conversing.

"Looks like Cape sitting there with Martin and that other does looks like Alex Brubaker. It's been a long while since we've laid eyes upon him. Don't see Brett though," Steve said as he continued looking in the direction of the Brubaker table.

"Nope, he ain't there. That is Alex, though. I wasn't expecting that. Shit, we have ourselves three Brubakers sitting among us way up here in this bow hick town. Quite odd, ain't it, to see them here? Wonder what it is they is doing here?"

"I s'ppose it is as strange to them seeing us here as it is for us seeing them. What it is that they may be doin' here is anyone's guess. We saw that one cowboy with Travis

Sweet and saw Martin alone earlier. Maybe they is running with that Travis fellow."

Scott nodded.

"It could be that way. In which case, are we even ready for such a confrontation? I'm sure we could handle Travis, but three Brubakers and one cowboy along with Travis, not to mention we don't know one way or the other if Brett ain't about. The math don't add up in our favour."

"What are you saying, Scott, that we tuck tail and leave and wait to find Travis another time, or what? We've been making our way here for the past few weeks. To turn around when we know he's here don't add up either."

"Nope, I ain't saying that. Travis ain't sitting with them so that means he's alone somewhere. I say we finish these whiskies and step outside, go have a look; see if we can't find him. If he's alone, we're close to a big payday."

"Yeah, so say we do find him and we fulfill our contract, if the Brubakers are running with him, you can bet they'll be looking for us."

"That is a conundrum, ain't it?"

"More than a conundrum I'd say. I'd say more like a neighborhood brawl, something we ain't danced in for a long time. It could be fun," Steve added as he shot back his whisky.

The Tellman brothers stood up and made their way to the saloon exit. Cape Brubaker though spoke up.

"Are the two you running back to the chicken-coop, Steve?"

The Tellmans stopped and looked back at the Brubaker table.

"Nope, jus' leaving a pig pen," Steve responded, as they stepped closer to the Brubaker table. "What brings swine like you to a place like this?" he questioned as he and Scott approached the table and stood there waiting for a response.

"You Tellmans must be full of whisky to dare step this close to our table," Martin responded his back facing them.

The four of them sitting at the table chuckled.

"Ahh, never mind the taunting," Alex began as he looked at Steve. "It has been a long time, Steve, Scott. Why don't you join us for a bit? I'm sure there is a lot we could catch up with," Alex smiled.

He was baiting them.

"I agree, c'mon fellows, pull up a stool," Cape added.

"I dunno, Steve. Sitting with three Brubakers and someone they ain't even cordially introduced us to smells no different than the pigs they is," Scott said with disdain.

"Awe, shit, sorry about that," Martin began with sarcasm. "This here is Colby Christian, a cousin of ours. Colby, those two chicken-shit cowpokes behind me is Steve and Scott Tellman. They grew up in a hen house near where we all once lived. They was the best neighbours one could hope for, ain't that right, Steve?"

"Your name is Colby, eh?" Steve questioned. "What kind of stupid name is that?"

The two brothers chuckled.

"You might wanna stop right there," Colby said as he turned and looked at the two of them.

"And why might I wanna do that?" Steve answered back with a snarl.

"Look, I don't know the two of you from dirt. Whatever it is that you two and my cousins here have going on, don't involve me none, but you keep pressing me and you'll soon find out why you best stop," Colby said with sincerity.

He hated what it was he might be getting into, but there was no way he was going to sit there while someone made fun of him for no reason at all.

"I think maybe you've been riding with Travis Sweet for too long and think you are someone we ought to look out for. You are that cowboy we met earlier t'day, ain't ya?"

"I am he, but I ain't ever rode with him," Colby replied.

I dunno the two of you was pretty cozy earlier, you his old lady then?" Scott chuckled.

Colby gently slid his chair out from the table and stood up, his rifle in his hand.

"I think I'm starting to see what kind of assholes the two of you are. Don't know when to shut up, eh?"

"Oh, geez, look at that, Scott, the cowboy stood up."

Steve stepped closer. The smell of whisky on his breath told Colby that he was drunk.

Colby stared him down.

"I tell you what, the two of you go sober up, come back then and I'll dance with either one of you or one after the other, whichever you think is fair. Hell, I'll take you both on."

Scott and Steve began to laugh.

"You seriously think that you could take us both on? You don't even know who the hell we are!" Scott Tellman expressed as he stepped closer to stand by his brother.

"Right now I know the two of you are drunk and stupid 'cause you don't know who the hell I am either and that makes you *stupid*. Your brother there, the way he's slurring words makes him *drunk*. So there you have it. I know you as drunk and stupid," Colby shot back with a crooked smile.

He knew what was coming next and as Scott was about to swing at him he put the rifle barrel between his attacker's legs and sacked him. Scott fell down and rolled on the floor as Steve took a swing, Colby though simply dodged the swing and stepped aside as Steve fell forward onto his knees. He tried to stand, but Martin punched him in the side of the head as he sat there smirking. The few patrons chuckled a bit while others simply left, not wanting to be involved in what looked like was leading up to a four man, two man brawl and possible gunfight.

"You best stay down there, Steve, or I'll smack you down again. Should've took Colby's advice and stopped. Hell, we was even nice offering to buy you two a drink and you go and start this shit. Some things never change, do they, Cape?" Martin questioned as he took swig from his glass of draft.

"Nope, some things always seem to be the same no matter how much time has passed."

Cape stood up and helped Steve to his feet. Scott on the other hand was squealing on the floor clutching his balls. Colby reached down and helped him up too. The Tellman brothers were now standing, one with a black eye from where Martin had slugged him and the other with a shrivelled up ball sack. They cursed the Brubakers and stumbled out of the saloon.

"That won't be the last time we see those two," Alex pointed out with a chuckle.

It was only by coincidence that while the Tellman brothers were stepping out of the saloon, that Tyrell was stepping in and they crossed paths.

The two brothers stopped and even after taking, a beating still couldn't resist taunting Tyrell.

"Hey, now, look at this, Scott. Here is Travis Sweet," Steve slurred.

"It weren't my intent to meet up with you. Now, if you'll excuse me, I have better things to do, then stand here and listen to your garble."

Tyrell began to walk away when Steve reached for his pistol and cocked it.

"Hold it right there, Mr. Sweet."

"Jesus Christ, Steve, what the hell are you doin'?" Scott asked as he looked back in pain.

"This here is our payday, Scott."

Tyrell slowly turned and looked at him, Steve certainly had the drop on him, and he felt idiotic to have turned his back on the two of them. There they were, though, one with a pistol pointing at him, cocked and ready to fire, the other standing there, confused, and debating on what to do next. It was the Heath Roy and Ollie Johnson thing all over again and in the same damn town too...*what were the odds.*

"The two of you going make use of them six-shooters or are you going to stand there?" Tyrell questioned as he looked at them.

"The truth is Mister Sweet, Barclay Atalmore wants you alive. He has plans for you."

Tyrell chuckled and shook his head.

"Now there is a name I ain't heard in a while."

"That's right. He and the others are due release from prison. He hired us from the inside to bring your ass to Big Muddy," Steve now admitted.

"Is that right?"

"It is. Now unbuckle your gun holster and hand it to Scott."

Tyrell shook his head.

"Nope, I ain't going to hand my guns over."

He continued his stare-down with the two brothers.

"I could shoot you right here and now," Steve said as though he had the guts to do it.

"I suppose you could. But, if Atalmore wants me alive, I guess killing me ain't an option. So, what are you gonna do?"

"Go on, Scott, take his gun belt," Steve gestured to his brother. "I'll keep you covered."

"Couldn't you have picked a better moment?" Scott responded as he slowly made his way over to Tyrell.

"Nope, nothing better than the present, go on take his guns."

Steve insisted again. Scott now pulled his own gun out and pointed it at Tyrell, as he slowly reached for and pulled out the two pistols from Tyrell's holster and tossed them to the ground. He stepped back cautiously as he kicked the guns closer to where Steve stood.

"There, now you're gonna do exactly what I say Mister Sweet. Step off that boardwalk nice and slowly and make your way over here. Scott, go grab us some rope. We got a hog to tie," Steve said as Scott grabbed his rope from the saddle.

"You ain't listenin', Mister Sweet. I said step off that boardwalk and make your way over here."

"You want me come and get me," Tyrell dared, "or pull the trigger."

He still had his two shot derringer under his left shoulder and knew he'd kill at least one of them if they decided to shoot. So far, though, it seemed neither one was up for the task or for that matter even capable. They looked pretty beat up to him.

"Don't tempt me, Mister Sweet. Scott tie him up. We'll drag him off that boardwalk since he don't wanna play nice."

The saloon doors swung open and out stepped the Brubakers and Colby. They could see exactly what was going on and they stepped up next to Tyrell. The Tellman brothers, now outnumbered, looked at one another knowing what their fate would be if they continued.

"What have we here, Travis?" Colby asked as he looked over to where Scott and Steve stood.

"Seems an old friend of yours, Barclay Atalmore hired these two to bring me to Big Muddy," Tyrell responded.

"Atalmore, well holy shit, huh, ain't that something?" Colby was quite shocked.

"Hold on a second," Steve stumbled with the words. "You know Atalmore?" he questioned Colby, his pistol still cocked and pointing at Tyrell.

"I know the whole crew of the Rebel Rangers. I rode with them," Colby made clear.

"Well then, you would know that this here son-of-a-bitch Travis brought them in," Scott stated.

"He brought me in too, yet here I am standing beside him and not you."

"You're a snitch then, eh?" Steve slurred, trying to build up his courage now that he and Scott faced five men.

"That I ain't. I happen to like Travis here better than the two of you."

Colby continued to stare at the two dimwits standing there.

"I think under these circumstances that the two of you might consider riding out of here while you can."

"You say you ran with the Ranger's yet here you are standing b'side the man that brought them in and the Brubakers too. That don't seem like the Ranger way."

"I don't ride with them no more. I ride with this crew; and this is our way. I reckon we'll give you one more chance to live another day if you turn around and swing up onto your horses. Other than that, do what you can with that pistol in your hand." Colby brought his rifle up and rested the barrel over his shoulder as he and the others looked on, waiting for the Tellman brothers to saddle up and get or pull their pistol triggers.

Steve let the hammer back on his pistol and put it back into its holster.

"C'mon, Scott, let's get," he said as he and his brother swung up onto their horses. "We'll see the five of you again, rest assured," Steve said as he and his brother rode off.

"There you have it, fellows. Sounds like we might have a go around with the two of them soon," Cape said as the five of them watched the two brothers heading out of town.

"Should've finished it up right here and now," Alex said as he looked at Cape.

Tyrell by now had gathered his pistols and put them back where they belonged.

"Either of you want to fill me in on who they were? Sounds like you all have a history?" he questioned as he made his way to where the Brubakers and Colby stood. "They're the ones that you and I came across earlier today, Colby. You know them?"

"Only met them myself, a short while ago. Alex and the others though have the history, not me," Colby pointed out.

"All right so, who the hell are they?"

"The Tellman brothers, Scott and Steve, a couple of wanna be gunslingers. Neither one, though, is much good, not unless they get the drop on you," Cape answered.

"They could be trouble though," Martin added.

"Especially if they're working for Atalmore, I guess they is due to be released soon, eh, Travis?"

"You were there the day they was sentenced, Colby. They got six months. Them mentioning Big Muddy tells me, that Atalmore and the bunch might already be on their way to meet up with them, since it is only a couple weeks ride. It wouldn't make much sense for the two of them to try to bring me to meet up with Atalmore if he and the others were being released in January. They've either been released early or they bent the prison bars," Tyrell offered as a possibility.

"I'd never put it past that crew to break out of prison. Could be you is right," Colby agreed.

"You ain't thinking 'bout running with them again. Are you Colby?"

Colby was silent for a few minutes as he contemplated. There was a time that he would've ran with them again, but being with his cousins, the only family he had left, for now suited him.

"Nah, I don't think so. I don't have much use for them anymore, Alex. I'm quite content being in the presence of you lot."

"This ain't gonna turn out to be a damn tear jerker is it?" Martin teased, "I ain't drunk enough."

"Shit, tear jerker it ain't, honesty it is. I may have ran with them Rebel Rangers for the past while, but I seem to get along quite well without them. Nope, I don't think they'll see me cozying up with them no more."

"With all that has happened here now, what do the four of you say to me buying us a round of whisky?" Tyrell questioned.

He wanted to fill them in about Cross offering McCoy's a run at keeping his assets safe and to keep things on the right side of the law at Gabe Roy's persistence to steal his land.

The four cousins looked at each other and shrugged.

"Sure, you can buy us a round, but it don't mean we're, as Colby would say, getting cozy with you. A friendly drink don't hurt none."

"That is fine by me, Alex, but we might be seeing one another a lot more in the coming days and weeks," Tyrell said as he stepped up to the saloon doors and entered, followed by the Brubakers and Colby.

"What the hell do you mean about that, Travis?" Cape asked.

They made their way over to a table and sat down.

"Pete Cross wants to hire McCoy's to help keep his assets, mainly his land, from being stolen by Gabe," Travis answered as he waited for the barmaid to make her way over to them.

"What! Why the hell would Cross want you on a payroll?" Alex asked somewhat perturbed. He didn't want to work alongside the man who killed his brother or for that matter the man who had maimed his right shooting hand.

"Yeah, I'd be a bit curious to know as well," Cape added, as the barmaid finally took their order of a round of whisky.

"I ain't sure why, myself, he'd want me there, but he offered up the job and I might take it," Tyrell answered.

"I dunno... I dunno if I'd want to be working alongside you. We have a history and we ain't by any means friends," Alex said as the barmaid set down a bottle of whisky on their table and five shot glasses.

"Folks work all the time together that ain't friends, Alex," Colby pointed out as he shot back his first hit of whisky. "B'sides, having him on our side ain't a bad thing at all. He wears a badge of law."

"Since when do you care about a badge of law, you have been on the wrong side of things since you was a kid," Martin commented. He himself was indifferent. Still he wasn't sure having Travis on their side was a good idea either.

"To set the four of your minds at ease, I ain't said yes yet."

Tyrell brought his shot glass of whisky up to his lips and shot it back.

"There would certainly be a benefit to me taking on the proposition though. It'll also help with the work I've been doing to see Gabe behind bars."

"Other than that what kind of benefit would there be, if'n you took the offer? And where the hell does that leave us?" Alex wanted to know.

"I reckon that'd leave you in the same position as you is in now. Cross never said he didn't need you folk. In fact, the only reason I might accept it is the fact that I'd working with the five of you. You might not wear badges, but you ain't broken no laws either. From what I have seen, and know you all are law-abiding and I know damn well you is all-good with guns.

To be honest, no matter what any of us feel toward the other, I personally believe we'd be damn good together at protecting Cross's land against a land thief such as Gabe. You'd all be legally protected, and if I got the go ahead from Ed, I could deputize you. If it were needed, nothing permanent, but whilst we try and hold off Gabe, and protect Pete's land."

"No damn way would I wanna be a lawman," Alex said, not sure, if he meant that or not. In a sense, the work he and his late brother Earl did was no different. The exception being they didn't follow regulations, they didn't hold the documents that legal Bounty Hunters had, they were civilians. They didn't need to follow rules. They were freelancers.

Sometimes the bounties they brought in were a lot, other times it barely paid for their horses feed and upkeep. For a few moments in time, Alex thought about Earl. It was a well-known fact that if Earl Brubaker was looking for you, you were found, and if you put up a fight, you simply died. His unorthodox ways of doing business was Earl's downfall. Alex began to realise this as he sat there surrounded by his cousins and the man who had killed Earl.

The thing that ate at him most of all was the fact that he knew that Earl never made a mistake when tracking down a bounty. So how could he have slipped up so badly and come across Travis and not Tyrell? Something was missing from the puzzle and he knew it. He recalled that Earl had set off to find a man named Tyrell. He knew it was Gabe Roy, who had hired Earl, even though he had tried to convince him to turn the job down. Earl, though, was adamant that he'd find Heath Roy's killer, the man who went by the name of Tyrell, Alex recalled how the two of them had argued about it.

Everyone knew Gabe Roy and everyone knew he was a cheat, liar, killer, and thief. Alex had a bad feeling about

Earl's association with Gabe, but he couldn't convince Earl one way or the other. That was the last time he saw Earl alive. Perhaps this was the reason Alex hated Gabe Roy so much. He also hated Travis for killing Earl.

"Hey, snap out of it," Colby began as he noticed Alex drifting. "Let me answer that question you had 'bout being a lawman. You wouldn't be. You'd still be the same asshole that you are, I reckon," Colby finished with a chuckle.

The table grew silent for a short while as the men sitting around it shot back more whisky and sat in thought at what it was they might all be getting involved with. On one hand there were the Brubakers and Colby Christian, all five quite capable of protecting Pete Cross's land. On the other hand there was Tyrell Sloan, aka Travis Sweet, a full-fledge gunslinger working on the right side of the law. In all actuality, all of them together working for the same cause, would undoubtedly put a stop to Gabe Roy's bullying of an old man and possibly see Gabe Roy's rise to wealth tumble over like a brick shithouse. *It would all be good.*

It was Tyrell, whom finally broke the silence and monotony.

"The first time you and I met, Alex, you drew your gun on me, trying to avenge your brother's death. Old Ed McCoy saved your life. If he didn't have that field kit with him, you'd have bled to death. You also know a little bit about the law and I will admit you're damn quick at pulling out your pistol. I reckon it took a lot of determination to learn how to do it so quick with the left hand. You also know that on that day, I could've killed you flat out, 'cause you fired upon an officer of the law, me. I didn't kill you though, because I knew you had your reasons. I don't condemn you one damn bit. Whether we are friends or not, it would seem to me we both want to see to it that Gabe doesn't steal Cross's land. Your reasons obviously vary from mine, but that don't mean we can't work at it together."

Tyrell shot back another whisky, and then continued.

"Colby, the first time I met you was when you had your pistol pointing at me, Buck and me had convinced Atalmore that your crew was surrounded by ten men."

Tyrell half chuckled as he thought about that. Colby though didn't see the humour.

"Yeah, you bastard, you and that big fellow, Buck, said we was surrounded by ten men, when we wasn't."

Colby shook his head.

"When I think about that now, I think how stupid we must've been."

"From what I remember you didn't believe it. In fact, you were certain that we was pulling your leg, it was Atalmore, who convinced you to toss down your pistol. You and that crew could have killed us and walked away. I also remember the look in your eye as you contemplated whether you believed us or whether to shoot.

The next time I saw you, you was doing community service work, pulling up the old boardwalk outside the Snakebite Hotel. You worked damn hard too, which tells me that you have strong character. Again, whether we're friends or not, there ain't no reason we can't work together for the same cause. As for the rest of you, I know nothing at all about you 'cept you are cousins of these two yahoos."

Tyrell chuckled as he looked back to Alex and Colby. Turning his attention again to Cape and Martin, he continued.

"I'm a pretty good judge of character and I think you two and your brother, Brett, are no different than any of us sitting around this table. I'd never try to come b'tween any of you. If I took this job, I wouldn't treat anyone of you any differently than I'm treating you now and I wouldn't expect to be treated any differently myself. We'd be acquaintances working for Pete Cross. That is all it would be. Once Gabe is halted or I get him sent to jail before then, my job here will be done and I'll head back to the Fort."

With that said and one last shot of whisky, Tyrell stood up from the table and tossed down some coins to pay for the bottle they had been sharing.

"That is it for me. I'm heading across the street to my bed. I've had my fill of rot gut."

Chapter 10

He was groggy when he woke that morning. The whisky he had drunk with the Brubakers and Colby the night before had obviously been enough. He wasn't quite sick but he wasn't quite well either. His head hurt and his gut burbled every now and again as he lay there, thinking about all he had said the night before.

His mind raced with the entire events of the evening, from the confrontation with the Tellman brothers to the half-hearted meeting with the Brubakers and Colby. Nothing was a blur; it was all fresh in his mind and he wasn't disappointed at how it all turned out either.

The Brubakers and Colby knew where he stood. The Tellman brothers were a bit of a concern, but not as big a concern as the possibility that the Rebel Rangers headed by Barclay Atalmore, may have been set free, or may have broken out of prison. His biggest concern in that regard was the fact that Atalmore had hired the Tellman brothers and chances were they weren't the only ones Atalmore had hired. For now, though, he would concentrate his efforts in bringing Gabe Roy to justice as had been his efforts so far.

Swinging out of bed, he looked at himself in the mirror and splashed water on his face from the washbasin provided. Looking out his second floor window, he glanced up and down the street for no particular reason, then slid into his boots, donned his hat and headed out. Today his hope was that he'd receive a wire from Ed in response to the wire he sent the day before. Making his way to the livery stable, he saddled up his horse and whistled for Black Dog. It didn't take long for the dog to appear. He ambled over to Tyrell and sat.

Tyrell scratched him behind the ear and smiled.

"I want you to stay close to me. We're going do a lil'
bit of everything today. First off, we're going to see if
there is anything from Ed at the telegraph office. Then
we'll grab some breakfast from Emma's Eatery. From
there we'll make it known to Gabe that I'm still here in
town. That ought to take the better part of the morning,"
Tyrell inhaled deeply, "and what a nice morning it is too.
The sun is shining, the wind ain't cold, and although there
is snow here and there and especially up in the mountains,
down here in Willow Gate we're about to turn up the heat
on one Gabe Roy."

Tyrell swung up onto his horse.

"C'mon, Black Dog, we got business to attend."

Heeling his horse, he and Black Dog headed over to the
telegraph office. He wasn't surprised at all that indeed
there was a telegraph for him from Ed. Tyrell looked the
wire over and smiled. *"Yes"* is all it read. Folding the
piece of paper up, he tucked it into his shirt pocket and
questioned the telegrapher if there was a Pony Express in
the vicinity.

"Nope, there surely isn't. Over northwesterly along the
old Gold Creek wagon road, leads you over to Hefley
Creek rail station. It delivers mail from east to west, which
is the only reason I can assume you'd be looking for a
Pony Express outpost," the telegrapher replied with a
smile.

"Gold Creek Road, northwesterly from there, you say.
Would you know how far from there that'd be?"

He leaned up against the counter as the man on the
other side briefly brought a map over so that he could give
a general estimation on how far it was.

"Hmmm, looks to be near thirty miles from Gold
Creek. Just have to stick to the road; it goes straight
through to Barrier. You can't miss the station, it'll have
train cars," the man teased with humour.

Tyrell chuckled. "Imagine that a Rail Station with trains," he responded as the two of them snickered. "All right, well thank you for pointing me in the right direction. I'll be seeing you."

Tyrell tilted his hat in respect and exited into the street. Black Dog as usual, lay close to the horse, and was up and ready to move as soon as he saw Tyrell approach.

"A change of plans has come about Black Dog. We're going on a trail ride to a place called Hefley Creek. We likely won't make the distance in one day, and we'll likely have to spend a night out, but we should be back here in a couple three or four days."

He swung up onto his horse and headed back to his hotel room to gather up his gear and reports he had on Gabe. He spent a few minutes scribbling out a message to Ed. From there, Ed would work his magic and send an arresting officer from the Mounted Police station in the Fort. He even teased in the letter not to send Constable Rick Bash. He filled Ed in on the fact that the Brubakers and Colby Christian were indeed in Willow Gate and that he was likely going to be working alongside them whilst he worked for Pete Cross. He briefly explained why.

He suggested that Ed look into two names, a man named Carl and another named Smitty, both hard-hitting cow wranglers from down south, and any other names associated with them. He reminisced for a moment, as he recalled that Ed employed a man who went by the same name. He wondered if they were at all related then shrugged his shoulders, it mattered little.

Satisfied with the letter, he tucked it into one of his saddlebags along with the few reports and such and then grabbed his bedroll, his rifle, and a change of warmer clothes. Exiting his room and making his way to the street and his horse, he secured everything, then he and Black Dog headed out of town toward Gold Creek and the Hefley rail station.

They had only passed Pete Cross's place when Brett Brubaker rode up to him. Slowing his horse down he pulled him to a stop.

"Good morning." Tyrell greeted.

"Morning to you too, Travis. You leaving town?"

"That is the furthest thing from my mind. I still got business here in Willow Gate, likely going to take Mr. Cross up on his offer. I got the *okay* from the Fort this morning."

"That is good to know. Pete and I had a real good talk on how he wants things run around here and I have to agree with him, having a man like yourself 'round here as we wait on Gabe Roy to pull his shit, ain't such a bad idea. Was able to decipher a lil' bit 'bout what the boys said last night when they showed up here finally, as drunk as they were and all. When I saw you heading out of town, I wanted to simply let you know, we'll work with you, not against you."

Brett leaned forward on his saddle and looked out across the lightly snow covered land.

"Pete owns a lot of land, Travis. You know the real reason Gabe wants it?"

"Prime land would be the only thing that comes to my mind," Tyrell answered.

"That be part of the reason, but not the only reason. The other reason is that Pete found gold and lots of it. Come spring he hopes to start mining it. Gabe somehow learned this one way or the other. He knows the gold here on this land is of the purest quality, upwards of twenty-five dollars an ounce. When the time comes, the boys and I are going to head the operation."

Brett paused as he looked back to Tyrell.

"It'll be the only decent and steady work any of us have had. So, having a cowboy such as you helping us reach that goal is appreciated, leastwise by me, I want you to know that."

"Jesus, Brett I wasn't expecting spew like that from you. And I mean that in the most respectful way. It means a lot to me to hear you say that and when I get done with my current business, I'll be sure to show up at Cross's place. You can let Pete know that."

Brett nodded and turned his horse back in the direction he came.

"All right then, I'll let you get back to whatever it is you got going on t'day, it was nice having this chat Travis. I'm looking forward to working alongside you in the coming days."

"Yep, we'll be seeing you," Tyrell replied as the two men now parted ways, Brett heading back to Cross's place and Tyrell continuing toward Gold Creek.

He shook his head somewhat taken back by the brief conversation; yet at the same time relieved by Brett's words.

Working alongside the Brubakers and Colby he knew wasn't going to be all roses. Undoubtedly, they would have their disagreements and, as long as it didn't turn deadly, neither he, the Brubakers or Colby would be any worse for wear when the doors to Gabe Roy's cell or his eyelids were finally, closed.

There was still a lot of work to do and a lot of risk involved, but in the end he knew, Gabe would be dead, or in prison, and all those that schemed with him or those he had in his back pocket would also, be exposed. *It'll be a good day when that happens,* Tyrell thought as he continued.

As Brett made his way, back to Cross's place and the corral, Alex met up with him.

"What did ya do, Brett, send Travis running?"

"Nope, I invited him with open arms to come along and work for Pete."

"Why'd you do a thing like that? You know how I feel about working alongside him," Alex spit out.

"That's 'cause you ain't thinking with a clear head. Last night you were saying the opposite."

"Yeah, well last night I was half drunk; I'm sober now."

"You and I both know, that having a lil' bit of law on our side can't hurt a damn thing. Keep your mind focused on the bigger picture, not the shit that is scattering your brain. Having Travis working for Cross, in helping us rid that piece of shit Gabe of ever being able to take over Cross's land, is a big plus for all of us. He gets this land, we can forget about heading any gold mining operation and we'll be looking for work. I myself like the idea of finally having some kind of security in life. I believe that is what will come from all of this, once it is all said and done. Your feelings of disrepute toward Travis is your own issue brought on by your own hubris," Brett pointed out as cordially as possible as he walked away, not wanting to have an argument over something so trivial.

Alex leaned up against the corral fence. He knew Brett was right on both counts. It was true neither one of them had ever been offered such an opportunity as what Pete Cross had bestowed onto them. It was also true that he acted hastily when he drew his pistol on the same man who had killed Earl. He should have thought that through. Still, no matter how long ago that may have been, Alex couldn't help but feel bitter toward Travis.

"Hold up a minute," Alex began as he stepped away from the corral and walked towards him.

Brett stopped and turned. "I don't want to argue with you, Alex."

"We ain't gonna argue about a thing. You made your points and now I'll make mine. Travis Sweet killed my brother Earl. Travis Sweet maimed my good shooting hand of which I used to make a living with."

Alex inhaled deeply he was going to lay it on thick, not because he wanted to, but because he had as much right to be heard.

"Now, if the same happened to you, whether it was your hubris or a vengeful thought, how the hell would you feel if, sometime later, that very same man ended up on the same chow line as yourself? Can you answer me that?"

Alex could tell by Brett's expression that he hadn't thought about it like that. The situation was changed now. He waited now for Brett's response, which seemed long in coming.

"You know what I'd call that, Alex, 'life'. That is it. That is all that is. Could you imagine the type of men and women this world would be full of if we constantly harped on yesterday? The world would be full of people like Gabe Roy, which is a damn fine example of a man that perhaps in life somewhere along the way got dealt a shitty hand and instead of accepting that and moving past it, he turned into a son-of-a-bitch. Could be I'm wrong about that analogy, but I know you ain't stupid and that you get the gist of it."

"That is all fine and dandy what you say there, but that is an explanation, not an answer to my question," Alex tossed back.

Brett looked at Alex and shook his head.

"To be honest, I ain't got a clue on how that'd make me feel. I ain't lived it and I leave it in fate's hand's that I never do. I do know this though. I'd do whatever it took to keep on living, I'd try not to be so hateful toward my shortcomings, and most certainly, I'd learn from them. Bad luck and misery come hand in hand, as does good luck and fortune, hard work and worthiness. It all depends on the hand in life we are given and the roads we choose to get us there."

Colby who was standing at his open window in his room above where Alex and Brett were conversing had listened to most of their conversation and he finally spoke.

"Shit, Brett, what are you doing? Writing a dime store novel?" Colby firstly teased. "I've been listening to both of you for the past while and I have to say, from up here and from what I was able to make out, I'd say you is both right. Alex is right to feel as he does toward Travis, and Brett is right, that not all things are as they seem and that the roads we choose to walk in life, are the roads that lead us in that direction."

Alex and Brett were both looking up at Colby as he said all that. They weren't sure what he was going on about, but most of what he said made sense.

"Are you still drunk?" Brett asked.

"Hmmm, I ain't sure, I could be a lil' bit I guess, but that don't matter none. You two should just accept whatever facts about each other that the other don't like. Life's battles ain't won by the hesitant or the weak. Usually the man who thinks he is the toughest crawls away cowardly, whilst those who follow him continue on to finish the battle. So, pull up your undergarments ladies."

With that, Colby fell over face down onto his bed.

"Yep, he's still drunk," Alex said as the tension between him and Brett dissipated. Even drunk Colby often made one think.

"C'mon, let's go get some breakfast. I'm buying," Brett said as they made their way back to the house, their argument turned upside down by Colby.

Pete Cross was sitting at his usual spot at the table a silver coffee urn nearby.

"Good morning, Brett, Alex. Please help yourselves to coffee. Renatta has breakfast cooking."

"Thanks, Pete."

Brett poured both he and Alex a coffee and sat down at the long oak table.

"Colby and Martin came in last night with Cape and Alex."

"Yes, I know, I still have yet to meet them."

"I also ran into Travis this morning. He said McCoy's has agreed to take on a security detail for you. Travis says he'll be by later to go over the details."

Brett took a swig from his morning coffee.

"That is good news. I want you to know that your work for me is not jeopardized by this."

Pete addressed both of them.

"I still need men like you. Travis's work for me is short term, yours can be for as long as you like. I think I still have a few years left in me."

Pete chuckled.

"Besides, there will be plenty of work once spring arrives. Let's hope we get there."

"We'll make it happen, Mr. Cross, we'll get there," Alex confirmed with little doubt.

Tyrell had finally made the distance to the Gold Creek road and he looked northerly, in the direction he needed to travel. Pulling out his pocket watch, he looked at the time. It was 9:30 a.m. He had a long way to go, thirty miles minimum. There was no way they would make Hefley by day's end.

Sucking on an eyetooth he looked out across the creek to where he had met up with Crying Wolf a few days earlier, he wondered if his friend had left the area and continued on to the Athabasca territory. In a sense, he hoped that he had, and at the same time hoped that between where he was now and where he was heading that he would come across him.

"Here is where we head northwesterly, Black Dog. Thirty some odd miles up this trail is Hefley. If things go well, we should be close by the time evening rolls around.

I hope the weather don't turn. It is nice now, but that could change. C'mon, let's get."

Heeling his horse's flank, they headed in the direction he needed to go. For a couple hours, they sauntered onward. At around noon that day they met up with a group of horsemen who stopped to ask him for directions.

"Hey, mister, you know how far we is from Willow Gate, by chance?" the first rider asked as the other three pulled up next to him.

Tyrell could tell by the garb the men were wearing that they were likely hired guns and more than likely looking for Gabe Roy. Chances were that they were the first in an array of gunmen that Gabe had hired to take Pete Cross's land. It was only an assumption, but he was confident that is who they were.

"Willow Gate, you say?" he questioned as though he wasn't clear.

"That is right. We was told it is around here somewhere," the second rider pointed out.

"You ain't from around here then I take it?" he questioned.

"Nope, we surely isn't. We've been riding steady for a couple of days now."

"I hate to tell ya in that case then, but you're miles away. You'll have to keep heading west past the Gold Creek sign, down the road some. There are two roads, one heads southwest and then due west. That's the wrong way. Keep on the southwest side of things for about two days ride and you'll come across it," Tyrell lied.

The directions he had given them would see the riders end up south of Willow Gate.

"Damn. I thought we was closer than that."

"Nope, you ain't. You're about two days ride away." He repeated again.

"Huh, well, all right. Thank you for the directions, Mister."

"You bet; good luck in your travels."

Tyrell watched as the four riders continued back the way he had come.

"That ought to slow them down a bit, eh Black Dog? I reckon they is looking for Gabe Roy. Likely they is part of the crew he is summoning up to pull the heavy on Cross, leastwise I hope they is, otherwise I gave bad directions to four horsemen."

Tyrell waved his hand through the air.

"Ah, I guess it don't matter much. They'll eventually figure it out. If they are who I assume they are; it will give us a couple extra days to get settled in with the Brubakers and Colby, before Gabe can make any hasty move."

Turning his horse northwesterly once more, he travelled for another two hours. Looking at his watch, he was surprised that it was only 2:00 p.m. The sun was warm, but it was slowly creeping closer to the western horizon. Daylight hours were certainly getting shorter. The four and half hours he had been travelling already were taking their toll on him and the horse. Deciding to rest for a few minutes, he pulled his horse up to the side of the trail and tethered him to a sapling.

"We'll rest here for a bit. Inside of my damn thighs is sweating. Can only mean one thing eh Buckskin, you're likely sweating to beat hell too beneath that saddle and blanket."

Tyrell lifted up the saddle stirrup strap and checked. Sure enough, the horse was sweating. He removed the saddle and set it down on the ground.

"There, that'll let you cool down some. Don't need you getting no saddle sores," he said as if the horse understood.

They rested for a half hour give or take. The horse had stopped sweating by then and so he saddled him up again and once more headed toward his destination. So far, the only passers-by he had come across were the four riders earlier that day. He hadn't run across anyone since. It was a lonely trail; there was no doubt about that and he shouldn't have expected anything else. Early fall always saw the trails and wagon roads between towns sparsely travelled. Folks weren't inclined to do much of that. By the time the horizon to the west showed its true colours as the sun began to set, he guessed he had travelled close to fifteen maybe twenty miles.

There was no way he could make it to Hefley before the sun completely set and so he found a small clearing along the trail where others had obviously camped. He was satisfied with the journey so far as well as the distance he had managed. He could've pushed himself and the horse to go further, but he wasn't in much of a rush. The little bit of solitude and serenity was something he looked forward to. He had a lot on his mind and the peace and quiet that enveloped him always helped him think.

The solace that the small fire he had burning offered him, put a lot of what it was he was trying to accomplish into perspective. Once the documents he had tucked away in his saddlebags were on their way to the Fort and McCoy's, only one part of his job would be done. There was still likely a second and third part. It would all come together, though, or at least that was his hope. Either way, he was free from being in the company of Gabe. It was something that had sickened him from the first day he took on the job. Now he could without prejudice, or influence, see to it that, his investigation into Gabe Roy would be forthright without distraction.

For one reason or another at that particular time, there was one thing he craved, and that was a cheroot, something he hadn't craved in a long time. He wondered then if perhaps he had a pack somewhere in his gear. He dug through his saddlebags and lo and behold, he found a pack. The package itself was old and mangled and the two cigars that the package held were stale and roughed up some, bent, flattened. As stale as they were, he lit that first one and drew in a lung full of smoke.

He looked at it as the end burned orange and he smiled at his good fortune in finding a couple. It didn't matter if they weren't perfect, hell nothing in life ever was. He was simply grateful that he could satisfy the stupid craving. In a sense, it seemed to give him a feeling of utopia. Here he was, out in the middle of nowhere, surrounded by beauty and silence, and although the feeling of utopia was, generated falsely by the smoke he inhaled deeply into his lungs he felt good.

His serenity though would soon turn deadly. The Tellman brothers had circled around Willow Gate and were making their way back along the same trail to fulfill their contract in seizing Travis Sweet and forcing him back along with them to Big Muddy. It was Black Dog, who alerted Tyrell of the oncoming travellers. Tyrell sat up and listened closely. Sure enough, in the distance he could hear mumbled voices and the clip-clop of horse hooves.

"I hear it too Black Dog, you best make yourself invisible. Until we know if who is coming is the friendly sort, you need to be on guard. Go, now Black Dog! Stay alert."

Black Dog understood every word and he slipped into the undergrowth, not far from Tyrell's side.

Tyrell waited with cautious trepidation for the riders to show and he tossed a couple more pieces of wood onto the flames to bring up the light. The flames danced this way and that as the sound of voices and horses grew closer. He wasn't going jump up and hide. Hell, he had no idea who the oncoming travellers were. All he knew is that there were riders approaching. Then as though the sounds were swept from earth, a din of silence enveloped the lonely trail. Tyrell squinted into the darkness and tilted his head, confused and perhaps a bit fearful of what might be coming. He slowly rose and peered down the trail.

A distance away in what looked like to be, in the middle of the road, a small fire gently glowed. He couldn't make out if anyone was near, and beyond the flames, all he could see was darkness. He was somewhat relieved as he'd much rather face the passers-by in daylight. At least then, things would be visible. He continued observing for a short while. Obviously, whoever lit the small fire couldn't see the flames from his. It was a bit further off the trail, and blocked from view. The bit of smoke that rose to the sky was hidden by the sheer darkness of evening.

For now, he knew there would be no confrontation between himself or those close by. As long as he remained quiet and didn't feed the flames of his own fire too much, there would be no reason for any confrontation by either party. It didn't mean he wouldn't be alerted to every sound he heard, he knew damn well that he would be. In the morning, there would be no way that a confrontation wouldn't take place. Until then, though, he'd certainly keep Black Dog and his pistols close. Meandering back to his fire, he sat down and signalled to Black Dog. The less he spoke the better and he was glad the dog understood his hand signals.

"Up the trail some," he began as Black Dog silently made his approach and stood idle by to listen, "a good distance away actually there is a fire burning. You know what that means; t'night we sleep with one eye opened. Not sure, who is down there and I ain't going to march down and introduce myself. At sunrise, we won't have much of a choice though. They're coming our way and we're going theirs. An introduction isn't going to be unavoidable."

He grew silent for a moment to break up any sound of his voice that the gentle breeze may carry.

"It can be for t'night, though," Tyrell finished in a soft and hushed voice.

He smiled as Black Dog came close and lay down to his right. He would not move from that spot. Circumstantial vigilance, bravery, and ability to maim, wound, and scare off or otherwise kill was not Black Dog's second sense; it was his first. Both the man and the dog felt this way about the other and it was that uncanny relationship between man and beast that some were lucky to possess that made their relationship that much stronger. It was never taught, borrowed, or stolen it had simply always been that way between Tyrell and Black Dog. It was a godly trust and always would be.

Tyrell stared into the low flickering flames of his fire, his mind fluttering with visions and thoughts, this and that's on what morning might bring. Was he prepared to take on a couple of hoodwinks who were on the same trail and had business in Willow Gate? He had already passed what he knew to be hired guns once that day. It was likely that those down the road were of the same type. Hell, it made perfect sense. A man with money to spare could certainly put the word out that he was looking for hired guns and in only a few short days, men would come running. He was betting himself that is exactly what Gabe Roy had done.

Only thing was, in this case, Tyrell would lose the bet. Down the road were Scott and Steve Tellman who were run out of Willow Gate the night before by the Brubakers, Colby Christian, and Tyrell himself. The brothers knew him as Travis Sweet and, in fact, were in Willow Gate the night before to bring him to Big Muddy. They wanted to get the reward that Rebel Ranger commander, Barclay Atalmore, had promised if they could bring Travis Sweet to Big Muddy, hidden in the southern Rocky Mountains, before winter settled in.

Things, though, went sideways for them when the Brubakers and Colby stepped into the picture. The Tellman brothers turned heel and headed out of town. They spent the entire day circling back towards Willow Gate and were now sober. Things weren't going to be as they were with their first confrontation. Their heads were clear now and their ignorance gone. They were confident that they wouldn't slip up a second time. Confidence is short lived, though, when you are face to face with a man such as Travis Sweet.

"You figure we'll be in Willow Gate by noon 'morrow?" Scott questioned as he and his brother stirred the coals of their fire with a stick as they sat.

"We'll be close, we ain't gonna simply run in and run out with our quarry. I managed a glimpse of the room key Travis had in his shirt pocket. He's staying at the Owl's Nest, room eleven. That'd be on the second floor I reckon," Steve smiled.

"That right there is damn good information. I never once thought about that. We could disarm him and hogtie him in his room. We only need to get in."

"That is the downside, Scott. Knowing his room number might not be as significant as we'd like. Knowing where he is staying," Steve nodded and grinned, "that is the plus side. We can watch his comings and goings keep our eyes on him for a while. A day or two at most ought to give us enough time to learn his routines and, when the moment is right we take him down. Our only obstacles, of course, are the Brubakers and that cowboy Colby."

"Yeah, the Brubakers, it is hard to say where they might be at any given moment. I say we simply keep our eyes and ears opened and wait for when we are sure they isn't 'round. That ain't such a big deal," Scott shrugged there wasn't much else they could do.

"Nope, you are right there, you certainly are." Yawning, Steve stood up.

"I think that is it for me t'day, Scott. I'm heading for bed."

Rolling his bedroll out near the fire, he laid back and put his hands behind his head. Scott tossed a couple more pieces of wood on the fire and followed close behind.

Tyrell, more cautious due to the fact that he knew others were close by, didn't bother adding any more wood to his fire that evening and instead wrapped himself up in a couple of woolen blankets. In the morning when daylight came, those down the road wouldn't be alerted to any smoke rising from his fire, giving himself a bit more time before the inevitable confrontation. Closing his eyes now, he drifted in and out of sleep for the first few hours, until finally giving in wholly to his need for sleep. He woke the next morning later than he had wanted and he could smell the smoke that drifted his way from those down the trail. Black Dog, unsurprisingly, was sitting vigilantly scenting the same smells.

"I reckon we best get, Black Dog. No time for coffee or biscuits this morning."

Tyrell gathered up his gear, saddled his buckskin horse, swung up onto the saddle, inhaled deeply at what might come, and headed down the trail. Black Dog, of course, headed into the bramble and walked in the bushes as Tyrell slowly made his way toward the unavoidable confrontation.

He recognised the two men sitting around the fire from a distance.

"Shit," he mumbled beneath his breath.

It was the Tellman brothers.

Scott noticed the rider approaching and he nudged his brother. "Look at that, Steve, ain't that Travis?"

Steve looked up and smiled.

"Damn right it is!" he blurted as he stood quickly with his pistol in his hand. "How nice of you to come our way

Mister Sweet, you'll now swing off of that horse of yours nice and slow."

Tyrell got his horse to stop and he looked on.

"Nope, I don't think so."

He knew what was coming and he knew death would come to the trail that day.

"For a man that has a couple of pistols pointing at him, you sure are cocky. Now get down from that horse; we ain't going to tell you again."

"You're going to have to shoot me off this here horse or put your pistols away and I'll carry on. You decide?" Tyrell said with over bearing confidence.

He knew damn well even if the two brothers had their guns pointing at him, he'd kill them both or die trying. Either way someone was going to die.

"Jesus, can you believe this cowboy. Thinks he can pull his pistols on us before we pull our triggers and shoot him. You ain't very well-schooled, are you Travis?" Scott said as though he were daring Tyrell to reach for his guns.

Tyrell shook his head and chuckled.

"I think it's the two of you that ain't been very well schooled. So, are we going to dance, or are you going stand there and wet yourselves?"

Black Dog by now was directly behind the two brothers and if Tyrell could keep them talking a bit longer he'd make his move. He crouched down and crawled on his belly a short distance getting closer to where their horses were tethered. Unseen by the brothers he crept closer and in an agile hop and skip, he startled their horses, which ultimately made the brother's turn their heads and look. That gave Tyrell a one-second edge to pull his own pistols. Turning back to look at their quarry they were staring down the two barrels of Tyrell's .45s.

Scott and Steve dove for cover. The sound of their gunfire erupted and echoed in the early morning sun as they pulled their triggers, missing him with every shot they fired. Tyrell though didn't miss. Moments later the smell of gun smoke and blood drifted in the gentle breeze. Still sitting on his horse, he slapped his pistols back into their holsters. The Tellman brothers lay on the side of the trail. Tyrell shook his head. He hated having to do that, but it was the nature of the beast. It was synonymous to the name he held. Swinging off his horse, he walked over to where the brother's lay. Kneeling down he checked to see if either one was still alive; then, with his fingertips, closed their cold dead eyes.

As badly as he felt about the confrontation, he knew it was going to happen. He didn't blame the Tellmans; he blamed Barclay Atalmore. If Atalmore hadn't sent them, they might still be alive or in the least, he may not have been the one who killed them. With rope found on the dead brother's horses, Tyrell draped them onto their saddles and bound their hands and feet beneath the horse's bellies. Then, pulling out a pistol he fired into the dirt and watched with saddening dissatisfaction as the horses took off heading west along the trail. Black Dog traipsed over to where he stood and he sat down next to his feet.

"You did good, Black Dog; I thank you for that. I ain't too happy I had to kill those two and I feel badly that I did so. I don't s'ppose they'll be the last, though. Others will come...they always do."

He grew silent as he scratched Black Dog behind his ear. With one last look westerly, he swung back up onto his horse and continued toward Hefley, his mind not quite clear. It was a shame things had happened as they did and he had to remind himself that he had given the Tellmans the opportunity to walk away. They had chosen not to and had paid with their lives. He always felt the same every time when forced to draw his pistols. Every time he gave those drawing down on him the same opportunity to walk away or run. Nine out of ten times, though, death was the outcome. There was no reason that it would ever change as long as he was Travis Sweet.

Chapter 11

The morning of November 27, he arrived at the Hefley rail station. There was small mercantile and cafe and, of course, the rail station. That was all there was; there were no hotels or saloons.

Tyrell made his way over to an old caboose that had a sign hanging on the door that read 'Rail Station'. He tethered his buckskin horse near the only water trough he could see and removed his saddlebags, tossing them over his shoulder he entered. A handsomely rough-looking woman sat on the other side of the counter behind a weigh scale. She looked up from what she was doing and offered a smile.

"Hello, mister. The train don't come by for another couple hours. If you're a passenger, you might want to wonder over to the cafe and wait," the lady said as he approached.

"I ain't a passenger, ma'am. Only need to get some documents sent to Fort Macleod," Tyrell responded.

"Let's see what you have. The train won't be going through the Fort 'til early next week."

The lady looked at a schedule.

"Tuesday, next week to be exact, I hope there ain't nothing alive in those saddlebags," she joked.

Tyrell chuckled and shook his head. At least she was joyful.

"No ma'am, there certainly isn't."

Setting his saddlebags down on the counter he pulled out the documents and whatnot and requested an envelope.

The lady reached under the counter and handed him a fair-sized envelope.

"The envelope is three cents," she said as she set it down.

He nodded and thanked her as he picked it up and put all his documents in. Licking the seal, he scribbled out where it was going and to whom it was addressed. Handing it back to the lady, she looked at it and set it on the weigh scale.

"That is three cents for the envelope, and five cents to get it to Fort Macleod by Tuesday next week."

She stamped it and threw into the shipping basket.

Tyrell thumbed through his front pants pocket, pulled out a dime, and handed it to her. The lady was about to hand back his change of two cents, but he raised his hand.

"No need for change, ma'am."

"Suit yourself mister," the woman closed the cash register.

"Is the food next door any good?" Tyrell asked.

"That depends," the lady smiled.

"On what?"

"On what you order I suppose," the lady answered.

"Would you recommend anything in particular?"

"I'm only funning with you, mister. All the food next door is good. I'll vouch for it."

She smiled again and wrinkled up her nose.

"All right, I'll hold you to your word. It is almost noon now. Can I buy you lunch?" Tyrell offered.

"It has been a long time since any man has asked me that."

The lady was quite surprised at his invite.

"But, if you want to buy lunch, I'll certainly take you up on that and I thank you kindly."

She stepped out from behind the counter.

"My name is Ann; and you?" she asked.

"Travis. My name is Travis, ma'am, and it is I who should be thanking you for accepting my offer."

"Travis, you can call me Ann; no need for that ma'am shit," she smiled again.

"Very well, Ann it is."

Tyrell gestured toward the door and opened it for her. He certainly liked her friendliness. She looked back as she stepped out and curtsied him and he chuckled.

"That is the first time a woman has ever curtsied me."

"We're even then, because you are the first man in a long time who has offered to buy me lunch."

"Well, there you have it," Tyrell responded with a smile as the two of them walked across the street to the cafe.

"Are you from around here?" Tyrell asked as they made the distance.

"I live here now. I ain't from around here. I've only been here a few years."

"And you, do you live around here?" she asked as they sat down at one of the few tables the cafe had.

"Nope, I come from down east, the prairies, the Fort mostly."

"I'm from Ohio, down south."

"You are quite the ways from home then."

"I am, yes, but that is okay. This is my home now."

She paused for a moment as she averted her eyes toward the cafe's kitchen.

"Customers out here; hurry up, John!"

She looked back to Tyrell.

"I'm sorry about yelling in your ear. John is sometimes slow. You got to holler for him most times."

"That is all right, I ain't in much of a rush. I ain't got no particular place to be," Tyrell said as John finally came to their table.

"Afternoon, Ann, Mister. What can I get for you?" he asked.

"Coffee would be a good start," Ann replied. "You want coffee don't you, Travis?"

"That'll be a good start I reckon. What have you got for food here?"

"Sandwiches, soup, and beans, mostly. I can certainly toss together steak and potatoes too. Anything you want Mister, if I got the supplies I can make it for you."

"Steak sounds good to me. A round of steaks for me and the lady, John, if that is all right with you, Ann."

"I never turn down a steak and especially one that John here makes."

"Good enough, I'll get them grilling right after I bring you your coffees."

John turned and made his way back into his small kitchen and fetched the pot of coffee that was sitting on the stove. He grabbed a couple of clean cups and returned to Ann's table. He set the pot and cups down.

"Here you go, fresh brewed."

The two of them thanked him and nodded.

"I'll get those steaks to the two of you shortly," he said as he went back to the kitchen.

Tyrell poured a coffee for both Ann and himself. He blew gently on the cup in his hand and took a swallow. He hadn't had a coffee all day and the one he was slurping on now was exactly what he wanted. Setting his cup down, he looked around.

"Is there only you and John around here?" he asked to make conversation.

"There is a bunkhouse full of train engineers and conductors down by the river. They switch with the other engineers, operators and conductors that bring the trains here from down on the coast, so there are always folks around. There are a couple of family ranches nearby as well, but all in all, I'd say there are no more than a dozen people here in Hefley at any given time," Ann answered as she too now took a sip from her coffee.

"I was wondering why it seemed so quiet around here; not many folks living here."

"There sure isn't, but that is all right. Those of us that are here are all friendly towards one another. You can't find that in the bigger towns and certainly not in the cities."

Tyrell nodded in agreement.

"You sure got that right."

They were finishing their second coffee when John brought them their steaks. Tyrell understood now what Ann meant about the steaks John grilled.

"Damn, that is some of the best steak I've eaten, quite comparable to what the Snakebite Hotel in the Fort offers up."

"I told you so. John certainly knows how to make them," Ann said as she wiped her mouth with a napkin she pulled from her blouse.

It didn't take them long to finish their meal and for a few minutes they conversed until Ann heard the train whistle blow.

"That is my calling. Thank you very much for lunch," Ann said as Tyrell stood up and pulled her chair out for her.

"You are very welcome, Ann. It was a pleasure sitting with you."

And it truly had been. Their encounter and the few words they shared were quite uplifting for Tyrell, who was until meeting her, not feeling too good about himself due the early morning clash with the Tellman brothers. Now though he was doing okay, thanks to that unlikely brush with Ann.

"I might see you again some time."

Tyrell smiled at her as she once more curtsied, him, smiled back, and exited John's Cafe. He watched her as she pranced across the street and up the stairs to the station.

"How did your meet up with Ann go?" John asked as he came to gather the empty dishes. "Was she glad to see you?"

Tyrell looked at John somewhat confused. "What do you mean, John?" he questioned as he sat back down and poured the last of the coffee into his cup.

John had a confused look on his own face now.

"The way the two of you were carrying on, I assumed you knew who she was."

"I don't think I'm following, John," Tyrell said as he brought the cup to his lips and took a swallow.

"That was Phoebe Ann Mosey? You know, Annie Oakley."

Tyrell almost spit coffee, shocked and surprised all at once.

"You mean, *the* Annie Oakley!"

"Is there another?"

"No, sir, there certainly isn't. I'll be goddamned. I bought Annie Oakley lunch. Now that is something that don't happen every day."

John a bit puzzled was now feeling like an ass. "Maybe I shouldn't have said anything at all. Ann don't like it getting around."

"No worries, John. I ain't about to go bragging that I had lunch with Lady Oakley. No sir that is something a man keeps to himself with pride and adornment."

"I sure hope you keep your word to that. If Ann ever found out that I blabbed to a complete stranger on who she is, without you recognising her, she'd peel a strip off my hide."

Tyrell chuckled. "You can set your mind at ease. My lips are sealed. I'll always only know her as Ann, but I'll tell you this, she is every bit of class I would expect from Lady Oakley."

Finishing up with his last slurp of coffee, he pulled out his pocket watch. It was 1:15 p.m. and he had a long ride ahead. He stood up, paid John for the lunch and coffee, and then headed across the street to where he had tethered his horse. As he swung up onto the saddle, he looked one more time at Lady Oakley, surprised to see her looking back. Tilting his hat in due respect and acknowledgement, he waved and could see her smile as she waved back.

He left Hefley that day grinning from ear to ear. He was the only one he knew that had met and ate lunch with the woman legend, Annie Oakley. It was something he'd not soon forget, but he'd certainly keep it to himself. He had no problem spewing his excitement and admiration he had for Ann to his horse and Black Dog though as they ambled along their way.

"I knew there was something special 'bout her as soon as I stepped into the station house, Black Dog. I tell you, when John filled me in on whom she was, I almost fell off my chair. I couldn't believe it! No sir, stuff like that doesn't happen often, and when it does, it takes you off guard, I tell ya. Goddamn, Black Dog, I ate lunch with Lady Oakley! Can you believe that? And we even shared a smile or two. I'll never forget this day for two reasons now. It sure brings a happy ending to how it started out."

Back at Cross's place, the Brubakers and Colby were playing a friendly game of five card stud. They had spent the majority of the day working on fences and scouting Cross's land for any incoming unwanted visitors. *Unfortunately,* none had shown up and the day had been rather boring for them as they hammered fencing staples and stretched wire. All four had been itching for some action, but none came. Now they sat at the big oak table. Pete Cross was snoring nearby in his lounge chair and Renatta was banging pots and pans in the kitchen. Lunch had already, been served and she was preparing for supper. It was Martin's turn to deal so he shuffled the cards and dealt the hands.

They were about to get their first card draw, when they heard the neighing of a horse. It seemed distant so they continued with the card game at hand. Then they heard it again, this time closer. Brett stood up and went to the door to see what all the commotion was. He was surprised to see two horses, without riders, but as he looked closer, he could see that there were men draped over the saddles.

"Hey, fellas we got a couple horses up yon with what looks like men draped across the saddles. We best go have a look. C'mon," Brett called as he stepped out onto the front stoop.

The others stood up and met him outside. He pointed up the road.

"It could be an ambush, I ain't sure. I don't see no one else around except them horses. I still don't like it," he pointed out.

"Where is that damn spotting glass of yours," Martin asked, "we might get a better inclination on what the hell it is all about."

"It's in my saddlebag. I'll grab it; you keep your eyes peeled."

Brett went back inside and came back a few minutes later. He brought the glass up to his eye and peered through it to where the two horses seemed to have settled. Indeed, there were men draped over the saddles. He couldn't tell if they were alive, nor could he see anyone else nearby.

"I can see that there are a couple men tied to them. Can't tell if they is alive or not, I don't see no one else around."

He brought the glass away from his eye and handed it off for the others to see.

"Shit, I don't know, Brett. Those fellas look like Scott and Steve. I don't like this one damn bit. It'd be like them two to pull a stunt like this. They don't seem to be moving, though. Hard to say from here if they is pulling shit or dead," Alex said as he handed the glass off to the next in line.

The horses now moved closer and the little bit of sunlight that still lit the sky gave Colby a better view.

"I don't know what you guys ain't seeing, but if that is Scott and Steve, I can assure you they is dead."

"How the hell can you tell?"

"Stains on their backsides and blood soaked shirts. That is what I see."

He handed the glass back over to Brett who took a second look.

"Uh-huh, yep, I can see that now. Should we go gather them or what? They ain't quite on Cross's land and we ain't by any means obligated."

"Jesus, what the hell is a matter with you? Damn right, we have to go and get them. I'd like to be sure they is the Tellman brothers," Martin blurted out.

He shook his head as he swung up onto his already saddled horse and sped off. The others shrugged their shoulders. It didn't take Martin long to make the distance and as he approached he could tell that indeed it was Scott and Steve Tellman. He swung off his horse, and looked back toward Cross's place, where he knew the others were watching him through the glass. He nodded his head confirming that it was the Tellman brothers.

"Well Martin confirmed it. It is the Tellmans," Brett said as he continued watching while Martin grabbed the horses by the reins and began to lead them back to the house.

"Shit, he's bringing them back. You know what that means?"

"Yeah, Martin gets to dig the hole," Alex chuckled.

By now, Martin had made the distance back and in tow with him were the Tellman brothers.

"Martin, what are we supposed to do with them?" Colby asked unenthused.

"I don't reckon we'll be giving them a funeral, but a couple words never hurt. B'sides, their horses ain't branded and there ain't nothing wrong adding a few extra head to the ones Cross already has," Martin answered back.

"What about the bodies, Martin? What are we supposed to do with them?" Cape questioned.

"We bury them. There ain't a soul within five hundred miles in either direction that will ever miss this lot. Their gear we can toss right into the hole with them."

Alex rolled his eyes and shook his head.

"You do know that the ground is likely froze, right?"

Martin stirred uncomfortably in his saddle and looked back at the brothers.

"Huh! I never quite thought it through, I guess."

"Nope, I don't figure you did; and how many years of schooling did you have, Martin?" Cape teased.

"Eight, which is six more years than you. I take it that none of you is gonna give me a hand in throwing dirt on these two?"

"You brought them here, you dig the hole."

"Yeah, I figured as much," Martin sighed.

"I tell ya what, we'll watch and help you toss them in, but we ain't digging."

"Thank you very much, Colby," Martin replied as he rolled his eyes.

"Ah, it is my pleasure, Martin."

A couple hours later, with a hole big enough for two bodies dug into the cold earth somewhere on Pete Cross's land, the Brubakers and Colby tossed the Tellman brothers in. Even though, none of them had reason to be saddened. There was nothing like dirt being tossed onto a grave that made one think.

"I wonder what took place to see these two dead," Martin was solemn when he said that as he continued to toss dirt onto the grave.

"Eight years of grade school and you can't figure that out? C'mon Martin, I'd put money on Travis that did this to them. I reckon he came across them or they him and the rest is history," Colby said right off the bat.

"There ain't no knowing either way 'less Travis says so. All we really know is that we've seen the last of Scott and Steve. And that don't hurt my feelings one damn bit," Cape pointed out.

"You know what Cape you can be pretty cold sometimes."

"It ain't summer and it ain't spring that is for sure, so yeah, I'm a bit cold. Hurry the hell up with that dirt tossing, Martin. I got a winning hand in that card game we got going."

"Christ, you ain't won a hand in ten rounds already," Alex replied with a chuckle.

"I've been letting you win. You are all damn cry-babies when you lose."

Colby shook his head and chuckled. "I can't believe were standing around the grave of your dear friends the Tellman brothers, talking about cards. Ain't anyone of you gonna say a prayer or two?"

"We was all kind of hoping you'd do that," Alex said with sarcasm.

"Sure, I ain't got a problem doing that. You almost finished Martin?" Colby asked.

"Almost, give me a minute."

"That is fine, take your time. We wouldn't want you hurting yourself."

Finally, Martin tossed the last bit of dirt onto the grave.

"There, all done. Damn, that wasn't easy."

He wiped his brow as Colby stepped forward.

"All right, let me say my piece." He looked down at the mound of dirt. "Rest in Peace you sons-of-bitches. There, all done, now let's get back to that card game."

Colby swung onto his horse and waited for the others to follow suit.

"Think we ought to let old man Cross know that we've buried a couple of hoodwinks in his back forty?" Cape asked as he climbed onto his horse.

"Nah, no point in saying anything to anybody, no one needs to know as far as I'm concerned."

Brett mounted his horse.

"Like Martin said, there ain't a bloody soul within five hundred miles or more that'll ever miss them two. B'sides the only ones that know they're dead is the killer and us. Strange though, how they did end up here, that right there is something. The Tellman brothers, not killed by us, but buried by us. I wonder what the odds were."

"Not very damn likely I would guess," Cape shook his head.

So it was settled, they'd leave it at that. In time, maybe they would learn who the killer was. Until then, it mattered little and none of them really cared. The Tellman brothers would have simply disappeared.

They made their way back to the house and turned their horses loose in the corral, then headed inside to finish their card game.

Making the distance back to where he had camped the night before with some hours of daylight left, Tyrell continued west until the sun cast eastern shadows, and the western horizon turned to crimson.

"All right, let's stop here for the night."

Pulling his horse to a stop, he swung off the saddle.

"We'll get an early start come morning and be back at the Owls Nest before noon tomorrow."

Removing his saddle and gear from his horse, he laid it on the ground. It seemed colder that evening than the previous one and he slipped on another jacket before he gathered wood and lit his evening fire. Setting his coffee pot down to brew, he opened a can of beans. Not bothering with a pot, he set the opened can on the fire and stirred the beans slowly.

His mind drifted as he looked into the flames. It was hard for him to believe that earlier that day he met Ann Oakley. He had only ever seen black and white photos and sketches of her and, as he thought about it, she didn't look anything like what the photos and sketches depicted. In the flesh, she was ruggedly beautiful, and robust. Her personality was jovial. The Ann Oakley portrayed in the newsprint was nothing like the Ann he had met. He wondered then why she would slip into anonymity. He shrugged as he thought about that. Perhaps her reasons weren't any different than his.

The beans now cooked, he sat back on his saddle that was near the flames and ate what he could. What was left in the can after he was done, he scooped onto the ground and let Black Dog finish. He was too lazy to gather a plate and the last time he had let Black Dog eat out of the can, the dog had slit his tongue on the serrated edge of the opened can. So, the ground would do. Black Dog didn't complain. After tossing more wood on the fire and pouring his second cup of coffee, a few flakes of November snow danced to- and- fro in the icy breeze that gently blew, rustling the dead leaves of birch and poplar while pine tree branches brushed against each other. Tyrell pulled his jacket collar up around his neck and tucked in his chin.

"I knew this was coming," he said quietly to himself as much as to Black Dog and the horse. "Sure hope it don't accumulate. I'm far from being ready for winter. I still have lots of work to do in regard to this, that and the other thing," he sighed as he paused. "Soon, it'll be over... everything that puts me here will meet its end."

Averting his eyes to the darkness that was always beyond a fire, he thought about the Tellman brothers. He had to clear his head on how their deaths came about, but not the reasons behind them.

The worst part was that deep down he knew others under Barclay Atalmore's command were very likely on the prowl for Travis Sweet and the Rebel Rangers themselves were out to seek revenge. That was what the entire story of the Tellman meeting and their deaths told him. Barclay Atalmore was behind it all. He inhaled deeply then looked back to the flames of his fire. He was relieved that there were no witnesses to the brother's deaths. No witnesses meant that not even Atalmore knew where Travis Sweet was and no one could say without his admittance, that it was he, who killed them. Secrets, though, don't always hide guilt.

He had no idea that the dead men's horses had ended up at Pete Cross's front door and that the Brubakers and Colby were the ones to find them. The odds of that happening were slim there were so many other places, that the horses could have gone. Both parties involved were guilty of one thing or the other. Tyrell killed them the Brubakers and Colby Christian buried them, and neither reported their actions to local authorities, which was law.

The two conundrums could in time clash. For now though, not the Brubakers or Colby, were going to say a thing about burying the Tellmans and Tyrell's lips wouldn't mutter that he was the one that killed them. Some things in life are simply better left alone. *It was what it was*, for now at least.

Suddenly and surprisingly, all at once, since Black Dog did not alert him, he heard a voice.

"A man huddled near a fire with a dog tells me one thing."

Then there was silence.

Tyrell stood quickly and looked around. The voice was familiar and he smiled when out of the shadows stepped Crying Wolf.

"You got to quit sneaking up on me like that, Crying Wolf. You might get lead in you," Tyrell chuckled. "Come, my friend sit down at my fire," he invited the brave.

"Yes. I will," Crying Wolf slowly approached. "What can this mean, you way out here and me coming to sit by your fire?"

"Coincidence, I reckon. Can't be nothing else, this isn't any dreamland." Tyrell replied, as Crying Wolf slid off the horse he was riding and tethered him next to Tyrell's.

"Travis, it is good to see you."

"I'm quite pleased to see you too, Crying Wolf. Can I offer you any food, I have beans and such."

"I am not hungry, but I did smell coffee."

"Yes, by all means."

Tyrell grabbed the pot and fumbled through his gear for an extra cup. Pouring Crying Wolf a coffee, he handed it to him along with an old tin that held sugar.

"Thank you," Crying Wolf said as he took both items, adding sugar to his coffee.

He handed the sugar tin back and Tyrell set it on the ground next to him. Crying Wolf gently blew on the tin cup in his hand and eagerly took a sip. He looked over to Tyrell, and squinted.

"The voices I have heard on the winds that have come and gone since we last sat together, tell me that Travis Sweet no longer works for the filth of a man named Gabe Roy."

Crying Wolf took another drink from the cup in his hand, as he waited for a response. Tyrell shook his head and while looking into the fire, he chuckled.

"It almost sounds like you knew that was going to happen."

Crying Wolf smiled, "I am not a shaman or a magician, but I have been told by the lives and faces of many what is good and what isn't. I knew you would not accept that man's ideals." He pointed at Tyrell and moved his finger from left to right, "the two of you could not have coexisted with the other for long." Crying Wolf grew silent for a moment as he contemplated. "Does this now mean I can kill him?" he asked.

Tyrell drew in a deep breath, not sure, how he should answer. He went with the usual spew, trying to convince Crying Wolf that by killing Gabe Roy in cold blood was nothing more than murder. Any unprovoked killing of any man, woman or child in the white man's world was exactly that, murder.

"Ahh, I see. If he is provoked, I could kill him and the white man would not be so quick to judge the killer."

"No, that isn't what I'm saying, Crying Wolf. For a white man perhaps, but as I told you before, the world we live in t'day would hang an Indian, whether he was the friendly sort or not, quicker than any white man. You must understand that. Even between treaties, government deals, the whole works, the white man's world has many grudges and not all of them have any bearing to truth. Most of it is prejudice. I know that and so do others, but not all of us. In fact, we'd be the few."

"Yes, I know. It is a sad world isn't it?" Crying Wolf questioned. "It is sad because what you say the white man feels towards us is what we feel toward the white man. There does not seem to be an in between, except for the odd meeting of, as you say; the few. You and I together are the few."

"You're right, I couldn't be sitting here with just any brave, and you couldn't be sitting here with just any white man, but that tells us, Crying Wolf, that there is hope, that one day, we can all quit with the shit and live our lives together."

The two men chuckled. It was true, perhaps one day it would be like that. For now, though it wasn't, and the *few* had to live with it.

"Let us talk of other things now," Crying Wolf suggested.

"Yeah, I'd agree." Tyrell looked over to Crying Wolf's horse. "Here is what I'd like to talk about, Crying Wolf. That horse you have there that you stole from me or traded with me some time ago, belongs to Brady McCoy. He lent it to me." Tyrell smirked, "Now he's going be quite upset at me if I don't have his horse when I make my way back to the Fort. So, rather than stealing that buckskin I'm riding in the morning, how about we do a fair trade. You take that buckskin of mine and I'll take back that buckskin of Brady's."

Crying Wolf looked at the horses. "I don't know if I like that one of yours. He looks ill."

"The hell he does. He's a mighty fine horse. I paid one hundred dollars for him. Do you know who I bought him from?"

"I hear certain things in the wind, but I don't hear where you buy horses," Crying Wolf smiled.

"I'll tell you then. That first horse you stole, the red dun, was Colby Christian's horse. You took it from him when you did the old *grabahorseshoot* some months ago east of here and west of the Fort."

Crying Wolf looked at Tyrell. "Ah, yes. That was due to necessity." He threw his hands in the air. "I had no horse then."

"I reckon that'd be the only reason why you'd pull that old trick. I'm glad it worked for you. It slowed down a handful of what could have been trouble for Brady, but that is another story. There is more to what I'm telling ya though and it is kind of funny." He paused for a moment. "Would you like another coffee? Whilst I continue?" Tyrell offered.

"Yes, I like coffee when tales around a fire are told."

"When you took Brady's horse and left that red dun, I didn't know whose horse it was, until recently."

Tyrell poured each of them a coffee and handed Crying Wolf back his cup.

"It was recognised by Alex Brubaker who happens to be Colby's cousin. I told him how it was I ended up with that horse. Ain't quite sure he believed me. Anyway, he took the horse back at gunpoint and made me take off my boots."

Crying Wolf was looking at him oddly. "Why did he take your boots?"

"I guess he wasn't impressed about the tale on how I ended up with that red dun. I had to walk all the way back to where I was staying at one of Gabe Roy's shacks, with no damn boots and no horse either."

Crying Wolf began to laugh he was amused by the story. His laughter as infectious as it were spread to Tyrell who then also began to laugh. Indeed, it was a funny tale and that was only half of it, there was more.

"So there is Travis, walking with no boots and the red dun, back where it belongs," Crying Wolf said between gasps of air and his laughter.

Tyrell nodded his head as his laughter petered out and he looked into the flames of the fire. He half smirked the more he thought about it all. It was a pretty strange and humorous tale.

"In a roundabout way, I s'ppose, but that is only part of the story. That buckskin I'm riding now is the second horse since then. The first one after that was one of Gabe's and it wasn't a very good horse. Then Gabe took that one away and made me walk from his ranch house outside of Willow Gate to the hotel where I'm staying. Here is where it gets interesting. I get my gear stowed away in my room and not but a few minutes later."

Tyrell paused to take a breath and then continued.

"Someone is knocking at my door. Turns out to be Colby Christian, he's made his way to Willow Gate after all this time, since the other four cowboys he was riding with had found their horses and three of them had already been in Willow Gate for a while. The five of them were short one horse, after that *grabahorseshoot* trick, so Colby doubles back with that cousin of his, Martin, to buy a horse from the Fort.

He does and eventually he and Martin make their way west to Willow Gate to meet up with the other three cousins they was riding with. He's at my door curious to know if I had seen them, I tell him I had and where he can find them."

Tyrell averted his eyes to Crying Wolf who it would seem had lost interest in the rest of the tale.

"Are you listening to me, Crying Wolf?"

"At first yes, but now I wonder. The beginning part was interesting, but now, hmmm..."

Crying Wolf brought the coffee cup in his hands to his lips and took a swallow.

"What do you mean? Shit, this here tale I'm telling you, Crying Wolf, brings me to the reasons I want Brady's horse back and want to make a trade," Tyrell said in an almost bruised voice.

"I see, okay, carry on. I will listen, but I still won't make a trade," Crying Wolf pointed out.

"Well then, forget it. I don't want to tell ya no more." Tyrell shook his head and smiled. "Let's talk about something else. You got any suggestions, Crying Wolf?"

"Let's go back to how odd it is that here you are and here I am again. I was not looking for you. Were you perhaps looking for me?" Crying Wolf asked.

"Nope, not at all I had to make a run to Hefley rail station to have some stuff sent to McCoy's. It is only by coincidence that here we sit and I am glad that we are, but I think here is where we'll part ways for the time being. Come dawn, I'm heading back into Willow Gate. I still have business there," Tyrell answered. "Yourself, what about you, Crying Wolf, where do you venture to from here?"

"The snows will soon come to stay, for now though they come and go. I too will do the same. I am not needed anywhere yet and I too have unfinished business."

Tyrell knew what his unfinished business was and since there was nothing he cared to do about it, there wasn't any reason for him to repeat what he had earlier told Crying Wolf. It was clear to him there were no preventable measures that he could take or for that matter wanted to take. All the documents he had accumulated regarding Gabe were no longer in his possession and he no longer was responsible for Gabe Roy's safety. For the remainder of the evening the two friends talked with poetic wit and shared stories of times gone past. Eventually, adding more wood to the fire for the final time that evening, Tyrell and Crying Wolf laid out their bedrolls and were lulled to sleep by the soft crackle of the burning wood and flames that warmed them as they slept.

Chapter 12

Tyrell rose the next morning long before a rooster's crow and ever so silently slipped his saddle onto Brady's buckskin horse, then he pulled out the receipt for the horse he was leaving behind and set it on a piece of wood, with a rock on top. Smiling with delight, he headed west. Crying Wolf, who had heard Tyrell rise that morning, watched him with one eye open and softly chuckled to himself as he watched Tyrell trying to be stealthy.

"I knew he was going to do that. It is better than trading," Crying Wolf said beneath his breath as Tyrell faded into the early dawn.

Before noon that Saturday, Tyrell was pulling up to the Owls Nest. Tethering Brady's horse, he grabbed his gear and made his way up the stairs to his room. The maid had been by, and his room was tidy with fresh sheets, and a clean pitcher of water. He poured some into the basin and washed his face. Looking in the mirror he realised he needed a bath and shave, and while he was at it he would get some clothes laundered. Then he'd head over to Cross's place to begin the next chapter in the fall of Gabe Roy.

While he was gathering up some dirty laundry, a note was slipped under his door. He opened the door to see who had slipped it under, but the hallway was clear. He opened the note and read it with intrigue. It was a wire sent from McCoy's. An escaped prisoner known as the Apache Kid had been spotted in and around the Fort. He had been stealing cattle along with a couple of other renegade Apaches. The reward for him was five thousand dollars.

The story had always been that, in October of 1889 after being sentenced to seven years in prison, he and a few other Apaches had escaped while being transported to

Yuma Territorial Prison and had been on the run ever since. They were now in the Canadians and a threat to all.

He was unsure why Ed would send him the telegram. How could he help? He was in Willow Gate. He tucked the note in his pocket, and made his way to the front desk. He requested a bath and was been told by the clerk that it would be ready within the hour. The handful of dirty laundry that he had, he dropped off at the hotel laundry and could pick it up by day's end. With some time to spare before having his bath, he entered the saloon and ordered some food and coffee. It didn't take long to be served and when he was done with his hotcakes and coffee, he returned to his room.

Only minutes later, the hotel clerk informed him that his bath was ready. With soap in hand and his razor, he slipped into the warm welcoming sudsy water. It felt good to clean the filth and sweat off his body and it felt even better to draw his razor across his whiskered face. Clean now, he dried off and slipped into some cleaner clothes, then made his way outside to where his horse was tethered. From there he headed over to Pete Cross's ranch. Making the distance a short while later, he met up with Colby and the others as they sat on the front stoop.

"Hello there, how are you all t'day?" he asked as he slipped off his saddle and tethered his horse.

"That ain't the horse I sold you," Colby noted.

"Nope, it ain't. I sold him to an old codger in Hefley. I was running low on funds and needed some riding cash, sold him for the same as I bought him. Then I bought this one for fifty dollars, so I gained back fifty dollars," Tyrell fibbed.

He didn't have the time to explain that it was Brady's horse, and that he had recovered it, from Crying Wolf, nor did it matter, he was just glad that he had got it back.

Pete Cross by now stepped out onto the porch as well, and greeted Tyrell.

"Mr. Sweet, it is with great pleasure that you are here. Come in and let's have a talk," Pete gestured to Tyrell.

"Thank you, and please you only need to address me as Travis," Tyrell said as he made his way up the stairs and into the old ranch house.

He followed Pete into the dining room and to the big oak table. Pulling out a chair, Pete sat down and gestured for Tyrell to take up a spot. Sitting, Tyrell removed his hat and set it on the floor next to his chair.

"Would you like a coffee?" Pete asked as he poured himself one.

"Yes, please. Thank you, Mr. Cross."

Pete smiled and poured him a coffee, then handed it to him. Tyrell took it and set it down in front of him.

"Brett tells me that, McCoy's has agreed to protect my assets and assist me in stopping Gabe Roy's ruthless attempt to try to muscle me into selling my land?"

"Yes, sir," Tyrell said as he brought the cup of coffee to his lips and took a slurp.

"The boys," he began referring to the Brubakers and Colby, "are all good boys but they aren't so inclined to abide by the law. Having you here may influence them otherwise," Pete chuckled.

"They'd have the right to defend your assets as long as they weren't the aggressors. They'd have every right to kill anyone who came down your road shooting. I hope it doesn't come to that, but I know what Gabe is capable of and I know he has sent for some hired guns. The Brubakers and Colby are all good with their guns; you may have been okay with them alone, but I want to sink Gabe Roy as much as the next man, and I have a feeling he isn't going to stop until he has your land, or he is dead or sent to prison, either outcome would suffice, I s'ppose. Having him tried by a judge feels better to me."

Tyrell took another sip from his coffee.

"The problem with that is that the law here in Willow Gate is on his payroll, which as you know, makes things problematic in getting him to trial. I have sent a request back to the Fort to have one of the lawmen from down that way to assist in seeing to it that Gabe does face a judge. That though, may be long in coming and until then you have my undivided support in protecting what is yours." Tyrell made clear.

"I am relieved to hear that. You are, of course going to stay here in one of the empty rooms upstairs, yes?" Pete asked with hope.

"If there is an extra room to take, I certainly wouldn't turn it down. I hope you like dogs because I have one, he's my companion, and if he can't stay, then nor will I. We'll stay at the Owls Nest."

"No, no, your dog is as welcome here as you are. He can even stay in your room if you like."

Tyrell chuckled. "That'd be up to him I s'ppose. He'll likely stay in the barn, he's not so inclined to be indoors much. B'sides, with him out and about, he'll always alert me of oncoming trouble."

The two men continued to converse, discussing strategies, and fees until their coffees were finished.

"I'm glad we had this talk Mr. Cross. I thank you for the coffee and I'll see you later."

"Yes, I'll have Renatta prepare your room," Pete said as he and Tyrell stood up from the table.

Tyrell donned his hat, nodded to Pete, and made his way outside.

The Brubakers and Colby were being acquainted with Black Dog and were throwing a stick for him to fetch.

"You all settled up there with Cross?" Brett asked as Tyrell approached them.

"Am too. I look forward to working alongside you all. We have some time to work things out between us and how we're going to face what is coming."

Tyrell swung up onto his horse, "You coming Black Dog, or are you content?" Black Dog looked up to him and darted to his side. "All right fellas I'll be seeing you later, got to gather my things from the hotel. We'll be back later t'day." With that, Tyrell and Black Dog headed back into town.

"I guess that is it then. Travis will be working here for the next while," Alex said with little enthusiasm, as the five of them watched him heading back into town.

"There ain't nothing wrong with that at all. An extra shooter for when the shit comes and one that is on the right side of the law only benefits us," Colby pointed out.

"Colby is right," Brett added.

"You two sure about that," Alex wondered.

"There ain't no reason to not be sure, I reckon. He's working with us for the same cause, and that is to protect Cross's land and Cross himself. I see nothing wrong with that," Martin said as he leaned up against the corral fence.

"Ah, Alex is sore at the fact he gets to work with him," Colby said with a smile.

"I'll tell you one thing, Colby, and the rest of you too. I won't be his puppet," Alex made clear.

"Puppet? None of us is going to be his puppet. Like, he told us in the saloon the other night, he ain't going to treat any of us differently than the way we treat him. He ain't our master; I will agree with that."

Colby nodded his head.

"I think we would all agree upon that, Cape. We do our job and he does his. It ain't any more complicated than that and trying to make it so is damn foolish. I for one am honored to be working alongside him."

"Honored? Why the hell would you be honored?" Alex asked repugnantly.

"He ain't the only one. I feel damn honored too. A man such as Travis, and what we know about him, and what we've been told about him... he is a man that deserves respect. There ain't no point in beating your head against the wall with what he has done to you and of course, Earl. As you know Alex there are very few folk that I respect and Travis, well, he's one of the ones I respect."

"You can respect him all you want, Martin. I always have a lump in my throat when I hear his name and working with him don't make that lump any smaller."

"I think we can all relate to that, but don't let it fog your mind. We all need to have clear heads when it comes down to the punch."

"I know, Brett. And my head will be clear when that time comes. For now, well let's say I ain't honored to be working with him. I'll only be doing that out of necessity."

"That is good enough for me," Cape said as he too now leaned up against the corral fence with Martin.

Colby and Brett nodded. "I think all of us would agree with that."

"Good, as long as you all understand it, that I ain't going to be no puppet and that I'll be doing my job as well as the rest of you. That is all I want you to be clear on."

"Yep, we is," Colby said with understanding and confirmation.

Their conversation now changed to better things as they went about their day.

At 2:00 p.m., Tyrell returned and settled in. The Brubakers and Colby were still out fixing fences and after finding out from Cross where they might be, Tyrell headed out to give his helping hands to the five of them.

They saw him from a distance riding toward them and they stopped working while he approached.

"Howdy. You need an extra pair of hands?" he asked as he got his horse to stop.

"What, you're gonna work in mending fences with us?" Alex asked.

"Why wouldn't I? I ain't no different than the rest of you. If Cross needs fences fixed, then we fix them," he said as he swung off his horse.

"Wasn't sure this'd be the type of work you'd be inclined to do while you are working for old Cross."

"I'm a hired man, not different than yourself, Alex. I don't need no special treatment. If stretching fence wire is a job needing done, then let's get it done."

Alex half chuckled and nodded his head.

"All right, we ain't gonna turn down no extra pair of hands. There is a lot of wire needing stretching. We need to get all the way up to there," Alex pointed.

"That is quite the distance, ain't it?" Tyrell responded with good vibes.

"It sure is. A few more days work, I reckon, before we make the distance. Then we move on to the barn and corral. Lots of work there needs doing too."

Alex turned back to the work at hand and the six men worked side by each until dusk. Finishing up, they gathered their tools and headed back to the house.

Gabe Roy had heard the news that Tyrell was working for Cross, and he wasn't at all impressed.

"So, what you're telling me Donavan is that son-of-a-bitch is now cozying up to Cross and the crew that is working for him?"

"That is right. That makes six men protecting Cross and his land and one that is on the right side of the law," Donavan repeated.

"Not the law that I own. Is there any garbage we can get on them sons-of-bitches that could get them out of the way? I don't care what kind of dirt you can dig up, Donavan, but Jesus, dig something up."

Gabe poured himself a brandy and shot it back.

"I should have expected that from Travis, but I don't care when we strike and believe me we will. The law here in Willow Gate will see it my way."

Gabe poured another brandy.

"Now go on, Donavan, bring me back dirt on those trying to defy me. I have a crew of men on the way, and I have paid them handsomely. They should be here by mid-week, so you have until then to find something out about those working for Cross."

Donavan nodded and exited Gabe's office.

Gabe, now alone, sat down at his desk with the bottle of brandy and a single glass. He was distraught and as mad as hell about the entire situation. He needed Cross's land for his own purposes and all the gold on it to make himself even richer. That was the thing about Gabe. He was greedy and was never satisfied with what it was he already had. He was always wanting more and always getting it. Getting Cross's land would be no different. Perhaps he should have thought about that, but greed is blind, and Gabe was blinded by it.

Chapter 13

Tyrell woke at dawn ready to face the day he made his way downstairs to the dining room. The others were sitting around the table slurping coffee and waiting for their eggs and toast.

"Good morning. I trust you slept well?" Pete asked as Tyrell pulled up a chair at the table.

"I did so. That mattress must be made from down, softest bed I've slept on for as long as I remember."

He looked at the others sitting at the table.

"What are we going to get up to t'day?" he asked as he poured himself a coffee and took a swallow as he waited for a response.

"We don't do anything on Sunday. We rest today and tomorrow pick up where we left off yesterday," Colby said as he too took a slurp from his own coffee.

"I see. Can I, by chance, have one or two of you to ride the range with me? I'd like to know how far Mr. Cross's land stretches and the fences that need mending."

"I don't mind showing you around, Travis."

Brett was the first to reply.

"The others, though, you can't count on them to do anything today. They'll sit around and swill coffee. They might step outside."

"That's okay. If you know the land, you can show me around. No need to impose on the others rest."

"I take my Sundays seriously, Brett. We put in six days of work a week and we go from sun-up to sundown most times. I don't wanna sit on a horse for two hours 'cause you know that is how long it'll take to show Travis around. I'm glad you volunteered," Cape smiled.

"I don't like not having something to do. Sitting around is boring."

"It might be, but Sunday is a day to reflect," Cape added.

"It sure is, uh-huh," Brett rolled his eyes and shook his head. "One can always reflect by doing one thing or the other. They'd don't have to sit idle."

"That is all right. If that is what they choose to do, it is fine by me, Brett," Tyrell said as Renatta hollered from the kitchen that breakfast was ready.

Martin stood up and went to retrieve the eggs, toast, and fried potatoes that Renatta had cooked. He brought it all back on a couple of platters and set it down on the table.

"Dig in, boys. Renatta made us a big breakfast today and damn it looks and smells good," Martin said as he slapped some eggs and fried potatoes onto his plate. When his plate was full, he dug in. "Yep, she out done herself again. Damn, she's a fine cook." Martin scooped up another fork full and brought it to his mouth as the others grabbed their servings.

It didn't take long before they were all mopping up the yolks on their plates with some freshly baked and toasted bread. Finishing their meals, they slid their plates to the sides and drank more coffee. Morning was burning up as they all continued to converse. Laughing, chuckling and, of course what is never missed they argued some. It was around 9:00 a.m. when they all helped with the cleanup, bringing their dishes and cups to the kitchen and getting a list of things Renatta needed from the cellar. She didn't care who brought her the things and she didn't care who helped peel the vegetables, but somebody was going to.

Of course, they argued whose turn it was to help her out, and all except Martin, agreed that it was Martin's turn.

"No, it ain't. I helped her earlier this morning, even brought the damn food to you to all. No sir, it ain't my turn. I say Colby does it. He ain't helped her yet and has been here as long as me."

Colby shrugged his shoulders.

"Sure I don't mind, no problem, but Martin, I think it is your turn to clean the barn."

Renatta jumped into the conversation.

"I don't care which, but if no one does it, then no food today."

She put her hands on her hips waiting almost daring someone to chime in. None did of course, and they decided that the three of them left behind would all chip in while Brett showed Tyrell around.

"Well now, that is settled. Travis, you wanna head out?" Brett asked.

"It is as good a time as any I s'ppose. Sure, take me on the tour."

A few minutes later with their horses saddled, Tyrell and Brett headed out into Cross's land. They started the tour at the creek that ran through the property. It was frozen around the edges, but, it still rolled by.

"Cross says this creek never freezes over because it runs too fast. It is here where we get our water and I think Willow Gate too, but I ain't sure. He says the creek is full of trout but I ain't saw a one. He also says the area we're standing on is a gold mine. It is this area that, he wants to start mining come spring. It makes sense I s'ppose. The water is fast and there does seem to be a lot of black dirt." Brett shrugged, "I ain't never worked at mining, none of us has, but Cross knows all about it. Says it straightforward. You dig dirt you clean dirt, and so on."

Tyrell nodded as he remembered how he had spent the first and last summer in Red Rock doing exactly what Brett was describing.

"I've done a little bit of panning and I can tell you it can consume you and drive you mad all at the same time. Do you know if Cross is going to bring in equipment?"

"Yeah, he mentioned a few different pieces of equipment, rocker boxes and a mule driven rock and dirt cleaner or something like that. I guess if me and the others are still here come spring, we'll learn the trade. He's talking about bringing in cattle too. He used to have quite the cattle operation I guess. Claims he got too old to keep up with it. It is easy to tell he ain't kept up with it, with the way all the fences and barn seem to have almost fallen down.

There is a lot of work to do now, due to neglect. It would have likely been less if Cross had kept things maintained. So, maybe he did become too old. It didn't help, though, when those he had working for him took employment elsewhere after Gabe came to Willow Gate and started chasing folks off and buying up the land. Old Pete though, he ain't ever going to leave here. He is as willing and quite capable to defend his land with his life, like the rest of us are. He loves it too much to have a bastard chase him off," Brett explained, referring to Gabe Roy.

The two of them, gazed up and down the creek as Brett continued to talk.

"He's got big plans, Travis, and has sited us at the helm of it all. Like I told you the other day, this could be a good beginning for me and the others. I ain't so sure Colby has taken an interest. The others, though, are all for it. Colby might change his mind, but I don't count on it. He's always been the one to take to adventure, I guess. Doesn't like staying in one place for long, but, that is Colby," Brett said as he now looked south up into the mountains.

"We can follow this creek right up into those mountains and still never find where it is coming from. I don't even think Cross knows off hand."

Turning their horses, they continued with their ride, stopping on occasion to chitchat and for Brett to point things out. It took more than two hours to show Tyrell the lay of the land and all its abundant splendors, but he knew it now. He knew the strengths and weaknesses of the boundaries. The fences, he knew, once repaired with barbed wire, would slow a herd of galloping horsemen hell bent on bringing harm to Pete Cross and his land, but it wouldn't stop those on foot trying to do the same. His request that day to have a tour of the land wasn't only for his benefit. The more he knew about it the better security he could provide Pete Cross.

They ended the tour a good distance away from where the Brubakers and Colby buried the Tellman brothers.

"And up over yon... a short distance away is much of the same as you see here, bramble, and whatnot. Not much point in going that way; maybe in the spring," Brett pointed out as they stopped.

Tyrell wasn't stupid though and he could sense a bit of evasiveness in Brett's voice. He simply noted the spot maybe he'd go that way some other time.

"All right, so have we about seen it all?" Tyrell questioned.

Brett nodded his head. "Yeah, that about covers it all it ain't by any means small. There is a lot of land here," he inhaled nervously another thing Tyrell was quick to notice, "Some as you can tell is well forested so logs could even be found, but mostly it is flat with pasture. Old Cross could farm wheat if he wanted to. He's got it all," Brett finished as he heeled his horse's flank followed closely by Tyrell.

"I thank you for showing me all this. I can see now why Gabe would want it. As you say, it has everything. It is indeed a damn fine piece of land, a lot of potential to do a lot from cattle rearing to gold digging, logging, and plain old farming grains," Tyrell mentioned as he caught up and they continued on.

"No problem. It was nice to get out for a casual ride; only wish it weren't so damn nip. I think we're gonna get a lot of snow soon. I hope like hell we get the fencing done. Working indoors on the barn when thing's is cold and the snow deep won't be so bad; that is, of course, if everything is still standing," Brett responded.

"What do you mean still standing?" Tyrell questioned.

"With the shit that is going on between Gabe and Cross, who is to say what might come of it when it happens? I know this much for certain we'll all be going down fighting if we go down at all. It will be one hell of a blood bath for one side," Brett assured.

The two riders grew silent for a few minutes. The only sound heard was the echoing of their horse's hooves as they sauntered on. By all accounts, Brett was right. There was going to be a hell of a gunfight when the time came. There was no *'if'*. It was coming and Gabe Roy would be the driving force.

"The other day after we talked, four riders stopped me up the trail some asking for directions to Willow Gate. They came across to me as hired guns. I told them they needed to head south for two days." Tyrell chuckled, "I reckon by now they're likely heading back this way. So, that is four men I can say might very well be on Gabe's hired list. That means more might be on their way.

I don't know how long it is going to take him to gather all those men he said he was going to get, but I would put money on it that it ain't going to happen for some time. The weather is changing and as you said earlier, the snow is going to fly soon. That might be our salvation. In the meantime, we're going to have to keep our eyes and ears open and make note of who we see coming and going. We learn that and we can stay one-step ahead. And one-step ahead is better than two steps behind," Tyrell pointed out.

"That it is indeed," Brett, concurred.

They continued talking about other things as they rode the last mile back to the house. Setting their horses loose in the corral, Tyrell noticed what looked like the horses that the Tellman brothers had been riding. Not completely sure, though, he wasn't about to ask and instead for now would pay no heed to the new horses in the corral.

"I guess we can go sit now, maybe have a coffee. The others, I reckon, are either snoozing or playing cards," Brett said as he and Tyrell walked toward the house. The sound of riders on the top road caught their attention and they slowed to have a look. There were two riders trotting toward Willow Gate and followed by them was a wagon and a couple more riders.

"Hmmm, what you make of that?" Brett asked as they continued to look.

"Hard to say from this distance, I saw a couple horse riders and the wagon. Could be nothing, could be something. Maybe later we should take a ride into Willow Gate and do some looking."

"We could do that, might even be able to get the others, to tag along."

"Someone should be staying here with Pete. You stayed that last time, so maybe it's your turn to go into town this time," Tyrell smiled.

"Good point, so you and I will go; maybe Colby or one of the others."

"Sounds good to me," Tyrell responded as they went inside.

It was quiet in the house except for the low voices of Cape and Colby who were sitting at the table. Martin was somehow conned into peeling potatoes and was in the kitchen with Renatta. Alex and Pete were sitting in the front room, talking between themselves.

"Did Brett give you a good tour?" Pete asked as he and Brett walked in.

"Sure did. Quite a lot of land you have here, Mr. Cross. I can understand now why Gabe wants it. I'd say your land has more potential than what Gabe currently has. Yours is prime land, his not so much," Tyrell said as he removed his hat and sat down in one of the big high-back chairs next to Pete.

"Yeah, but the upkeep of it all certainly isn't an old man's game. That is why I'm glad to have found Alex, Brett and the others. They're hard workers. They've been fixing fences and slashing brush since the first day I hired them."

"I won't deny there isn't a lot of work to do around here, and having young men like them helping out, I'm sure it won't be no time before it'll all be fixed up," Tyrell replied as the lunch triangle was rung.

"I think Renatta has lunch ready now, shall we." Pete gestured toward the dining room as he rose from his chair. "Come on, men, I'm sure we could all use a bite to eat. Renatta doesn't make big lunches on Sunday, but certainly spoils us at dinner."

The four of them made their way to the table and sat down. Martin, Cape, and Colby we're already putting their sandwiches together. A plate of ham and roast beef sat in the middle of the table and a pot of beans and beside all of that were two loaves of bread. There were pickles in a bowl and a dozen or so boiled eggs. The silver coffee urn as always had fresh coffee in it and some cream and sugar were in two small bowls with spoons.

"That all looks mighty tasty, I must say," Tyrell said as he cut two slices of bread and stacked it with the meat and pickle. He grabbed a couple of cold, hardboiled eggs and peeled them, then slopped a ladle of beans into a bowl. The others did the same, and soon they were all enjoying their lunch and talking among themselves.

"Cross sure has some nice land, eh Travis?" Alex asked as he poured a coffee to wash down his first sandwich.

Tyrell waited until he finished chewing.

"He sure does. There is a lot of potential to it."

Tyrell carried on with his sandwich and beans. Thirty minutes later they were all slurping coffee letting their food digest.

"Brett and I are going to head into town a little later. Any of you want to tag along?"

"What the hell are you going there for?" Colby asked as he picked his teeth with the fork.

Tyrell told the tale about the four riders, the two riders, and one wagon he and Brett had seen earlier.

"I guess then that is a plausible reason. Maybe they is part of Gabe's crew. Sure, I'll tag along," Colby said as he put the fork down on the plate. "The others I reckon ought to stay here though in case something is up. Three here and three out there, that makes sense," Colby said, "b'sides I did find it boring sitting here t'day. I should've tagged along when you rode the land."

"All right, so you, Brett, and I will go have a look later on before dusk. I ain't so inclined to head off yet. I have to let the old stomach digest that food, eggs, and beans. Riding a horse after that too soon might mean trouble." Tyrell smiled as he poured another coffee.

The others chuckled they knew exactly what he meant.

"I tell you though it was a damn fine lunch. A man could get used to that in a quick hurry." Tyrell took another swallow from the cup in his hand. He looked at Pete and smiled. "And you say Renatta spoils us at dinner."

"She sure does, Sundays especially. Four course meals followed by pies and whatnots. In late winter we'll be seeing a lot of soups and stews."

"How long has she been working for you, Pete, if I ain't prying?" Tyrell asked out of curiosity.

"A long time, she was the second cook I hired when I was running cattle and had a cattle crew working here. I saw no reason to terminate her after the last man rode out. She has kept me company for many years Travis. She was young when she first started. It was even before Gabe moved this way; a year or two before then I'd guess."

"How long has Gabe been here, I always thought he'd been here forever?"

"Oh, I'd say Gabe bought that house of his back in the mid-1880's, then started building his hotels and buying all the land he laid his eyes on. I don't know why he wanted it all," Pete waved his hand through the air. "It wasn't any of my business until he started throwing hints at me that he wanted my land next. He's been trying get his hands on it for three or four years now."

Pete brought his coffee to his lips and took a slurp.

"He'll never get it though as long as I'm alive. I'd rather give it away then sell it to him," he said with sincerity.

"I bought this land as a young man and cleared most of it alone. Built this house with my own hands and started cattle rearing shortly thereafter. Then I got old, Gabe moved to Willow Gate, ran off my workers, and well, the rest is history."

"No wife or kids, Pete?"

"None that I know of," Pete said cheekily with a smile. "I never found the time to settle down, was too busy keeping busy. I do regret not taking a bride, but a man's needs and desires, can always be bought with a couple of dollars. Kids, though, I often wondered about what it would've been like to have some." Pete grew silent as he thought about that. "I think I would've liked to have had kids, but, could never really find the right woman to help me with that." Pete sighed, "When my time comes and it will 'cause it always does, I'll leave all this to someone, probably Renatta."

Tyrell smiled and nodded. "I'm sure she'd like that."

"I think she deserves it. She's had to put up with this old man for a long time as I said. At present I can't think of anyone else more deserving."

It was left at that, and a short while later, Tyrell, Brett, and Colby headed into Willow Gate. They pulled up their horses to the Owl's Nest Hotel and entered the saloon. There were a few familiar faces, but the place was certainly not humming with patrons. Sitting at a table, they ordered a jug of draft beer. The saloon was quiet and when their draft came, they poured themselves a glass and conversed. Tyrell reached into his vest pocket, pulled out his last cheroot, and lit it with the candle that sat in the middle of the table. He inhaled a lung full of smoke and exhaled.

"I don't see anyone I don't recognise. We should've headed over to the Gold Nugget instead. That'd be where anyone looking for or working with Gabe would be."

"Could be that is true, but we're here now. Got a half jug of draft to finish, who knows, maybe someone will come in before we finish. If not, we could always go have a look in the Nugget before we head back," Brett pointed out as they continued with their drink.

"I s'ppose you is right. B'sides, I like this place more than I like the Nugget," Colby said as he looked around.

"Me too," added Tyrell as he finished his first glass of draft and poured a second.

"When did you start smoking, by the way? I ain't saw you light up b'fore?"

"Back when I first started working for McCoy's. A bounty we had brought in, hung himself on my shift. Drove me to smoke, I guess. I gave it up for a while and only found this pack the other day among all my gear. Was having a craving out on the trail; were only two in it."

Tyrell looked at the cheroot between his fingers. "I might have to pick up another pack, though. I have kind of missed it."

"How long did you go without?" Colby asked.

"Months I reckon."

"Well then, you couldn't have missed it that much."

"No, probably not," he looked again at the cheroot. "There is something about having a cigar when you're out on the trail and sitting around a fire, I s'ppose... or sitting in a saloon." Tyrell shrugged. It was what it was. He really had no idea why he wanted it, but he did, and so he'd have it.

The barmaid came by and asked if they wanted a refill.

"Nah, we really ain't looking at getting drunk," Tyrell said with a smile as he looked at her.

"If you fellows decide, just give me a shout," she said as she traipsed off.

"You bet we will, thanks," Tyrell said behind her.

Finishing up with the last of their draft, they stood up and exited into the cool late afternoon. Across the street they now noticed that tethered to the horse rail were three unfamiliar horses.

"Looks like the Nugget has got some business, should we wonder over?" Tyrell questioned.

"Might as well. We might get a look at who is there. I don't see Gabe's horse, though," Brett pointed out.

"Nope. I don't see that mare he rides either. It don't mean he won't be there soon. C'mon, let's go have a quick shot of whisky," Tyrell said as the three of them headed across the street to the Gold Nugget.

Tyrell, Brett, and Colby pulled up to an empty table and sat. They looked around at the men and women, noting that most of them they had seen in and around Willow Gate, except for the three strangers. They were new. Dressed in hired gun garb and sporting shiny six-shooters around their waists.

Tyrell nodded. "I'd say those three are hired guns," he said softly as to not bring attention to himself and the two men sitting with him.

"I wouldn't disagree. They got the guns and look to be gunmen," Brett said as the barmaid came by to take their order. They ordered another jug of draft deciding to stay away from the whisky for now.

"I haven't seen you in here in a while, Travis. I heard that you and Gabe had a falling out of sorts," she said as she looked at him.

"I s'ppose it was that, yep, a falling out," Tyrell smiled.

"You must be crazy then coming in here."

"Why is that? Ain't this a public saloon?" Colby asked.

"It is and I don't have a problem with you men being here. Gabe though, well, he might. So it is a jug of draft, right?" she said as to change the subject.

"Yes ma'am, and three glasses," Tyrell replied.

"I'll get it for you right away."

She pranced off, returning only a few minutes later she set the jug down and the three glasses.

"Those three over there," she said in a soft voice, "they're here waiting for Gabe."

"Uh-huh, so, Gabe is going to be showing up soon."

"I suppose. If he sees you here, Travis, he's going to make a stink."

"That is fine. There ain't no law that says I can't be here, he can make as much stink as he wants. I don't care none." Tyrell waved his hand through the air.

"I don't want you fellows breaking up my bar any."

"No worries, Chalice. We ain't here to start no rumble. Only want to drink our draft and we'll be gone," Tyrell confirmed.

"Drink it fast then, because Gabe will be here soon," Chalice, said as she turned and made her way back to the counter bar and began cleaning glasses.

"So, as we suspected, them three is here for Gabe?"

"I think we already knew that, Colby. They are hired gunmen as sure as the day is light. I know they ain't the four I sent south, so that makes seven men we can assume are to be working for Gabe. Not sure when the other four will get here, but, they will," Tyrell filled his beer glass again and took a long swallow.

"We should take them three out to the woodshed and dust 'em," Colby half-joked.

"We can't do that. Remember, to be within the law we can't be the aggressors. They start something with us, though, and we'll defend ourselves."

"Well then let's get 'em to start somethin'."

"Once Gabe gets here and he sees I'm here, he may very well get them to try something. Until then, though, we're simply patrons drinking draft, so drink up."

By the time they had finished their jug of draft, Gabe still hadn't showed up so they left and headed back to Cross's place, with the knowledge that three gunmen were indeed in Willow Gate, waiting on Gabe.

Finally making their way back, they turned their horses loose in the corral and headed inside. Dinner was still a few hours away and the others were lounging around.

"You find anything out?" Cape asked as they sat down.

"There were three gunslingers waiting on Gabe. They weren't the four I sent south, which means them four ain't made it to Willow Gate yet. Still, we can assume that Gabe has hired seven men so far, a far cry I know from the twenty he claimed he could round up," Tyrell commented as he removed his hat.

"We should bring the fight to them, rather than wait. We take out those three and all of a sudden, Gabe ain't so powerful no more," Alex pointed out.

"I'll tell you the same thing I told Colby earlier. We can't be the aggressors if we want to be protected by the law. They have to make the first move."

"Why don't we then make them make their move?"

"Nope, I don't think that'd be any wiser. We wait, Alex. That is all we can do, for now at least."

"So, we know there are three gunmen sitting in Willow Gate hired by Gabe to bring a fight to us and we can't do a damn thing about it until they all come galloping down Cross's road? That don't make a lick of sense whatsoever to me," Alex said with disappointment.

"I agree with Alex," Colby started. "If we know what is coming, and we know who is behind it, why the hell can't we stop it b'fore it happens?"

"Sounds to me like the two of you simply have itchy trigger fingers. Whether we know, what is going on or not, those men and Gabe haven't done a damn thing yet. They are innocent of any crimes right now. We can't go to Willow Gate on assumptions that those men are here to cause Cross harm. We'd be found guilty of one thing or the other, right quick and even more so here in Willow Gate, since we all know Gabe owns the law around here. We have to wait for them to make their move. Then we have the right to protect what is Cross's. Until then, starting any shit at all simply won't fly," Tyrell made clear.

"I s'ppose you is right, but I don't like it one damn bit."

"I don't reckon any of us do, Alex, but it is what it is and until Gabe and his horsemen come stomping down that road there ain't a damn thing we can do about the gunmen sitting in Willow Gate," Tyrell responded.

And so it was left at that.

For the rest of the day, the Brubakers, Colby, Tyrell, and Pete talked about better things. When dinner was finished and their evening coffee served, they sat at the big oak table and conversed about this, that, and the other thing, sometimes nothing at all. Then, one by one, they retreated to their rooms.

Chapter 14

On Wednesday, Tyrell went alone into Willow Gate to see if anything from Ed had been wired to him regarding the information he had sent via rail. Sure enough, there was a telegram for him. The information had made its destination, and the Mounted Police of the Fort had gone through it all and as requested by Tyrell they were sending two redcoats to arrest Gabe Roy and to take over the Willow Gate Mounted Police detachment.

Two of the best, it read, were being sent. On the list was Special Constable Rick Bash's name as well as Lieutenant Bob Cannon's and tagging along with them would be Riley Scott. They had already left east for Calgary and would be arriving at the Hefley rail station the following week, and from there make their way to Willow Gate.

Tyrell was unsure why Riley Scott was tagging along. It didn't make much sense. Riley wasn't a redcoat. There had to be a reason, though, and not until the three of them made the distance to Willow Gate would he know. Somewhat curious on what it all meant, he was satisfied and comforted in knowing. Swinging onto his horse he headed back to Cross's place and the days that lay ahead. Although help in the form of Bash, Cannon, and Riley Scott was on the way, the work in protecting Pete Cross and his land from Gabe Roy was far from over.

Pulling his horse up to the corral, he turned him loose and walked to the house. Meeting up with the others in the front foyer, he told them the news.

"Bash, Cannon, and brainwashing Riley Scott, now those are three names I was hoping I'd never hear again," Alex said with disdain.

"Any lawman that is on the right side of the law is better than the two-faced law we have here in Willow Gate working for Gabe," Brett pointed out.

"I dunno, I think it is all right that them three is coming here. They can wash the Willow Gate law up and having Riley here ain't a bad thing either, Alex. He could certainly be a plus in our pockets," Colby said as he stood up from the stool he was sitting on and donned his hat.

"Anyway, whatever Bash and Cannon can do about Gabe Roy, if he ain't dead by the time they get here, is better than what the current law can and will do. So, I ain't going to take issue with it at all. Right now, though, we have more wood to chop for winter and fences that need attention. C'mon, let's get at it," Colby said as he stepped outside.

Since he was the first to get going with the day's chores, he took up the axe and started chopping wood. The others could deal with the fences. Today he was going to swing the axe and splitting maul until his hands blistered and his shoulders ached.

By Friday, Tyrell, along with the Brubakers and Colby Christian had managed to repair all the dilapidated fences and had gathered and chopped enough wood they needed to get through the winter. They were moving onto the barn next. They spent Saturday cleaning the old barn and making minor repairs to it so that it could, at least withstand the winter snows that now began to fall.

"I knew this shit was going to come sooner than later. Damn, I hate snow," Tyrell said as he and the others took a break and looked out the big open barn door.

"It keeps coming down like it is now, by 'morrow we'll have a foot of it. Sure glad we got the fencing and wood gathering done when we did," Colby mentioned as he leaned against the door frame and continued his gaze of the field of white that now covered what was once fall brown.

It was Martin, who noted Black Dog barking up a storm and he looked in the direction the dog was barking.

"Hey, look alive, we got riders comin' down Cross's road. They is movin' fast too."

The others moved quickly to where they could see and sure enough, there were riders approaching.

"Gabe Roy ain't with them. What the hell do you s'ppose that means, Travis?"

"I ain't sure Colby, but we best make an appearance." Tyrell said as they all now stepped out of the barn and made their way closer to the house.

"Them riders don't look like they're here for pleasantries," Alex said as they made their way to the front of the house and took up positions.

The riders slowed to a halt and looked at the men standing on the porch. The first rider gave a hand signal and the men riding with him pulled up their rifles and pistols and pointed them at those on Cross's front stoop. The Brubakers, Colby, and Tyrell pulled their weapons at the same time and were pointing them right back at those on horses. The day was going to turn bloody if things didn't turn around.

"State your business," Tyrell said as he pulled the hammer back on his pistol.

"You must be Travis, the leader of this group of amateurs."

The man chuckled, as though it were the funniest thing he had seen.

"As you can see, we have you out numbered. We have eight men and you have six. Now toss them weapons down," the first rider demanded.

"No sir, we ain't gonna do that. What is your purpose for being here?" Tyrell responded.

"We're here on behalf of Gabe Roy, to seize this land. It is in arrears of payments."

"Bullshit, to that," Colby said. "This land is clear and free and belongs to Pete Cross."

"Old man Cross might have implied that to you all, but he ain't paid this land off yet. Now, we're going to take it by force if the six of you don't toss down them weapons."

"Already told you once that ain't gonna happen, so turn your steeds around and hightail it back to where you came from," Tyrell once more made clear.

Instantly all hell broke loose, as Pete Cross fired at the riders from an upstairs window, knocking one rider clean off his horse. The others remained on their saddles and tried to shoot back, but their horses in a panic reared up making any clean shots impossible. Gunfire now erupted all around. Bullets ripped into the house as wood splinters fell to the ground. More shots in quick succession came from upstairs and another man fell hard and fast from his horse as his limp and bloodied body crumbled to the ground.

Tyrell and the others darted for cover in all different directions, finding cover behind whatever they could. Spotting one of the men, Tyrell brought his pistol up and planted a lead pill into the man's chest. The man stumbled backward and with a quivering hand, his pistol moving to-and- fro, fired aimlessly into the air as he fell to his death. The surviving riders jumped from their saddles and found cover themselves. Martin watched one man ducking behind a shrub of trees and with instinctual precision shot the man in the throat, severing his spinal cord. Reloading quickly he brought his rifle up once more and picked off another man who was trying to swing back onto a horse.

The remaining riders knowing that they were over gunned by those who were once on the porch and who now had found cover, and whoever it was shooting at them from inside the house, grabbed their horse's reins and swung up onto their saddles, firing at whatever they thought to be those firing at them. One of the bullets ripped into Colby. He slumped to the ground for a quick second and then grimacing in pain, he rose and looked in the direction he knew the bullet had come from.

He could see that the remaining riders had turned their steeds and were heading back the way they came. Raising his rifle, he knocked one of the three off his horse, as his bullet passed through the back of the man's skull. Only two out of the eight managed an escape. The peacefulness of the day had been broke by the sounds of gunfire and the freshly fallen virgin snow was now crimson with the blood of six dead or dying men.

"Anyone hit?" Tyrell hollered as he peeked his head above a stack of wood, making sure that it was all clear.

"One is... yep, think I've been hit in the gut, goddamn son-of-a-bitch..." Colby yelled back before he faded into darkness. Alex and Brett ran to where he lay, followed closely by the others. His shirt and jacket were soaked in blood and he was still spewing it out. Tyrell quickly ripped Colby's shirt opened to see where he had been hit and he shook his head. It didn't look good. Alex brought his ear to Colby's face and he listened for any sign of life. It seemed like forever and then he heard it. Colby was alive.

"He's alive, he's alive! Let's get him inside," Alex said with haste as he and the others picked him up gently and carried him inside. They laid him down on the big oak table and looked at his wounds. Renatta quickly brought a washbasin and cloths. They tried to staunch the flow of blood as best they could. Pete by now was standing over Colby, his field kit in his hand.

"He is lucky, it passed through, he'll live," Pete said with conviction. "We need to get this bleeding stopped though. He's losing a lot and fast."

Pete reached into his field kit and brought out his stitching needle. The others stepped back and watched Pete go to work.

"You sure he's gonna be okay?" Martin asked with dire concern.

"If I can get this bleeding to stop, he'll have a chance. Now enough, no more talking!" Pete said as he went to work using all the surgical skills he had. The others watched in awe as the bleeding slowed to a trickle.

"We need to get him over now, so I can mend the exit wound," he said as the others rolled Colby onto his side. "There, there, right there. Yes, I can get it from here."

It took a few minutes longer due to the exit wound's torn and tattered flesh. Finishing, Pete looked at the wound and wiped it clean.

"There, I think that has got it. Let's get him propped up on his side, so I can bandage him up."

Stepping back, he wiped his brow as the others put pillows and blankets under Colby's side so that he wouldn't roll over onto his back while Pete bandaged him up.

It didn't take long before Colby was breathing normal and not the laboured breaths he had been taking. Still unconscious but safe to be moved, the Brubakers and Tyrell carried him up the stairs and laid him down on his bed. Renatta was already there and ready to keep monitoring him, a washbasin, clean bandages, and cloths within a hands reach. She sat in a chair next to the bed.

"It is best we let him rest now," Renatta said. "I will stay and keep the wounds clean."

The others nodded, relieved that Colby would be looked after and that he would survive. Following one another back down the stairs, they exited outside and looked at the bodies of six dead men.

"What the hell are we supposed to do with these pieces of shit?" Alex asked as he kicked one of the dead.

"By law they need to be brought into the Mounties, identified and buried," Tyrell said as he looked around at the bodies scattering the ground. "You can bet that the Willow Gate law is going to come down hard on us."

Tyrell inhaled deeply.

"We have one chance to avoid that fiasco and one chance only."

"What might that be Travis?" Brett asked as he looked into Tyrell's eyes.

"We don't take them to Willow Gate. We take them to Hefley, which is a two day ride. Granted their bodies may stink by then, but that is our best bet. We could get lucky enough that Cannon and Bash would be close to Hefley by then. We turn the bodies over to them."

"How likely do you think it'll be that we'll make that distance without being tracked down by the Willow Gate law? Hell we'd be leading six horses with dead bodies draped over them. Now that don't look at all as suspicious now does it?" Alex questioned and pointed out with sarcasm.

"I think I have the answer to that. We turn their horses loose and load up the dead into a wagon. We'll send two riders. Two riders and a wagon is less likely to look suspicious," Martin responded.

"Except for the heap of dead in the back," Alex pointed out.

"Shit, that is easy enough to conceal, Alex. We'll throw some loose hay over them."

"That is what I was scheming," Tyrell said as he knelt next to the dead man they were hovering over. He looked through the man's pockets searching for some identification and finding none, moved onto the next. Out of the six dead, he found only two pieces of ID.

"Who we have here is one Ted Mackenzie and one Jeremiah Neufeld."

Tyrell shook his head.

"Ain't never heard of them. We can assume though Gabe knows them. The others, well, they're John Does. I'll keep these ID's for now." Tyrell put the ID's in his pocket.

"Let's get the wagon loaded and gear packed for a two day ride. We'll decide who goes once that is done," Tyrell said as they went about the task of hitching up the wagon.

That done they loaded up the dead, tossed some loose hay overtop, and gathered enough gear for two riders to head for Hefley. It took less than an hour to finish the disguise and by then they knew that it would only be a matter of time, before the law, or more riders showed up.

They decided that Tyrell, being on the law side of things would be staying behind along with Cape, Martin, and the recovering Colby. Alex and Brett would head to Hefley. Tyrell told them how to get there and what to expect when they got there. Once there, if they didn't come across Bash, Cannon or Riley, that they'd hold up somewhere and wait. It was anyone's guess now on how any of it was going to play out.

"I guess we're set then," Brett said as he and Alex swung up onto the wagon.

"You got ammo and weapons?" Cape asked as he stood near the wagon.

"Yeah, we is pretty much loaded for bear. Got enough fire power to take down anyone who wants to stop us, I reckon."

"Let's hope like hell it don't come down to that. One good thing is if the snow keeps falling, our tracks is going to be buried. There's less chance of being tailed then, I figure," Alex said as he snapped the reins and the wagon creaked on up the road.

"Keep your eyes peeled! We'll try to slow down anyone that suspects what it is we're doing," Tyrell yelled after them.

"We will, Travis," Brett yelled back as he and Alex continued onward.

"You think this is going to work, Travis?" Cape asked as they watched Brett and Alex now turn the wagon in the direction of Hefley.

"As long as they get a few hours ahead of anyone that might be on their way here, I think it will."

"And if not?" Martin questioned.

"If not, then I guess we'll have another mess to clean up. The way the snow is falling right now is going to make it tough for anyone to follow them. Even the bloodstained snow where the bodies fell will soon be covered. I reckon this snow fall is a godsend."

For a few minutes, the three men stood in silence as they watched the wagon vanish from sight.

"All right, they're onto the trail now. I say we fortify as much of the house and barn that we can. If there are more men saddling up right now in Willow Gate and are going to make another run at us, we best be ready," Tyrell said as they turned heel and gathered up what they could to fortify the house. Next, they moved on to the barn and fortified it as much as humanly possible with bales of hay. Any protection against ripping bullets was better than none. It took the rest of the day to secure it all. Once done, they stowed weapons and ammo at every fortification point.

As the last bit of daylight faded into dusk, the three of them along with Pete and Renatta remained on high alert. Black Dog too was vigilant, making his rounds between the barn and house. Tyrell knew that he would be the first to alert them if he heard the voices of men and the hooves of horses coming from a distance. It was possible that any other attack, if one was coming, would come at night. They waited, taking turns sleeping and going between the barn and house. As a new dawn came, they let their guard down enough to enjoy some food and coffee.

"Damn, that was a long night. Sure glad it stayed calm," Cape said as he poured himself a coffee.

"We was ready though," Martin responded as he took a swig from his coffee. "I checked in on Colby earlier. He's talking a little bit now. Wanted to be armed so I gave him his rifle and a six-shooter. He's happy about that. I think he's going to be okay," Martin smiled.

"I am sure Colby will be fine. He was lucky that the bullet didn't hit anything I couldn't fix."

"Where did you learn all that stuff, Pete?" Tyrell asked out of curiosity.

Pete inhaled deeply as though it was something he'd rather not talk about.

"During the Indian wars, I was a medical officer for a horse cavalry that was sent into the Indian territory. I saw a lot of death, wounded, and the like. I sewed together more men than a tree has apples and helped bury as many too." Pete grew silent as he reminisced about that time. It was long ago, but it still haunted him, all that death, and blood.

Noting he had hit a soft spot, Tyrell quickly made it a point to apologise.

"Ah, no worries Travis, it was a long time ago. Every now and again, I'm often reminded of that time. This time was no different."

Alex and Brett, who had spent an unpleasant night sleeping under the stars, were beginning to come to life. Brett tossed some wood onto their fire and brought the flames up. To the east, a pallid yellow sun was rising and the morning air was frigid. The sky was clear and the snow had stopped, but it had laid down enough over the course of the evening that any tracks they left behind were long buried by at least six inches of fresh snow. Brett rubbed his hands above the flames and warmed them.

"It was damn chilled last night weren't it?"

"Only after the snow stopped, I couldn't sleep worth shit. Mind is boggled about Colby gettin' shot and all. Think he'll be okay, Brett?"

"You was there when Pete stitched him up."

Brett stood up now, feeling distraught too.

"I sure as hell hope he's gonna be okay. Things wouldn't be the same without that son-of-a-bitch here on earth."

"You're right there, they wouldn't be."

Alex looked westerly, back the way they had come.

"Travis says two days ride to Hefley. It means we'll be spending another night out."

"We could probably do the distance in less time, if we ride from now until we get there, right through the day and into night."

"That don't make any sense, Brett. We don't know the trail. It's hard to see a trail at night when you don't know where it is."

"We light the wagon lanterns when it gets dark. The snow will brighten things up enough that we should be able to stay on the trail. Shit, it is a wagon trail after all, Alex."

"I s'ppose that is one option," Alex replied.

"What do you mean one option? It is the only option if we want to make the distance by early twilight. Wouldn't have to spend another night sitting around a fire wrapped up in our bedrolls. We keep going 'til we make the distance."

"You think the horses would be able to maintain that pace, Brett? They is pulling six dead men and a damn wagon."

"We ain't going to be running them. I reckon they'd do fine. We can stop and rest every now and again. We just wouldn't stop to camp out. I'm pretty sure we can manage that."

"What if we were to go down the trail a bit further, find a clearing somewhere and off load the pieces of shit in the wagon and then carry on? I could see us making the distance b'fore it is too damn dark to see, then. The horses won't be pulling all that extra weight, except for your fat ass and mine."

Alex smiled it made perfect sense.

"That is a good idea, Travis didn't say we needed to have them bodies with us when we got there, only that we needed to turn them over to Bash and Cannon, which we will do. Easy enough to hide 'em along the trail and hope no one comes across them. We can lead Bash and Cannon back this way to where we off load 'em and let them take it from there."

It was so obvious that it was funny and the two of them chuckled.

"That is right. See two options, I vote for number two," Alex smirked.

Brett nodded. "I'd say I like option two as well."

"All right, then, let's get to it." Kicking snow over their fire, they loaded up their gear, hitched the horses back up to the wagon and continued toward the Hefley rail station. A mile or so later Brett slowed the horses and wagon to a stop.

"Right here looks like as good of a spot as any we've seen so far, to unload the stink from the back. We got this big cedar sticking out here like a sore thumb, easy enough to remember. They'd be off and below the trail some, and hard to see unless one looked over the bank."

"Yep, looks good to me, we can throw some hay and snow over them too, that'd give it the look as though it were bramble. Good eye, Brett," Alex said as he slid off the wagon seat and stepped down, followed by Brett.

They didn't take too much time tossing the bodies out and they cared little on how far down the bank they rolled, as long as they couldn't be seen it was good enough. They threw some hay and snow over the mound and took a quick second look to make sure the bodies weren't noticeable. Satisfied, they climbed back onto the wagon and carried on.

Their first extended rest was four hours later when the sun was high in the sky. They had travelled, they guessed, over five miles by then and there were easily that many hours of daylight left.

"I think we're doin' good, since we unloaded the wagon with all the manure, we had in the back. I don't think we would've made it quite this far yet, if we were still loaded. You had a good idea there, Alex," Brett said as he climbed off to relieve himself and to stretch.

"An empty two-horse pulled wagon can travel at a walk near twenty-five miles a day give or take. Some have even made it further," Alex began as he too now slid off the wagon to relieve himself.

"I knew if we lessened the load we could do that too." Buttoning up his fly, he continued. "We might make that place Hefley b'fore having to spend another night out. Today we'll triple the distance we travelled yesterday. I'll bet we'll do it before it gets dark. That'll mean the furthest distance to Hefley from that point would be like five miles, which we could certainly do in the dark with the wagon lanterns lit."

Alex leaned on the side of the wagon and he looked around.

"Glad it stopped snowing leastwise. I hope we don't see any more until we get back to Cross's place."

Brett now came out from behind the bushes he had been squatting behind, pulling up his pants and buttoning them up.

"I don't think we're going see any snow today; the suns too warm. That don't mean the evening is going to be warm though. As long as we keep moving easterly we should make Hefley before any cold does set in."

Brett reached for his canteen and took a swallow, while Alex fed the horses a few handfuls of grain.

"You should probably slap down those eye reflectors over the horses lids. Keeps them from being blinded by the brightness of this damn snow. It sure is white, ain't it?"

"Yeah, the high sun certainly makes it blinding," Alex responded as he followed Brett's advice and pulled the horses eye reflectors down. "There, that ought to help them see a bit better."

He walked over to where Brett stood.

"You really think we'll make Hefley t'night, Brett?"

"I don't see why not. Since leaving Cross's place yesterday, we've already made half the distance and it ain't quite noon yet. I think if we really want to make the distance, we'll make it. Might entail a short while travelling in the dark, but that is what the lanterns are for."

"But, we ain't gonna make any more distance without them wagon wheels turning. You want me to take the reins for a bit?" Alex asked.

"By all means have at her. You take the reins now and we'll switch again later on down the trail. Let's get," Brett said as he climbed up on the passenger side while Alex slid in to the lead seat.

He snapped the reins and clicked his cheeks and the wagon slowly pulled to a start. They had to stop on a few occasions to knock the snow and ice that built up in the wagon wheels as they travelled. The warm sun melted the snow while the cold air turned the wet into ice.

Switching wagon masters after another extended rest, they carried on through dusk. The wagon lanterns flickered and swayed this way and that with each step the horses took. Finally, in the distance they could see the Hefley rail station lights up ahead, blocked every now and again by the blowing branches of the pine and cedar trees that were on either side of the road as the evening winds blew.

"That's got to be Hefley," Brett said as he pointed.

"I reckon so. It ain't too much further ahead. Goddamn! Am I glad to see that," Alex said as he stirred in his seat.

They had pushed themselves and horses too, but it had paid off and none was any worse for wear. Pulling into Hefley rail station a few minutes later, they tethered the horses to the horse rail and made their way up to the station house.

The door was locked, but they could see inside that there was a man lying on a cot inside a small room. They banged on the door a couple of times and finally the man sat up and looked. He waved his hand at them acknowledging that he had seen them, then stood up and made his way to the door and unlocked it, keeping the chain in place.

"What is it you want? We ain't open until five a.m.," the man said as he looked at them.

"We is coming from Willow Gate, been on the trail all day. Any chance you can let us in? It is a might cold out here," Brett replied.

The man gestured with his chin across the street.

"You might be able to get a bed over at the eatery or in the least have a warm place to sit 'til morning."

"There ain't no hotel 'round here?" Alex questioned.

"Not here in Hefley, nope," the man answered.

"What the hell are folks supposed to do if they is waiting on a train?"

The man shrugged. "Like I said, your best bet in finding a place to stay until morning is over at the eatery. John might allow that. I can't let you in here during non-business hours."

"All right, are our horses and wagon okay where they are for now?" Brett wanted to confirm.

"The horses and wagon is fine there, yep," the man answered back.

Brett and Alex nodded their appreciation as they turned heel and headed across the street. The eatery door was locked too, but there was a rope and bell outside so they rang it. A few minutes later, the door opened and a man armed with a rifle greeted them.

"A little late or too early for the train, ain't ya?" the man said as he looked at the two of them.

"We ain't here to cause harm. Are you John?" Brett asked.

"What of it?"

"The man at the station said you might allow us sanctuary 'til morn."

"I might. What is your business here in Hefley at this hour?"

"We're waiting on a train coming in from Calgary with two Mounted Police redcoats and an old bounty hunter on it. We've been on the trail since yesterday."

"Where are you coming from?"

"Willow Gate," Alex responded.

"Willow Gate, uh-huh, was a cowboy here a week or so ago, was from Willow Gate too. What are your names?"

"I'm Brett and this is Alex?"

"Uh-huh, all right Brett and Alex, I'll let ya's in." John opened the door fully and let the two of them inside. "The train coming from the east and Calgary ain't due here as far as I know until early evening tomorrow. It comes from the east every Monday. You're gonna have yourselves a long wait, I think. The snow might even slow it down some. But, you're welcome to sit and wait, gets you out of the cold leastwise. I can have coffee made if you like, but that is all I'll offer at this time of night. I won't be sitting up chit-chatting with you either. So, you want coffee?"

"That'd be kind of you. Thank you," Brett responded.

John waved his hand through the air as went toward the small kitchen to perk coffee, while Brett and Alex sat down at a table.

"That damn Travis never told us there weren't no hotels here," Alex complained as he looked around the small eatery.

"Nope, he didn't, but it is damn awful kind of John to offer us shelter here," Brett replied as he removed his hat and set it on table. "A lot warmer in here then it'd have been out there, that is for sure."

John showed up a few minutes later and set the pot of coffee on the table with some cream and sugar.

"Ain't sure either of you use it, but there is some cream and sugar too. I'm heading back to bed. You is welcome to lay your bedrolls out on the floor if you like, but at five a.m. tomorrow, the morning train arrives and the switch over of conductors and engineers takes place. There will be a few folks in for breakfast."

"We'll be up and about by then, John," Brett assured.

"All right, well, g'dnight I guess."

"See you in the morning," Brett and Alex said in unison as John went back to his room to sleep.

"Here we are, Alex... Hefley rail station, we got a roof over our heads and a fresh pot of coffee to warm us up. I'd say it wasn't a bad day after all," Brett poured himself a coffee and lit the candle that sat in the middle of the table. All was good.

Chapter 15

At 5:00 a.m., Monday, as John had warned, the small eatery at Hefley rail station got busy. The few tables in the place filled up quickly. It was easy to tell that most of the patrons were train personnel, the way they were dressed and all. There were two passengers only, and they were heading east. This was the morning breakfast stop and crew change over. They sat down at a table opposite where Brett and Alex sat. They nodded at the pair and the two men nodded back.

"Small place this Hefley is, isn't it," one of the men commented as he looked at Alex, and Brett.

"Not much more than a train stop," Alex answered back.

"I heard the food is good here, though," the man smiled.

"We can attest that the coffee certainly is. We're still waiting on our breakfast so can't say much about the food. It smells good," Brett took the time to respond.

"That it does, yes sir."

The man turned back to his travel companion and the two of them carried on conversing.

Finally, Alex and Brett's eggs and pancakes arrived. They thanked John and dug in, and, as rumours had it, the food at that little eatery was everything that was said about it. It was simply good.

"Jesus, it's like John made these out of air, so fluffy and soft. Damn good," Alex said as he continued shovelling his breakfast into his mouth. Neither of them spoke. They were enjoying the savoury food too much to talk.

Meanwhile, the west bound train coming in from Calgary that Cannon, Bash and Riley Scott were on, had been slowed down to a crawl as it traversed into the Rocky Mountain passes that were deep with snow. Constable Rick Bash looked out his side window.

"Never would have thought there'd be this much snow. It really slows the train down, doesn't it?"

"We got to consider as we inch forward that the train is pushing all that snow with the cattle catcher. I'm sure once we start to descend we'll pick up speed. Right now, the conductor is taking it slow to be safe," Lieutenant Bob Cannon responded.

"Better safe than sorry, I guess. I ain't travelled much on trains, but there ain't no way we could've made it to Willow Gate in less time. It's a little nerve racking going by rail, though," Riley said with uneasiness as he looked out the window.

He turned his head quick once he realised how high up in the mountains they were, "Jesus, we're a long way up ain't we?" he questioned with a look of both apprehension and surprise on his face.

Bash and Cannon both chuckled.

"We are, yep, but don't worry, Riley. We'll be descending after a mile or so. There is one tunnel and once we go through that, we'll be down low," Cannon said as he continued his gaze out the window quite amazed by the scenery.

"A mile at this pace though, might take a while, and I really don't like it one damn bit," Riley added nervously.

"Calm down. We are as safe as we would be if we were riding saddle horses through here," Bash pointed out as he tried to help Riley relax a bit.

"Shit, I need whisky," Riley said as he looked around. "Where the hell can I get a whisky?"

"Unless someone has a bottle with them or a flask, you're out of luck getting any whisky on this train, Riley. Take a couple of deep breaths; you'll be fine."

"No I won't, Cannon, I'm damn petrified. I ain't ever taking a train again! Leastwise not one that heads into the damn Rockies, no sir, I won't do it! If I can't ride my horse then I'll be staying put."

Riley shook his head. It was obvious he wasn't joking. After forty-five minutes of fear and gruelling nervousness for Riley, the train finally entered the tunnel. He sighed in relief only after the train made its way through and they were descending to lower altitudes.

"There, that is better, why the hell didn't one of you tell me we'd be way up there in the Rockies. I'd have stayed at the Fort if I had known it."

"How many times have you been through the Rockies, Riley?"

"A number of times, but I was on a damn horse."

"Even so, you should've known the train has to weave its way through," said Cannon as he smiled and shook his head.

"Maybe I should've, but I didn't. And neither of you two warned me, you bastards," Riley half chuckled.

"No more worries, Riley. From here on, we're through the mountains. It's all prairie and low wooded areas now. You could take this time to change your undershorts."

"Shut the hell up, Bash. I don't need to change my undershorts, but I might need to have my heart checked. The damn thing almost blew up in the mountains."

The train sauntered on.

The patrons at the small eatery in Hefley slowly, one by one, were soon gone. Brett and Alex were the only ones left. With nowhere to go and with nothing to do until the west bound train arrived, they got bored quickly.

"This waiting stuff is a real piss off. There ain't a damn thing to do and we still have hours to wait. What are we gonna do for the next ten or so hours?"

"I dunno, Alex. There ain't much we can do except wait," Brett shrugged, there was nothing they could do but wait.

"Maybe, John has a deck of cards or something," Alex began.

He turned his head toward the kitchen and asked loud enough for John to hear him.

"Hey, John, you got any cards?"

"Cards," John responded, unsure that is what was asked.

"Yeah, a deck of cards, we got a long while to wait before the west bound train arrives and we're getting bored. So, you got cards?" Alex asked again.

"Sure do, you boys want to get into some five card stud?" John responded with excitement, hoping he could play along.

"Sounds like you are a poker player, John. Are you?" Brett asked with a smile.

"I play a lot of solitaire, not often are there folks here for more than a couple hours at a time and most times they ain't bored 'cause they ain't waiting on trains. I'd certainly enjoy a couple of hands of stud," John said as he grabbed the deck of cards from the shelf. He pulled up to their table and made himself comfortable.

"Shall we cut to see who deals?" he asked as he shuffled the cards. He did some fancy shuffling and Brett and Alex smiled.

"That right there is some pretty fancy shuffling. You must be a poker player?"

"Aw, shit, I played a little bit in my younger days and playing as much solitaire that I play on a daily basis, it don't take long to learn a few eye catching shuffles. Are we going to cut the deck to see who deals, or what?"

"Nah, they're your cards John. Go ahead deal 'em out. We ain't playing for money though are we?" Brett wanted to be sure, since that hadn't yet been established.

"Stud, without money is like a bull without nuts, Brett. C'mon, you know that. I say we play for a few bucks," Alex commented.

"That is fine by me. I just wanted to be sure. I have a couple bucks." Brett reached into his pocket and pulled out a couple of five- dollar bills and a handful of coins.

"I'd say I have twelve to fifteen bucks. I'll play 'til that is all gone. What do you got Alex?"

"Six dollars 'cause I need you to borrow me the money."

"You want half of what I got, so you can try and pay me back by winning?"

"Why not, you know I'm good for it," Alex smiled.

"Yeah, I s'ppose so, all right there you have it, John. We'll play for cash. The stakes ain't high, but it'll help pass time."

"I don't mind that the stakes ain't high. Good conversation and winning a few bucks from out of town folk, hell, there ain't nothing wrong with that," John smiled as he shuffled the cards again and dealt out the hands.

Three hours later and under seven hours of waiting still ahead, both Alex and Brett sat in the eatery, penniless. John though was kind enough to keep them fed and full of coffee.

"I can't believe he beat us that quick. I ain't got a dime left. Son-of-a-bitch," Alex complained with a slant of humor.

"I ain't got that either. I think John played us," Brett said as he shook his head and snickered. "All fun and jokes aside, it's been a couple days since Colby got stung by that bullet, I wonder how he is doing?"

"I have been thinking the same lately. Pete was certain, when he fixed him up, that he was gonna be all right. Colby is a stubborn son-of-a-bitch and won't die unless he wants to."

Alex smiled trying to put the worst-case scenario out of his head. Not being at Pete's place, neither of them knew for sure.

"I hope you is right Alex. I've seen folks with bullet holes b'fore, which were fixed up, and things still went awry, infections mostly."

"True as that might be, I like to think he's going to be okay. We ain't going know nothing 'til we make it back to Cross's place."

"You is right, Alex. We got another day maybe two b'fore then. That'd give him four days of healing and I reckon that if he's all right when we do make it back, then he's going be fine."

"And if he ain't, you don't think he's going be, or what?" Alex questioned with a sneer. He didn't want to think that Colby wasn't going to be all right. He wanted to believe that he would be.

"I dunno, Alex, he was shot, shit. We ain't there at this very moment to know either way," Brett responded wishing now that he had never brought it up.

He wanted to be assured as much as Alex that Colby was fine, but since neither one knew, it was a touchy situation for the both of them.

The truth was Colby was doing as well as anyone who had taken a bullet two days earlier. He was up and moving around although slowly. The fact that he was mobile proved he would recover.

"How are you feeling t'day, Colby?" Martin asked as Colby pulled up a chair at the big oak table after slowly descending the stairs.

"It hurts a bit, but I ain't losing blood no more. Renatta has been keeping the wound clean. She put some damn iodine on it earlier on and that hurt a hell of a lot more than it hurts now. I can tell you that," Colby said as he slowly sat down and Martin poured him a coffee.

"Thank you, Martin. Where is Travis and Cape?"

"They is out doing something; was gone when I came back in from tending the horses. You figure Brett and Alex made it to that Hefley place by now?" Martin asked for Colby's opinion.

"Travis did say it'd take two days ride. I reckon they is close by now if they ain't already there." Colby took a swallow of his coffee. "What about Pete, where is he?"

"He headed into town earlier. Had banking to do or something like that."

"Shit, he shouldn't have gone alone. That is asking for trouble."

"I think that is where Travis and Cape are too, they likely tagged along with him, I s'ppose. They wouldn't have let him go alone, I don't reckon."

"You ain't sure?"

"Only speculation, since they isn't here and I knew Pete was heading into Willow Gate." Martin shrugged.

"I figure any of us going into town under these circumstances ain't playing with a full deck. Gabe and his henchmen is going be on the lookout for them. We should saddle up and go into Willow Gate too," Colby suggested.

"You think you could ride? You was only shot a couple days ago."

"I think I'd be able to ride. B'sides I've been stuck in bed for a couple days, I could likely use some fresh air." Colby began to stand, "Nope, I don't think I'll be getting into a saddle yet." Wincing he sat back down, "Damn, that hurt some."

"What did you expect, you stupid son-of-a-bitch? Of course, it hurt. You was shot." Martin shook his head.

"You don't need to keep telling me that, Martin. I'm the one was shot and I feel it." Colby took another swallow of his coffee. "We've had quite the adventure, getting here and all, then, that gunfight the other day, I'm glad we is all still standing."

"I wouldn't argue that point. We sure have had an adventure, if you wanna call it that. I call it a hell of a time; not so much an adventure." Martin took a swallow of his own coffee.

"Ah, shit, it was an adventure, Martin, and here we are t'day, living under Cross's roof, working on Cross's land. It all turned out."

"Not really, you could've died or anyone of us for that matter when Gabe's henchmen showed up," Martin pointed out, "but we didn't so, yeah, as Alex would say, there is that."

"Yep, there certainly is that," Colby chuckled. "What time is it now any way?"

"It ain't morn' no more. Ain't quite dusk and lunch has already been served. I guess it is near three o'clock or something like that."

"How long has Pete, Cape, and Travis been gone?"

"They ate lunch and so they was here then. I cleaned up the barn some and when I came back they was gone. I can't be certain on when they left. Only know they wasn't here when I came in from the barn."

"They've been gone for at least a couple hours, then."

"I guess so," Martin shrugged.

"If they ain't back soon we best start worrying," Colby said as he reached for the pot of coffee to pour himself another. Reaching for it caused him some pain and he grimaced. Noting this, Martin slid the pot closer. "Thanks, Martin." Colby poured a cup and offered to pour another for Martin.

"Nah, I drank enough already," Martin responded.

It was around that time that the front door opened and Pete, along with Cape and Tyrell, made their way into the kitchen.

"Jesus, Colby, what are you doing out of bed?" Tyrell asked as he sat down and removed his hat.

"Needed to get mobile Travis, two days of lying in a bed on my back was boring after the first."

"Boring or not, you could rupture those sutures," Pete pointed out.

"They ain't split open yet, Pete. I think you did a mighty fine job." Colby took a sip from his coffee, "Where the hell did the three of you end up?"

"I had business in town. Renatta was aware. Cape and Travis accompanied me."

"Yeah, that is what we reckoned. Is there anything new in the Gate?"

"Nope, was pretty quiet actually." Tyrell poured himself a coffee. "Didn't see hide nor tail of Gabe or those two men that took off. I reckon Gabe has gone into hiding or is so defeated that he's sitting in his private room at the Nugget, likely hung over. He probably hit the booze right after he learned that the men he sent didn't quite make it back," Tyrell chuckled.

He was partly right regarding Gabe, but the two men that went running when the bullets stopped flying were strung up in a tree a good distance away from Willow Gate, put there by Crying Wolf who had watched the entire battle unfold. When the two men made a run for it, he tracked them down and killed them. Then he strung them up and chased their horses away.

He wasn't camped too far away from Cross's place and was like a shepherd overlooking the activities and waiting for a clear shot on Gabe Roy. It would happen sooner than later he hoped. For now, he was content in keeping an eye on Travis. The only one who knew he was near was Black Dog and he had visited Crying Wolf a couple times already. If he could speak, perhaps he would've told Tyrell, but then again, he and Crying Wolf had an understanding. It was as if Black Dog knew exactly why he was there and he didn't have any complaints about that at all.

Back at Hefley, Alex and Brett were getting ready to go outside and feed their horses, when John stopped them.

"You fellows want something to do? There are a few more hours before the west bound train arrives."

The two of them stopped and looked at John.

"And what might that be?" Brett asked.

"I could use a hand in cleaning the barn out back."

"What, you want us to shovel shit?"

"It wouldn't take too long. We only got five horses stabled," John answered with hope that they'd help.

Bret and Alex looked at each other.

"We ain't got anything to do and sitting around don't make time go any faster. Sure, we'll give ya hand John. But it'll cost you twelve dollars," Alex snickered.

John chuckled and shook his head. "You still can't get over the fact that an old timer like me beat your asses in stud."

"We ain't so sure it was a fair fight. You're a damn good poker player. You might have took advantage of us," Brett smiled.

"I did not, would never consider such a thing. Nope, I won fair and square."

"I reckon you did, John."

"I'll still pay you twelve dollars, though, if you clean the barn."

"So, you'll give us back the money you won, if we clean the damn barn?"

"I will too," John said with sincerity.

"Nah, you keep those dollars you won it. Alex was only making jokes."

"I don't mind paying Brett."

"That is all right John. We need something to pass the time and digging in shit might be that something," Alex responded.

"All right, well, the barn is out back, the shovel is in the corridor, and the wheelbarrow is leaning against the wall," John said with a smile, relieved that the two of them agreed to help.

"We'll get to it. C'mon, Alex, let's get the shit moved," Brett said as the two of them stepped outside.

The first thing they did was check up on their horses. They being okay, they fed them a couple scoops of grain and headed to the back of the eatery where the barn stood. Finding the tools they needed, they began cleaning the stalls.

"Hard to believe here we is, in some bow hick rail station, cleaning a damn barn whilst we wait for the west bound train, quite the change of events Brett."

"Ah, giving old John a hand is all right. He's kept us full of coffee and food. It is the least we could do for the old codger." Brett grabbed the wheelbarrow now that was full of horseshit, and wheeled it outside to the pile and dumped it. It took a little more than two hours to clean the barn and that meant the westbound train was two hours closer.

"There, well that takes care of that shit," Alex made a pun and chuckled. "That weren't so bad, other than the shit stuck on the soles of my boots." He looked at his boots and shook his head. Using the shovel, he scraped them clean. "I guess that'll do. Well, Brett, we've been at this for a while, killed some time and now we wait again."

"Yep, now we wait again. I don't reckon it'll be much longer, though. She's gotta be near three o'clock by now. The train should be here in a couple more hours. I guess we go sit." Brett shrugged his shoulders. The two of them made their way back to the eatery and the table they had been sitting at.

John came over, poured them fresh coffee, and set down some pie. "I made some apple pie, while you were cleaning the barn. Hope you like apple pie?"

"Damn right we do. Thank you very much John, for the pie and coffee," Alex said as the two of them dug in.

"I appreciate your help. This is my way of showing it," John smiled.

"And we appreciate you letting us sit here while we wait for the train."

"There ain't nowhere else for you to sit."

"Yeah, I s'ppose you is right there John," Brett responded between chewing and drinking. "You make damn fine pie, you know that?"

"I've been told that a time or two," John replied as he watched them eat and enjoy the pie and coffee for a couple of minutes. "I best get back to the kitchen and get ready for the incoming train and the supper rush. Enjoy your pie and coffee," John said as he turned and went back to the kitchen.

"What do you figure, Brett? Is this the best damn pie you have ever eaten or what?"

"I certainly would not disagree. It's damn near as good as what Renatta makes on Sundays," Brett responded as the two of them continued with their snack and coffee. For the next couple of hours they wandered around outside and stepped into the small mercantile that was adjacent to John's eatery. The shelves were stacked with souvenirs, canned goods, some tack, horse reins, halters, that type of thing. There were wooden barrels of potatoes, apples, and dry goods. For a store as small, it was well stocked.

"You folks need anything or need any help?" a rustic looking woman asked as they looked around.

"No ma'am, we is waiting on the train is all. Spent the night at John's and been there ever since. Jus' looking around if that is okay?"

The woman smiled, "John took any money you had, huh?"

Both Alex and Brett looked at each other then back to the woman behind the counter.

"What do you mean?" Brett asked curious to know how she knew.

"John, does that to every 'out of Towner' that needs to wait for the train. I wouldn't put it past him that he asked you to clean the barn too."

"Jesus Christ, he did do that!" Alex said as he shook his head.

The woman began to laugh, "He does that to everyone," she said.

"Everyone?" Brett questioned as he made his way closer to the counter.

She was smiling as the two of them approached, "You might only know him as John, but the truth is he's an old time gambler. Was one of the best, if not the best in these parts, right down into the prairies and south of the Rocky Mountains, you folks were beaten at stud by John Hardin."

"And who might that be?"

The woman leaned on the counter, "as I said he was one of the best gamblers to ever step foot on God's green earth. He can also shoot like a son-of-a-bitch."

Brett and Alex were taken back by the woman's use of an expletive. She noted their surprise, and waved her hand through the air.

"Ah, don't you worry about the way I speak. I mean every word of it and I'm as much of a lady as any. I just see no point in being all frilly."

The two of the only nodded.

"No worries, ma'am, we have no doubt that you isn't a lady. You was saying John next store at the eatery is a gambler, by the name of John Hardin. Ain't never heard that name b'fore."

"Nope you wouldn't. Folks around here don't talk much about their pasts, nor will John."

"I guess that is all right. Nothing wrong with that, I reckon. Everyone has a past that they may not want to talk about. It don't matter none. I think John is a hell of a nice old codger. We figured he was a gambler when we sat down to stud with him." Alex shook his head and snickered. "The way he could shuffle them cards was pretty much a giveaway. It is good to know leastwise that we was beaten by an old professional gambler, as we assumed he was?"

"Your assumptions are correct. That is enough about John. What brings young men such as yourselves to Hefley?" The woman wanted to know. She was curious and felt like conversing.

"We is waiting on the west bound train, coming in from Calgary. There are a couple of redcoats and another friend of ours on it. We've been asked to escort them back to Willow Gate," Brett replied. It didn't matter if he said that or not because that is exactly why they were there.

"Huh, I wouldn't have taken you two for lawmen?" the woman pointed out with surprise.

"No, you wouldn't, ma'am, 'cause we ain't lawmen. We work for Pete Cross. He has business with the redcoats."

"Oh Jesus, you work for Pete? Well it is about time that he hired himself a new crew. Pete used to come by here every second week or so, he and Renatta both. She still works for him, doesn't she?"

"Yes, ma'am, she does."

"I'll be. I think that is wonderful and it is good to know that Pete still has his land. Does he plan on putting cattle back onto it?"

"I have to say that it is interesting to know you know him and Renatta. That is quite the thing. As far as we know, he does have plans to do that, yep."

"Good. It will be nice to have him shipping his cattle through here again. There aren't many ranchers around anymore. Most have turned to farming cereal grains, fruit, and that type of thing. Pete was the life blood of this area before he turned away from ranching all those years ago."

"The life blood?" Alex questioned with curiosity.

It was interesting to both he and Brett to learn these things about Pete Cross.

"He sure was. Most folks at all points east and west of here bought his cattle. Now they buy them from the auctions down east, the prairies mostly."

The three of them continued talking for a few more minutes when in the distance the whistle blew and the westbound train grew closer. Saying their goodbyes to the nice woman behind the counter, Brett and Alex, exited the mercantile and headed over to the old caboose that was used as the station. It didn't take long before they could see the westbound train chugging along the tracks. Finally, it pulled up to a screeching halt and hiss. Then the doors opened and a few passengers stepped out, none of whom were Cannon, Bash, or Riley Scott. Alex made his way over to the counter and asked if the train had come from Calgary. It had.

"They say this train did come from Calgary," Alex said as he made his way back to Brett who was still looking out the window.

"Wonder where the hell them redcoats and that Riley fellow are? I don't see them."

The train now slowly pulled ahead and once more stopped. Then the shipping doors opened and out came Bash, Cannon and Riley Scott leading horses.

"There they are," Alex said as he pointed. "Shit, I was starting to think they wasn't on it. C'mon, Brett let's go meet 'em. They is going to be quite surprised to see we is here to escort them."

The two of them stepped out onto the passenger platform and watched until the three men they had been waiting for were off the livestock and shipping platform. Then they approached.

"Lookey here, Brett," Alex said with a smile when Rick Bash recognised him.

"Alex?" Bash was surprised to see him.

"Is too, Bash."

By now, both Cannon and Riley Scott made the distance.

"Hello Cannon, Riley," Alex began as he acknowledged them.

"Jesus Christ, what are you doing here Alex?" Cannon asked right off the get go.

Riley seemed surprised too but not really caring, he wasn't feeling too well. The train ride had made him nauseous.

"We was instructed by Travis to meet you here. Some of Gabe Roy's henchmen came a calling the other day. We killed them," Alex said as though it were second nature.

"Killed them?" Cannon questioned wanting to be clear.

"There was eight; two got away. Travis said we needed to hand over the dead to the law for identification and whatnot, except, well," Alex shrugged as he caught his breath, "we all know what kind of law we have in Willow Gate, so, we loaded them onto the wagon and headed here. Travis says we need to hand them over to you since you is the law."

Both Cannon and Bash looked around trying to see a wagon full of dead men.

"Where are these dead you're talking about, Alex?" Cannon now asked with authority, not seeing any close by.

"Well," Alex began as he scratched his face. "We off loaded them down the trail some."

"You what?" Bash questioned with anger and disbelief.

"They was slowing us down so we tossed them over a bank and covered them up with some hay and such. No worries, Bash. We know where they is."

All Riley could do was chuckle. It was simply too damn funny not to. Cannon and Bash on the other hand weren't so impressed and didn't think it funny at all.

"What the hell are you laughing at Riley? This isn't funny." Lieutenant Bob Cannon said with a frown.

"It is too, Cannon. Jesus, think about it," said Riley, smiling and snickering.

"I certainly see nothing funny about them throwing six dead men over a bank along the trail."

"Like they said, Bash, they were slowing them down. Think about that. I imagine their horses were having a hard time pulling the dead weight of six men and the two of them plus gear," Riley pointed out.

"Yeah, that is exactly how it was," Brett interjected.

Cannon and Bash both shook their heads.

"The two of you broke some damn laws, right off the top, by simply tossing them over a bank."

"What frigging laws are you talking about, Bash? We ain't leaving them there, if that is your concern, in fact we is gonna hand them over to the two of you. I don't think we broke no law whatsoever," Alex said with disdain.

"All right. The two of you can stop with the damn bickering right now," Cannon voiced. "We have a two day ride ahead of us and we best start getting along. Tell us more about what happened and when."

"I think I'd much rather wait 'til we get on the trail to tell you about it." Alex said as he turned heel. "C'mon Brett, let's get the wagon."

"Right behind you Alex," Brett replied as he caught up. Bash, Cannon and Riley Scott, sat on their horses and waited. They didn't speak two words to one another as they waited the few moments for Brett and Alex to gather their wagon.

Finally, Alex and Brett pulled up to them in the wagon and stopped.

"All right, here we all are; now let's get," Brett said as he snapped the reins and the wagon slowly started off again heading west to Willow Gate followed by Constable Rick Bash, Lieutenant Bob Cannon and bounty hunter extraordinaire Riley Scott.

The three horse riders pulled up alongside the wagon as they traversed.

"You were going to fill me in on what happened and why there are six dead men along this trail," Cannon said as he looked over to Alex.

Alex told the tale.

"What makes any of you think it was Gabe Roy that sent those men?" Bash asked now that the story on how it all came about was told.

It didn't take long for Alex and Brett to explain it all and finally Bash accepted the fact that they had been sent by Gabe Roy and that the killing of the six men was justified. Even Cannon agreed to that.

"See we didn't break no laws whatsoever, now did we, Bash?" Alex questioned with a sneer as they sauntered on.

"Don't start, Alex. Technically, you did break a law, and that law is desecrating the dead. We're going to look the other way this time, though, since the law in Willow Gate as we know is corrupt and those that are dead were the aggressors. You're all damn lucky that Travis was involved and that he had already informed us of what was going on between Gabe Roy and Pete Cross," Bob Cannon pointed out.

"So you all knew this and still made us explain it?" Neither Alex nor Brett, were amused.

"That, Alex, is called clarification."

"You can call it whatever you want, Bash. I think it is bullshit."

"You're lucky I don't call it a confession."

"Like I said, Bash, call it whatever you want, confession, clarification, I really don't give a damn. I just wanna make it back to Cross's place and check up on my cousin. I don't give a care on what you think. Once we turn over them dead to you and Cannon and we're in Willow Gate, I won't care if I ever see you or Cannon again. As for Riley, well, I really ain't got much of a sweet spot for him either, nor do I know why he is here at all and I don't really care. So when all this is over you three can kiss my ass." Both Alex and Brett chuckled as Brett snapped the reins and sped the wagon up.

The five of them carried on until it was too dark to see. Settling in for the evening they sat around the fire and conversed as friendly as they could to one another. No arguments ensued. They were simply five men sitting around the fire swilling coffee. Talking about this, that, and sometimes sat in silence. The flames from the fire kept them warm and the sounds of night kept them alert. Finally, they rolled out their bedrolls and slept.

Chapter 16

Riley was the first to rise that morning. He stoked the coals of the past night fire and melted some snow for coffee. He was having his first cup when the others came to life. "How'd you all sleep last night? It was a trifle cold wasn't it?" he asked as they all made their way to the fire and warmed their hands.

Pouring themselves coffee, they sat.

"Damn right it was cold last night. I can't wait to be off this damn trail and under a roof," Brett responded as he took a swig from the coffee in his hand.

"I'd agree with that," Alex replied as he now stood up and relieved himself behind some bushes.

"We have one more night out and the sky is clear. Likely going to be another cold one tonight," Bash commented as he poured himself a coffee.

"Once the sun is up Bash, she'll warm up," Cannon said with hope.

An hour later, they were once again on the move. They travelled a few miles until Brett and Alex slowed their wagon down.

"We're getting close to where we stowed them dead," Alex said as he and Brett started looking over the edge of the road. It didn't take long for them to spot the pile of hay, although it was lightly dusted with frost and snow.

"There they is," Brett said as he stopped the wagon. Hopping off along with Alex, the two men walked over to where the hay was and they kicked most of it off. By now, Cannon, Bash, and Riley were standing on the edge of the road looking down to where Brett and Alex stood.

Alex looked up to Cannon. "Here you go, Cannon. We graciously hand these dead assholes over to you and Bash," he added as he and Brett began to walk back up to the road, thinking that was all they needed to do.

Cannon stopped them. "No use in coming up with your hands empty. We'll need to load them up again onto the wagon."

"You and Bash feel free to do so. I ain't touching them frozen bodies," Alex said as he and Brett continued to make their way back to the wagon.

"You two threw them over; you two bring them up," Bash said as he looked at both of them.

"Nope, don't think so. We did our part. We handed them over to the law. Now you is the law, ain't you, Bash? You and Cannon both, I say we ain't got a damn thing anymore to do with them. You can load them onto the wagon if you like or leave them as they are and let the worms and crows eat 'em. I don't care either way," Alex said as he leaned on the back of the wagon.

"I could demand you to load them up," Cannon said with authority.

"Demand away, Cannon. I still ain't going to do it. Nope, we is done with them."

"Jesus Christ, Alex," Cannon said as he shook his head. He knew he was wasting his breath. "All right, Rick, come on let's get these dead men loaded up."

Not even Riley wanted to help but he did. It took a couple of minutes to load them. The bodies were frozen from the cold and rigor mortis, and a couple of the dead men's arms and legs were in a peculiar way, that made loading them into the wagon a pain. Cannon simply broke the limbs of the dead men that were discombobulated with a sickening snap and crack.

"That right there was one of the sickest things I've ever seen, Cannon. Did you have to break their bones?" Riley asked with disgust.

"How else would we have been able to load them?" Cannon questioned with authority.

"I don't know. Maybe you could've gently tossed them into the wagon. Breaking their limbs like that was sickening," Riley commented.

"I would agree with that and you say we desecrated them dead by tossing them over the bank. What is it called what you did?" Alex questioned.

"No point in questioning that," Brett pointed out. "If Cannon never did that to them bodies, their arms and legs would be sticking up in all different directions. They is loaded now, so I say we get."

Brett hopped back up onto the wagon and waited a few moments for Alex to follow suit. Then he snapped the reins and the wagon loaded with the six dead men once more headed west, followed closely behind by the three riders on horses.

"I guess we can be grateful for the cold, otherwise them dead would be a stinking up these woods," Alex mentioned as they sauntered on.

"And the dead festering under the heat from the sun for four days would certainly stink," Brett said with a snicker.

The convoy carried on throughout the day with the wagon in front and Bash, Cannon, and Riley trailing behind. They had made good timing in spite of stopping to let the horses rest and having a break themselves. Cannon took out a map and looked at the distance they still had to travel.

"I think by this map we are about twelve miles from Willow Gate," he began as he looked at the mountain range. "We still have about three maybe four hours left of daylight. I see the wagon has lanterns. We could carry right on through the evening and make Willow Gate by early twilight or dawn at the latest. What do the rest of you think?"

"It makes no never mind to us," Alex replied. "I'd much rather do that then spend any more time on this trail. The wagon does have lanterns."

"All right, so we'll carry right on through," Cannon wanted to be clear.

"Don't see why not. We can go at least until the horses decide they've gone far enough. We can always rest up along the way," Riley suggested.

Back at Cross's place the others were sitting at the big oak table, having their late afternoon break and talking among themselves.

"Sure feeling a lot better t'day," Colby said as he cut himself a piece of cake that Renatta had placed on the table. "I'm damn itchy though," he added as he put a piece of cake into his mouth.

"That is to be expected and is a good sign that you're healing," Pete pointed out.

"I had no doubt that I wouldn't heal up, but ain't there anything I can do to stop the damn itch?"

"I'll have Renatta put some salve on the wound the next time your bandages need to be changed."

"Will it stop the itch?" Colby asked as he put another piece of cake into his mouth and took a swallow of coffee.

"It will certainly slow the itching down."

"Damn it, Pete, I want it take the itch away completely," he said as he moved in his seat trying to get comfortable with hope that the itching would subside.

"There ain't anything that'll make the itching stop. Not until you're healed completely," Tyrell cut himself a piece of cake.

"Travis is right you'll have to live with the itch for a few more days I would think. The salve will help."

"Shit sakes, I guess any help is better than no help." Colby continued to eat his piece of cake and drink his coffee. How he wanted to take the bandages off and scratch the living hell out of the wound. He had never been so damn itchy in his life. And to top it all off, he hadn't been outside in four days. He was bored and itchy all at once. "Maybe if I get outside and do something it'll take my mind off it. I'm damn bored. Is there anything to do?"

"I don't think you should be doing anything strenuous yet. You split open them sutures and it'll only take longer to heal and you'll have to live with the itch longer."

"So, I got to stay itchy and bored until I heal. No way, I want something to do, anything!"

"You could always help Renatta in the kitchen, I'm sure she could find something for you to do," Martin said with a smile. He knew what it was like helping her out. It wasn't easy and she was always ready to beat someone down with the broom handle if they didn't do things her way.

"Yeah, maybe you could do some dusting or peel spuds," Cape added.

"When I think about it ain't it your turn, Cape, to help her out?"

"It is, but I don't mind you taking over. You said you was bored and needed something to do."

"Uh-huh, I did say that and I am as bored as a chicken sitting on a roost."

"You get busy with Renatta and you're boredom will soon change to fear," Martin said as he and the others chuckled.

"What is there to fear in peeling spuds or sweeping a floor?"

"You'll find out," Martin smiled.

Colby spent the rest of the day helping Renatta. He peeled spuds, swept the floors and helped wash dishes. The others went about their day in repairing the barn and other things that needed fixing. At five o'clock, they stopped for the day. Retreating inside, they sat down in the lounging room with Pete. Supper was served at its usual time of five-thirty. By then Colby was no longer bored and had a new respect on what it was that Renatta did on a daily basis. As they all sat down to eat, Black Dog began to bark aggressively outside and the men stood up to see why the dog was barking. In the distance, they could faintly make out a dozen or so riders heading into Willow Gate, hell bent for leather.

"Shit, what do you make of that Travis?" Cape asked as they looked on.

"I haven't seen that many men heading into Willow Gate along that road in years," Pete pointed out.

"If I made an educated guess, I'd say we best prepare for another onslaught of riders coming down your road, Pete. Those men are likely hired gunmen," Tyrell said with concern.

"You think they might make their move in the dark, Travis?"

"I wouldn't put that past Gabe, he's desperate now. Short six men already and now he has a dozen or more. This might be the big one let's get in position and wait, it is all we can do now." Tyrell inhaled deeply. They were only six strong, including Renatta and Pete. If a dozen men were blazing guns at them, he knew their odds weren't good.

"Colby, are you able to shoot?" Martin asked.

"Am so and I won't miss either. C'mon let's get barricaded and loaded up," Colby said. "I'll take the high ground from the barn. Martin you, Pete, and Renatta, head upstairs. You and I, Martin will have a better chance at knocking men off their horses if we is up high."

"I'd have to agree with that," Tyrell said. "Don't do no shooting though unless they shoot at us. Remember, we don't want to be the aggressors. Cape and I will head into the barn with Colby. Pete, you load up all your rifles. Can Renatta shoot?"

"Yes, she can," Pete, responded.

"Good, the more fire power we have the better. All right let's get into position," Tyrell said as they all headed in different directions. This was it. This was the big one.

They had one ace in their pocket that they didn't even know about, and that was Crying Wolf, who by now had also noted the riders heading into Willow Gate. He swung up onto his horse and headed toward Cross's place staying hidden as well as he could as he made his way there. Now hidden behind a clump of trees, he waited. No one knew he was in the vicinity, no one, that is, except for Black Dog who knew exactly where he was. Somehow, Black Dog knew not to give up Crying Wolf's position and so he never went to him. Instead, he stayed with Tyrell as he made his way to the barn rafters and loft.

From up there, Cape, Colby, and Tyrell had a good view of both the main road at a distance and Cross's road. No one coming down Cross's road would go unnoticed Crying Wolf who had a quiver full of arrows and a .45 Colt revolver, was as ready as anyone, and his target would be Gabe Roy, if by chance Gabe rode with the twelve men that had stormed by, and who were indeed hired guns.

Gabe had paid them well and they were more than willing to kill for him. Only thing was, neither Gabe nor the twelve gunmen knew what it was they would be facing when the hour came to strike. Four hours east, making their way westerly to Willow Gate, were, Bob Cannon, Rick Bash, the Brubaker cousins and Riley Scott. If they could make the distance to Gold Creek before Gabe and his hired gunmen made their move, then Gabe and his men would be facing them as well. Four hours, though, was a long time to wait. No one knew where the convoy was or how close they were. Time dragged on. Minutes turned to hours as the men waited.

The evening grew dark and a cold northerly wind came in gusts and with it came the snow. Flakes the size of quarters fell from the sky and accumulated quickly. In a sense, it was a godsend. The moonlit sky brightened up the now snow-covered fields and roads of Pete Cross's land. The only downside was the cold.

Wrapping themselves up with their heavy felt coats and dusters, the men at Cross's place sat huddled in the barn and waited. Crying Wolf sought shelter beneath a big cedar tree, and he sat with his back to the tree. Cold as he was he rubbed his hands together and draped his woolen blanket over his shoulders.

If Gabe weren't with the riders when they came, he would do as much damage to the men as he could and then make his way to Willow Gate and search for him. That was his plan and he would stick to it. One way or another, the reign of Gabe Roy was going to end. If he hung for his deed at least he would hang knowing Gabe was dead. The wind and snow slowly dissipated, but the evening air was frigid and the men remained cold.

"You still think them men is going to make a move t'night, Travis?" Colby asked.

Tyrell shook his head unsure, "Hard to say for certain. All we can do Colby, is wait and hope like hell the cold alone don't beat us down."

Tyrell could see his breath as he talked. It was indeed cold and it seemed to be getting colder by each passing minute. Gathering some loose hay they covered themselves up with it as they continued to wait. The hay at least kept them from freezing, but it was a far-cry from the warmth, they wished they could have. It was a numbingly cold. Even the barrels of their rifles and pistols they held close took on an icy frost.

"I'm going to head over to the house and grab some blankets and whatnot. It won't take more than a couple of minutes, at least then we could stay warm," Cape suggested.

"Good idea. Go ahead and do that," Tyrell said as he looked at him. "You hear running horses before you make it back, take cover and start shooting, or get your ass back here, and we will all shoot together," Tyrell said with a smile, trying to make light of the possible confrontation.

Cape stood up and made a dash toward the house. A couple minutes later, he returned and handed out thick woolen blankets and gloves. "Pete says these is the best he has."

"It is a lot better than what we have now," Colby said as he draped his blanket over his shoulder and slipped on a pair of wool gloves. The blankets and gloves did help warm the men up. The cold frigid air no longer hampered their vigilance and improved their moods.

"How long do you figure it has been since we've been sittin' out here?"

Tyrell reached into his pocket and pulled out his pocket watch, using the light from the moon he looked at the time. "We've been here for a while. It is two a.m. The sun will be rising in a few more hours. Maybe we're going to get lucky and Gabe and his henchmen ain't going to show."

"That wouldn't hurt my feelings one damn bit," Colby mentioned. "They don't come t'night though, they'll likely be here sometime 'morrow. Could be too that by then Brett and Alex will be here and the redcoats, and Riley. That'd certainly improve our situation."

"It would, but until then, it is only us against what might be coming," Tyrell responded as he looked out the loft window. How he hoped too that Cannon and Bash as well as Riley showed up before Gabe's henchmen.

Five miles east the Brubaker cousins, Cannon, Bash, and Riley were taking their last rest before making their final push to Willow Gate. They had lit a small fire and were warming themselves up.

"Goddamn, I can't believe how damn cold it got," Riley mentioned as he warmed his hands above the flames.

"Yeah, it sure came in fast. We'll soon be in Willow Gate. Things will get better then," Bash, pointed out as he too warmed his hands.

The others leaned in toward the fire too and took in as much of the warmth as they could before finally tamping out the flames.

"Well, we've rested now, have warmed up some and it is now time to make the distance to Willow Gate. Looking at my map my best guess is we're about five miles east of it. We should be able to pull off the remainder of the distance in three hours or less," Lieutenant Bob Cannon said as he swung up onto his horse while the others followed suit. "Let's make tracks men."

With that, the convoy carried on.

They were near Gold Creek when they heard what sounded like a hundred guns firing!

"Shit, that has to be at Cross's place. Goddamn!" Alex said as he looked at Brett.

"How far away is Cross's place from here?" Cannon questioned.

"Less than a mile," Brett said as he sped up the wagon. The bodies in the back bounced around and a couple fell out, but, neither Brett nor Alex, cared as they made haste toward Cross's place. Bash, Cannon, and Riley, took the lead and headed as quickly as their horses could carry them toward the echoing sounds of the gunfire. From the road as they drew near, they could see down toward a solely standing house.

"That's got to be Cross's place." Riley said as they galloped toward the carnage going on. Men were dropping from their horses like flies being sprayed. Their best guess was that there were at least twenty men.

"We're going to be heading into a hail of bullets, try not to take any lead!" Cannon hollered as the three riders rode straight into the ongoing battle, their pistols firing at the men that seemed to have outnumbered them two to one.

Cape noticed the three new riders approaching their guns blazing. "Jesus, who the hell is they?" he yelled as he continued to fire at the men trying to surround Cross's house, and throwing flaming torches at it.

"I'll be damned, that there is Riley Scott. The others must be Bash and Cannon. Wonder where the hell Alex and Brett are?" Colby hollered back as he too kept firing at the men running this way and that.

Gabe's henchmen, now noticing the three other riders firing at them, decided it was best to head for the hills. Out gunned as they were it seemed, they were losing the fight.

"We got to get the hell out of here!" one of the men said as an arrow found its mark and pierced his heart. He fell from his horse as the last thing he would ever see were two more of his companions falling to deaths embrace.

Crying Wolf now slipped into the shadows, found his horse and headed toward Willow Gate. Bleeding from the two bullets that ripped into him and full of vengeance and hate, the wounds didn't slow him down.

Not until the gun smoke settled and the surviving attackers had turned tail and vanished into the darkness, did any of them know that Crying Wolf had been there.

The quick thinking of Martin and Renatta seeing that their attackers were high tailing it out of the battle slipped out the backdoor and threw snow onto the back porch of the house that was on fire. It didn't take long for everyone, including Bash, Cannon, and Riley Scott to join the two as they doused out the fire. They didn't speak many words until the task was done. Finally, the flames died down and the fire was out.

"Jesus Christ, Riley couldn't you and the others have got here sooner?" Tyrell joked as he looked at him.

"Nice to see you too, Travis. Quite the battle was going on here."

"Second one," Tyrell responded as he made his way over to where Riley and the others were standing, "Nice to see you, Bash, Cannon, and you too you old son-of-a-bitch. Where the hell is Brett and Alex?" Tyrell asked as he acknowledged the three of them.

It was then they heard the wagon approach. Brett and Alex jumped out and ran over to where everyone was standing.

"Here they are," Riley said as he smiled at Tyrell.

"What a frigging homecoming this is," Alex said as he and Brett approached.

"Some of them dead got arrows in 'em," Brett pointed out.

"What?" Tyrell asked with confusion.

"Three of the dead is sporting purple feathers sticking out of 'em."

"Shit! We don't know nothing about that. I know what it means though. It means Crying Wolf was here."

"Crying Wolf?" Riley asked with as much confusion. Tyrell nodded.

"Why the hell would he be here?" Riley questioned. Tyrell explained.

"So while you were working for Gabe, he was here to kill him?"

"I reckon that was his reason. I did manage to convince him not to. Thought he had left the area completely 'til last week when I sent them papers to you folks in the Fort. I ran across him on my way back. As far as I knew, he was heading back home. I guess not," Tyrell shrugged.

"Right now a renegade Athabasca is the least of our worries. We got dead to account for," Cannon said.

"Nope, I think he is a concern and the dead is the least of our worries. If he managed to get away without dying somewhere, you can bet he's gone looking for Gabe."

Tyrell spit to the frozen ground. He was certain of that and at the same time grateful, that Crying Wolf had helped send some of the attackers to hell. That, in itself, as far as he was concerned, if Crying Wolf did kill Gabe before he could be stopped, should work in his defence.

"I can't believe one man such as Gabe Roy can be the root of all this. If this Athabasca you know as Crying Wolf kills him, I wouldn't give a shit," Cannon said with sincerity, even though he knew it would be murder.

A half a mile away Crying Wolf had fallen off his horse. The bullets he had taken during the battle had finally slowed him down. Lying in the snow, he looked up to the sky. If he was going to die, he didn't want it to be there.

Finding the strength to stand he gathered his horse, then, as though he knew what his fate was going to be, he headed into the mountains. It was only by coincidence that Crying Wolf and Gabe Roy were about to meet up.

Gabe had high tailed it from Willow Gate the moment he sent the men to take out those at Pete Cross's homestead. He told Neeada that he was going on a business trip that was all he said to her early that morning.

Now he was heading into Crying Wolf's path. Crying Wolf had seen the lone rider from a distance. He halted his horse and tried to focus. Not more than a hundred yards away there was a man on a horse. Crying Wolf wondered for a moment why a man would be running at a full gallop in such conditions. Then he realised who it was he was looking at.

No pain or loss of blood would slow him down now. He set chase. The rider, who he now knew to be Gabe Roy, turned his head and looked back at Crying Wolf as he fastidiously approached. Aware now that he was being chased hard and fast, Gabe heeled his horse's flanks with great urgency, and whipped him with the reins in his hands to get the horse to move faster. The horse stumbled due to an unseen obstacle and Gabe Roy fell to the ground as his horse galloped away.

Standing and disoriented with a pistol in his hand, he got his bearings. Spotting the Athabasca warrior gaining ground, he began firing at him. Crying Wolf feeling the sting from another bullet, pulled out his own .45 Colt Ranger pistol and returned the fire.

Gabe fell to the ground and going prone he once more sent lead toward the oncoming rider. Crying Wolf now within hand-to- hand combat range, jumped from his horse and rolled around with Gabe in the snow. The two men fought with aggression and purpose to survive. Crying Wolf getting control pulled a bruised and beaten Gabe to his feet. He stared into Gabe's eyes his own eyes cold and black. He shook Gabe like a rag doll, his teeth clenched. "My name is Crying Wolf. You raped my niece and murdered my brother. For that you will pay."

Gabe now realising who he faced, pulled out a small derringer pistol from his vest pocket and fired into Crying Wolf's chest. Crying Wolf stumbled backward and as Gabe was about to fire again, he thrust himself forward and knocked Gabe to the ground. This time he put the cold steel blade of his knife on Gabe's throat.

"There are no bullets that can stop the rage I have for you," Crying Wolf hissed with hatred as he drew the blade across Gabe Roy's throat. Gabe gurgled and twitched as he tried to speak, but his words were lost in the gentle breeze of late fall. *Justice had been served.*

Crying Wolf stood up and looked down at the man known as Gabe Roy dead at his feet. He chanted a few words and then he himself fell forward in dizzying pain and exhaustion. His world spinning as visions of his brother and niece palpitated his memory, like a carousel the memories kept spinning and spinning until finally, he fell to the cold ground unconscious.

Things back at Cross's place hadn't even ended yet and Gabe Roy lie dead.

"Where is Pete? Anyone seen Pete?" Colby asked with concern.

"Shit!" Martin said as he ran into the house. He made his way up the stairs and to the last known place he had seen Pete. There he was, sprawled out on the floor. A bullet had ripped through his chest, but he was still breathing and able to talk. Martin ran to the window and yelled. "I found him, he's been hit." Turning quickly he knelt next to him and looked at the wound. "Jesus, Pete, you took one to the chest."

"I don't think it hit anything important, I can still breath," Pete said as he passed out from loss of blood. By now, the others were standing near and they helped get Pete onto a bed. Renatta went to work on him right away and stopped the flow of blood.

"The bullet went through. I need rags and his field kit," she said as Bob Cannon removed his field kit from his belt and handed it to her.

"Use mine," Cannon said as he handed it to her.

Renatta took it from him and opening it, she took out the stitching needle and cat-gut. Digging in the entrance wound, she repeated what Pete had done to Colby a few days earlier, although Colby's wound was less dire, the same basic idea would work on Pete. It took near thirty minutes before she was successful. She and the others sighed in relief when Pete, burbled a few words.

"That is a good sign. I think he is going to be okay," Renatta said as she stepped aside.

Cannon now stepped up to the bed and looked at Pete. "He's breathing regularly. His pulse is a bit slow, but he will live to see another day. Now that we have taken care of the wounded, we need to check on the dead. Come on, Bash," Cannon said as he and Bash exited leaving the others in Pete's room.

"He and that other man, they are the redcoats?" Renatta asked.

"Yes ma'am. That was Lieutenant Bob Cannon and Special Constable Rick Bash. This here," Tyrell began as he pointed at Riley, "is Riley Scott. He works for McCoy's as well."

Riley tilted his hat to show respect to Renatta. "Ma'am," he said as he acknowledged her.

"Will all this trouble with Mr. Roy stop now with these new men here?"

"That is why they are here, Renatta. Cannon and Bash are going to take care of the law in Willow Gate, and Riley, well I ain't sure why he is here, but I'm glad he is. I reckon it won't be long before folks in Willow Gate can go back to how their lives were before Gabe Roy stomped into town. I'd say his days are numbered, Cannon and Bash will clean that mess up," he looked over to Riley, "I ain't sure why you are here though Riley, don't get me wrong it is damn good to see you and I'm glad you are here."

"I'm here because you and I, when this is all sorted out, need to head into Indian territory McCoy's has been asked with high regard to track down the Apache Kid."

"That is why that wire was sent to me with his name. Jesus, I don't know if I'll be up for that. Do we have any leads on where to even start looking for him?" Tyrell asked with little enthusiasm.

Renatta left the room to gather more rags and water to keep Pete's wounds clean. As soon as she left, Colby spoke. "The Apache Kid, you say?"

"That is right," Riley responded.

"I can tell you both this, Atalmore, would know where he is. The Apache Kid and Rebel Rangers have on occasion been in cahoots with one another, I can also tell you, he ain't gonna be no easy man to take down. He's a killer and has a crazy side to him."

"That is another thing too Travis. Atalmore and the others did escape the prison in Calgary a few weeks ago. Rumours have been heard that they're gunning for you."

Tyrell shook his head. "This day can't get any better. It has been one damn thing after another ever since I agreed to work for Gabe. There has been more killing than any man needs to see in his lifetime," he said as he paused for a moment. "I knew Atalmore was out and about. In fact, he sent a couple of gunmen my way a while ago, the Tellman brothers. Brett and the others know them." He ended it there as he contemplated on whether or not he should fill the others in that he had killed both of them.

"Funny thing about the Tellman brothers, a week or so ago we found them draped over their horses. They both was killed," Brett said, figuring it was best to let Tyrell and Riley know that.

Tyrell nodded. "I know. It was I who killed them." He too figured it was time to come clean. It took a few minutes to explain what had happened and where it took place.

Riley sat down on a chair and sighed. "So, they was here looking for you, and found you when you headed to Hefley. They pulled their pistols on you and you killed 'em."

"Had no choice really," Tyrell added as he sat on the foot of the bed.

Alex shook his head and smiled. "Goddamn, we all figured it was you that killed them two desperados. Now we know."

"I'd rather have not said anything, but under these circumstances, I figured it best to be known." Tyrell looked at Alex, "If you found them, what did you do with the bodies?"

"Martin dug a grave and we tossed them in. There was nothing more we wanted to do for them," Colby said as though it mattered little.

"Wait, you didn't report them to the law?"

Alex chuckled. "What law? There ain't no good law here in Willow Gate, not yet at least. We keep this among ourselves and only us will ever know."

"Shit, like I said, this day couldn't get any better." Tyrell shook his head wondering now if he should have said anything at all.

"I think Alex makes a good point. We don't need to say a damn thing to Cannon or Bash," Riley suggested.

Tyrell nodded. "I s'ppose we don't, but we ought to."

"Hell no. We gave them a real nice *Christian* funeral," Colby said with a snicker.

"A Colby Christian funeral that is," Cape added with his own smirk.

"There ain't no need making jokes, this is a serious situation," Riley made clear.

"Shit Riley, c'mon, Travis killed them in self-defense and we found them and buried them. There ain't nothing more to it than that. Let a sleeping cow sleep," Alex pointed out. "Ain't any of us in this room is gonna say a word 'bout it."

The room grew silent for a few brief moments as the men contemplated the situation. The only good that had come about while they all conversed was the fact that Riley and Tyrell had at least a lead now on how they might be able to track down the Apache Kid. That was by finding Atalmore and his crew, a task they knew would be difficult, but it was a lead and one more than they had.

Tyrell sighed and inhaled deeply. "I reckon for the time being we'll keep this among ourselves. It's likely the best thing to do for now. All right, let's go help Cannon and Bash with the dead," he said as he stood up and checked one more time on Pete. Satisfied that he was still breathing they exited Pete's room.

Making their way outside, they met up with Cannon and Bash who were looking over the dead and checking to make sure there were no wounded survivors.

"They're all dead there isn't one that is breathing. Fourteen in all, and we're missing two from the stack of dead in the wagon," Bash mentioned.

"We knew that. They fell out down the trail some when we was making our way here," Brett said as though he cared.

"Why didn't you stop and toss them back in?" Bash questioned with annoyance.

"We didn't have time, Bash. We were in a hurry to get here."

"You know what that means?"

"Do so. Means you and Cannon need to go find 'em. They ain't far I can tell you that. We is done with it. We turned them over to the law like what is to be expected. It ain't our problem no more."

Bash shook his head. "Shit, we're going to need a couple more wagons. Do you fellows know how many men you've killed since Colby's release?" he questioned as he looked at the Brubakers and Colby.

"We didn't kill all these though. We had help, and we were in the right to do so."

"Always the wise guy, eh Alex?"

"Speaking the truth is all," Alex responded.

Cannon interjected again. Bash and Alex could argue for hours and he needed to end it right there and then.

"Both of you need to stop with this bullshit. We have fourteen dead laying on the ground, four in the wagon and two down the trail some. This arguing shit stops now. Let's clean up this damn mess and put things right and into perspective. The two of you just stay the hell away from one another," Cannon made clear with authority.

"Suits me fine," Alex, said as he turned and walked over to the front porch and sat down.

"All right, let's get our heads screwed back on and get busy with what it is that needs doing. Rick, take a couple of horses and head down the trail, and gather those two missing dead. Travis and Riley you two can give me hand. Does Pete, by chance, have another wagon?"

"He has a flat deck, in the barn," Brett pointed out.

"All right, you go get that rigged up. The rest of you can go sit down and let the law deal with this pile of shit we all seem to be mixed up in."

It took some time to clean up the mess of dead, and when it was finally, accomplished and the two wagons were loaded, the investigation into the identities of the dead began.

"Well, that is done. We have twenty dead and a bunch of unanswered questions. Not one of these dead has any identification and some don't even have faces." Cannon inhaled deeply. "This is one of the damnedest things I have ever come across. We know nothing about these men. We have a son-of-a-bitch with money that, by the look and sounds of things, has bought off the Willow Gate law and sent some hired guns to try and muscle Mr. Cross out of his land." Cannon looked at the two wagons stacked with bodies. "And they're all dead. What a mess!"

"I did find some identification on two of the first eight that were sent," Tyrell reached into his pocket and handed them over.

Cannon looked at the identification and read out the names, "Ted Mackenzie and one Jeremiah Neufeld, they're two names I'm not familiar with. What about you, Rick?" Cannon questioned as he handed the two pieces over to Bash.

Bash looked at the IDs and shook his head, "Nope, never heard these names before either. There might be some information we can find in the archives, but as of right now, these names don't ring a bell with me at all."

"How is that out of twenty men only two are found with ID?" Cannon was exhausted by it all.

"Not many folks do carry ID, Bob, and especially those that are hired guns," Riley pointed out.

"You'd think though out twenty there'd be a few more than two with identification."

"I have taken many men in for their bounty and I can tell you very few have any identification. The only way to identify them is by their scars or pistols and the witnesses that know them. I'd say you and the law have your work cut out," Riley said with empathy.

"I'd say so, and we haven't even got to the bottom of the barrel yet. We're going to need a lot more lawmen working on this I think. First things first though. We need to clean up the law in Willow Gate and then apprehend Gabe, if he isn't dead by then." Lieutenant Bob Cannon grew silent for a moment as he contemplated what it was that still needed doing. "I guess that is it, then. Come on Bash, let's go to Willow Gate."

"You want us to tag along, Cannon?" Tyrell asked.

"Not just yet. I'll send Bash this way once we clean up the law and get these dead put in the ground. I'll need all of you to come in then so we can go over everything that has taken place. As for Riley, I believe his business is with you. Neither he nor Ed has said anything on why he came along at all."

"You're right. My business in coming here is with Travis. For now we'll leave it at that," Riley said as he looked at Cannon.

"All right, well, I guess Rick and I will be in touch over the next couple of days. For now, we have our own business to deal with, bringing in Gabe Roy and those officers of law that have been paid by him to look the other way."

With that, Bash, Cannon, and two wagons stacked with the remains of twenty dead men left for Willow Gate. Their work cut out for them.

Chapter 17

At 9:30 a.m. that day, as they watched Cannon and Bash head towards Willow Gate, Tyrell, the Brubaker cousins, Colby and Riley, made their way back inside and checked up again on Pete. He was still unconscious and Renatta was at his side patting his brow with a damp cloth. She looked up to the men and nodded with a smile.

"He has spoken many words. It is only now that he is resting." She looked back at Pete and continued to wipe his brow with the cool cloth.

"It is a relief to hear that. So, he is going to be okay, Renatta?" Tyrell asked.

She nodded. "Yes, he is a strong man. He will live, I think."

"Good, we'll leave you to it for now. We have repairs to make and I'm afraid there are some windows smashed, so the light coming into the house until we get glass ain't going to be much. We'll have to close the shutters for now against the weather."

"Pete has many panes of glass stored in the barn, all cut to fit these windows. It is not the first time they have been smashed," Renatta said with a sigh. She was exhausted from no sleep the night before and the turmoil of that Wednesday morning.

"All right, we'll go look. Maybe we'll be able to replace the panes." Leaving the room, the men ventured to the big oak table. "Have any of you seen those panes of glass Renatta mentioned?" Tyrell asked as they sat down.

"I ain't saw them," Martin replied as he looked at the others. "What about you, you seen them?"

"I don't reckon they'd be stacked in a corner, they might be up in the rafters in the tack room though. I have seen something up there stowed in thick cardboard," Cape mentioned.

"That'd be what they'd be stored in. Before we get to that, I'm going to make coffee. I think we could all use some," Tyrell responded. Standing up he made his way into the kitchen. Returning a short while later with a pot of coffee, he set it down and poured himself a cup. "Might not be as good as Renatta makes, but it's better than no coffee." They all agreed and poured themselves some.

"I guess we'll have these and then get at it. We got a lot to go over Travis, and a lot of work to get this house fixed up."

"I'd say so. Quite the thing that went on here this morn, I was sure pleased to see you, Cannon and Bash show up. It has been a while, Riley. How have things been back at McCoy's?" Tyrell asked now that they had the time to spend and finally talk more than only a couple of words to each other. He looked over to where Riley sat.

"Things got slow over the past while. Tanner is still up north, and I ain't sure you know otherwise, but Matt works with us now too. Ed sent him to find old George, so he could hand over a pouch of nuggets that Brady got from some fellow whilst, he and Matt worked their way back east.

The fellow told Brady that old Whisky Tooth saved his kin from a blatant Indian attack. I guess it is his reward to old George. Oh yeah, and there was a Lee Griffith, a United States Ranger, looking for Matt. Brady sent a telegram to Buck Ainsworth and arranged for Matt to head up to the Yukon once he gets them nuggets delivered, to avoid the damn Ranger." Riley shrugged as he took a swallow from his coffee.

"Jesus, Matt Crawford working for McCoy's. That is interesting. I never knew that. Who came up with the idea to send Matt into the Yukon?"

"That would've been Brady," Riley answered.

"Huh, ain't that something. That was damn quick thinking to avoid that Ranger. I guess Matt got the exoneration we were hoping he'd get, then?" Tyrell questioned wanting to learn more.

"Nope, he never got exonerated like we had all hoped. The judge stayed all the charges he was allegedly accused of up here in Canada. The Police Commissioner said it'd be fine for Matt to work with us, as long as he don't work on the cases that involve him. Like this Gabe Roy thing that's been going on. As well, he couldn't help Tanner none either, since he's a witness to Emery's death."

The others sitting at the table listened as both Tyrell and Riley reacquainted themselves. There was a moment of silence as Tyrell looked around the table and contemplated. Everything that had taken place up to then had come in full circle. Gabe had been exposed the Willow Gate law had been exposed, Matt Crawford was freed, the Brubakers and Colby Christian were alive and well, and Riley Scott was sitting next to him. Bob Cannon and Rick Bash were now in charge of the Willow Gate Mounted Police. *It all seemed so surreal.*

"Who would have ever thought that we'd all be sitting here together, yet here we are, me, you, the Brubakers and Colby, not to mention that even that damn Bash, and Cannon, is here about. Life is funny ain't it?" Tyrell pointed out as he took a swig from the cup in his hands.

"I'd say the odds of us all being together under the same damn roof, working for the same damn cause, is a bit peculiar to say the least, uh-huh. But, we is and I'm glad we is all still breathing too," Riley answered back.

"I don't s'ppose that'd be the case though, if'n Travis here wasn't working for Gabe at the time Gabe came here that first time. We'd likely have only seen each other," Alex looked at Riley. He still didn't like him that much, nor did he have much of a like for Travis either. It was odd, though, as far as he was concerned that there they all were. "Life is funny. I'll give you that, Travis, but things only turned out this way 'cause of what it was we was all doing. If we were doing something else, things wouldn't be as they are now. That is for certain," Alex took a slurp from his coffee.

"I agree. Things then would've been different, but they ain't, and so to me it seems odd is all."

"It seems odd to all of us sitting here, I reckon."

"The big eye in the sky works in mysterious ways," Martin chuckled.

The seven men sitting at the table continued to converse until the last of that morning's coffee had been poured. Then making their way out the barn they found the panes of glass that, were stowed in the tack room and went about replacing windows. Tyrell took notice to where Black Dog seemed to be spending time and he wandered over to him.

He knelt next to the dog and looked at the ground beneath the big cedar where Black Dog was sniffing. He could see a speckling of blood in the snow. The way Black Dog was behaving, Tyrell knew it was likely where Crying Wolf had lain in wait, and by the look of things, had been wounded. "Shit, Black Dog, looks like Crying Wolf took some lead."

Tyrell looked around as he and Black Dog followed the blood trail. "Here is where he got onto his horse. Looks like, he headed toward Willow Gate." Tyrell looked in that direction. A distance further, he spotted more blood, which, he believed to be Crying Wolf's as well. *Damn, looks like he took another bullet here,* he thought as he continued to investigate.

By now, Riley was standing next to him. "Looks like someone lost a lot of blood and headed toward Willow Gate," Riley observed as he knelt down and looked closer.

"It wasn't any of the men that came here with their guns blazing. I think this is Crying Wolf's blood. He must've been hit a couple of times. There ain't much blood under that cedar," Tyrell gestured with his chin, "which I assume is where he was held up. Here though, there is a lot more."

"Maybe we should saddle up and follow his trail," Riley suggested.

Tyrell nodded. "Yeah, that might be an idea. It is the least I can do for him since he helped put a stop to those henchmen of Gabe's. It has been a few hours since and he could be anywhere or worse lying dead somewhere." Inhaling deeply he looked once more in the direction Crying Wolf and his horse travelled.

Riley looked up to the sky. "I think another winter storm is coming. If we're gonna follow this trail, we best get to it b'fore the snow hides it."

"All right, let's do it, Riley." Making their way back to the house, Tyrell told the others what he and Riley were going to do.

"I'm feeling up to the task. You two don't mind if I tag along, do you?" Colby asked.

"I ain't sure, Colby. You think you're all right to ride?" Tyrell questioned.

"I ain't split open any stitches and I feel okay. I'd say I can ride. B'sides, we got all the windowpanes replaced and I ain't left here since the first day I showed up. I could use some away time."

"All right. The three of us will try to catch up to Crying Wolf. The rest of you stay alert. Who knows what else might be coming."

"I can't believe you is going after a damn redskin," Alex said abruptly as though he were perturbed by the idea.

"He ain't any redskin, Alex. His name is Crying Wolf and he put a stop to a few of Gabe's henchmen. Those men might have been the ones that killed either of us, if it hadn't been for him. Think about that," Tyrell said as he looked at him.

Alex remained silent and didn't respond. He only shook his head and spit to the ground. Then turning, he made his way back to the big oak table inside and sat down. He was joined, a short time later by Brett, Cape, and Martin.

"They is off," Brett said as he sat down. "Travis said if they find Crying Wolf and he's alive, they'll be bringing him back here."

"I figured as much," Alex said with disdain.

"I reckon if he's wounded and can be saved, why the hell wouldn't Travis want to bring him here for help? Shit, he took out a few men that was shooting at us. I reckon whether he's a redskin or not, the least we could do is patch him up."

Alex nodded, "Yeah, I s'ppose so. It don't mean I have to like it."

"Nope you don't. Neither of us has to like it, but it is the right thing to do," Cape pointed out as the room grew silent.

Lieutenant Bob Cannon and Constable Rick Bash were at the Willow Gate Mounted Police station. The two wagons full of the dead were hidden from view in the Mounted Police barn and only a few folks knew. Cannon sat down at an unoccupied desk and withdrew from his saddlebags a legal document. There were only two constables at the station and he had already introduced himself and Bash to them. They were now sitting across from him, curious to know why he and Bash were even there.

"This document will explain why Special Constable Bash and I are here."

Cannon brought the document up within reading distance and read it aloud. The document simply explained that he and Bash were now in charge of the Willow Gate jurisdiction, and that all officers housed there were thereby demanded to stand down and their badges confiscated.

"There you have it. The both of you are required by the Police Commissioner to hand over your badges and are under arrest until we can get to the bottom of who is and who isn't on Gabe Roy's payroll."

The two men stirred uncomfortably in their chairs.

"What... what exactly does that all mean?" one of them asked.

"There is no simpler way of putting it. You are both under arrest. You will hand over your badges and weapons. You will hang up your red tunics, and you will both be guests at the jail that you were once in charge of, Bash, arrest these two," Cannon said as the two constables looked up to Bash.

"Under the laws of Canada, you are both now relieved of your duties as law enforcement officers and are under arrest. Please stand up, remove your weapons and badges, and set them down," Bash said as he waited for the two constables to stand up.

Standing and without saying anything further, the two men removed their badges, and weapons, and set them down on the desk. Bash then walked them to a cell and locked the door behind them.

Returning to the front of the station, he pulled up to the desk where Cannon still sat.

"That takes care of that," he said as he looked at their weapons and badges. "So, we have here one constable, Steve Larry, and one acting sergeant-at-law, Brock Wilde."

"Let's find their arrest records and work histories," Cannon said as he stood up and made his way to the file cabinet. He looked through it for a few moments then returned with their records. He handed one of the documents over to Bash, who went ahead and began reading.

"Sgt. Wilde has an astounding arrest record, has been the acting sergeant since 1887 and up until May 1889 he's been quite active in upholding the law, but since has only arrested two men, both for assault, drunk and disorderly conduct. Other than that there has been no arrests done by him. That does seem odd, doesn't it?"

"Considering all things and the time that has elapsed since his arrival to Willow Gate, I'd say it is mighty odd. Constable Larry has a decent record too. He has only been here since September 1891, three months ago. He has made four arrests. From this writ, I'm not sure he knows anything about the corruption. We'll have to look into his name more. Sgt. Wilde, though, is a different story. He has been here for four years. If anyone is involved with the corruption that has become an everyday occurrence here in Willow Gate, I'd put my money on Wilde."

"Since the time of Gabe Roy's presence here, I assume there is a list of law officers that have at one time or another been assigned here. We're going to have to look into all those names."

"Yes, we are, Rick, and I assign you to do just that."

Cannon tossed Constable Steve Larry's work history onto the desk.

"For now, we need to put this arrest warrant we have for Gabe Roy to use. Let's make sure one last time that our guests are secured and go and find Mr. Roy."

Both Cannon and Bash stood up. Bash checked on their prisoners and satisfied that they were secure, he and Cannon headed out to look for Gabe. They had the directions to his house and that was the first place they went.

Pulling their horses up to the horse pole, they swung off their saddles and tethered the horses. Making their way up the stairs to Gabe's front door, they knocked. It took only a few moments for the door to open.

The woman answering the knock hesitantly looked at the two.

"Yes, can I help you?" she asked unsure why two mounted police officers were standing on the stoop.

"Good afternoon, ma'am. I'm Lieutenant Bob Cannon and this is Special Constable Rick Bash. We have an arrest warrant for Mr. Gabe Roy and a premises search warrant for this residence. Please step aside and let us in," Cannon said as the woman moved out of the way.

"Mr. Roy is not here. He left early this morning. What is this about?"

"We're not at liberty to reveal that, ma'am. What is your name?"

"I am Mr. Roy's house maid. My name is Neeada," the woman answered.

"Neeada, we're going to have a look through this house, here is the search warrant."

Cannon showed her the legal document and then had her sit down.

"Sit here until we have finished with our search. Go ahead, Bash. You take the upstairs rooms and I'll go through the ones down here," Cannon said as he and Rick began their search for Gabe.

It took thirty minutes for them to confirm that Gabe was nowhere in the house and that Neeada was alone. Next, they questioned her.

"Did Mr. Roy tell you where he was going?"

"He said he was going on a business trip. That is all he said to me."

"Is there a particular place that he may have gone?"

"I do not know where Mr. Roy goes. Sometimes he is gone for days other times it is weeks, but he always comes back. I'm sorry he doesn't speak much to me about his business."

The unrelenting questioning continued and in the end, it was clear to both Cannon and Bash that Neeada knew nothing about where Gabe may have gone.

"Well ma'am, thank you for your time," Cannon said as he and Bash now exited the house and swung up onto their horses.

"That certainly didn't prove be fruitful, did it?" Constable Bash mentioned.

Cannon shook his head as they turned their steeds and headed back to the station, "No, it sure didn't, Rick. We'll have to get another warrant to look into his financial affairs, I guess. I don't think there are any folks around that might know where Gabe went, and those that do, it is pretty much certain they aren't about to give up the information," Cannon replied as the two of them carried on.

"Here is a thought," Bash began. "We have a lot of work ahead of us, from finding Gabe to investigating law corruption and proving it or disproving it, we have to identify those dead stacked on Cross's wagon hidden in the Province's barn and their correlation with Gabe. There is a lot we have got to do," Bash stopped there as he inhaled deeply.

"That sounded more like a statement, Rick, than a thought." Cannon already knew what it was they needed to do, and the man-hours it was going to take to accomplish it all, so what Rick was going on about seemed moot to him.

"What I was thinking or going to suggest is we could hire McCoy's to give us a hand in tracking Gabe down. All the work we're going to be doing in investigating the law that has been hereabout since Gabe made Willow Gate his home, is likely going to be extensive and time consuming. Add that to getting warrants to look into his financials and we're up to our necks with a ton of work."

"You didn't honestly think it was going to be easy, did you, Rick?" Cannon questioned.

"I knew it was going to be a headache. Folks like Gabe always seem to manage one thing or the other to make things difficult, but what makes it more overwhelming is what we came upon this morning at Cross's place. So, there is even all that to look into. It'll take at least a week for the Province to send more Mounted Police this way once we send a wire that we need the extra help. A week from today could put Gabe Roy well into the States, in which case he'll never see any justice here in Canada."

"So, what you're getting at is we already have two of McCoy's men at our disposal, both Travis and Riley. Is that what you're trying to say?"

"Exactly."

"And you couldn't have said it in less-words?" Cannon chuckled. "To start, we don't know why Riley even came this way and it seemed not even Travis knew. We can assume they must already have business with one thing or the other. Chances are they can't drop that business to help the Province's law enforcement officers in looking for Gabe Roy. Travis has already done his part investigating him and we have all that information. That is the reason we are here in the first place. Although, your thoughts are plausible, I don't think they are possible at this moment. Besides, that is why we have officers of law. We'll get the help we need and until then we do our job."

"I guess that is all we can do then, isn't it?"

"It is, Bash, it is," Cannon repeated.

Finally, making the distance back to the Willow Gate Mounted Police station, they led their horses over to the corral and turned them loose. Next, they entered the barn. Taking out their notepads and pencils and began the gruelling task of writing down the descriptions of the dead men stacked like cord wood in the back of the two wagons.

They looked for identifying marks such as scars, broken and rotting teeth, eye and hair color, clothing, weapons, etcetera. Anything that could identify them they wrote down. Their hands now stinking of death, and their lungs filled with the putrid smell of soiled pants and blood, they closed their notepads and exited the barn. It was all part of the job and it was the worst part, identifying the dead.

Neither spoke until after they had cleaned their lungs with fresh air.

"That part of this job never changes does it, right down to the smell and the cold dead eyes we look at," Bash said as he continued to inhale deeply.

"It could have been far worse. It could be August."

Somehow, both men found the humour in that although it was a solemn type of humour. They chuckled.

It was around this time that Tyrell, Colby and Riley who had gone looking for Crying Wolf, came upon his horse, but not a sign of Crying Wolf. They took the horse by the reins and led him along as they backtracked, the horse's trail. A mile later and sitting with his back to a tree sat Crying Wolf. Tyrell swung off his horse and checked on him.

"He's still breathing," he quickly opened Crying Wolf's vest and buckskin jacket to look at the wounds. There were four holes three big, and one small that he could see. With every breath that, Crying Wolf took blood spewed out from one of them. Tyrell knew that at least one bullet had hit his lung.

"Shit, he has been hit in a lung he is losing blood with every breath he takes! C'mon, we have to get him onto a horse and make for Cross's place. I'll double behind and keep pressure on the wound. It might slow the bleeding down." Tyrell stood up and with help from Riley and Colby managed to get Crying Wolf onto a saddle and he swung up behind. He put as much pressure on the wound as he could with the palm of his right hand and with his left held the reins to his horse. "All right, let's get."

Heeling their horse's flanks, the riders hurried off back the way they came. It took less time to make the distance back than it took to find Crying Wolf. They helped him off the horse and carried him to an empty room. They laid him on a cot. Renatta immediately did all she could to slow the bleeding and to make it easier for Crying Wolf to breathe. She wasn't sure if what she did would help, but, for the time being, it was better than what anyone else could've done. Pete, the only one with any medical experience was in his own life or death struggle, so it was up to those who knew a little, or those who knew nothing on how to treat Crying Wolf's wounds.

Chapter 18

It was early morning, when Rick Bash showed up at Pete Cross's place he was greeted by Renatta when, he knocked on the door.

"Constable Bash, please come in," she said as she stepped aside and gestured for him to enter.

"Thank you, ma'am, are Travis and the others nearby?" Bash asked as he wiped his boots on the entrance rug, to remove the mud and snow.

"They are having morning coffee. Please, join them. They are in the dining room."

Renatta pointed in the direction. Bash checked once more that his boots were clean and made his way to the big oak table.

"Good morning, fellows," Bash said as he sat down at the table.

"Good morning to you too, Bash. Want a coffee?" Tyrell asked.

"Thank you, Travis. Sure, I could use a coffee."

Tyrell poured him a cup and handed it to him. "I take it your visit is business?"

"Yes, it is. We have sorted out the Willow Gate law and have had the bodies of all the dead transported to Calgary. It took a long time getting them identified and we're still not sure what names belong to whom. The Calgary law will have to figure it out." Bash took a swig from his coffee.

"Transported?" Riley questioned as to be clear.

"Yes, I only got back last night. We sent them by train through Hefley."

"Sure glad I ain't on that train. Twenty dead can't smell like roses."

"They ain't riding in the passenger car, Riley. At least I wouldn't think so," Tyrell said with as much surprise.

"Of course not, they were loaded into the livestock car. They were also put into body bags and tied shut," Bash said as he took another swig from his coffee. "By the way, I brought back one of Mr. Cross's wagons; the other is still back in Willow Gate. How is Pete faring?"

"He's still breathing and able to talk when he isn't passed out. We also have another houseguest. We tracked down Crying Wolf. He had one of his lungs blown out. He's doing all right too, thanks to Renatta." Tyrell took a slurp from his own coffee. "I guess now is the time we're supposed to give you and Cannon our statements of events?"

"It is, but there isn't any need for you folks to have to come into Willow Gate to do that." Bash took out his note pad and set it on the table. "I can take your statements here."

"What about Gabe? You have him locked up?" Riley questioned out of curiosity.

No one could know then that Gabe was lying out in the forest, having been dead already for five days. During that time, the crows and animals had their way with his corpse so that it no longer resembled Gabe Roy.

"Unfortunately, no, he seems to have given us the slip. His housemaid, Neeada, claims he took off a few days ago, likely last Wednesday."

"So, the same day he sent that last bunch of men here?" Colby shook his head.

"I assume, yep," Bash confirmed.

"Now, ain't that typical of that slime bucket. He's running free and three of us have all taken bullets. That pisses me off," Colby pointed out.

"The law will catch up with Gabe, Colby. We're looking into his financial affairs and trying to decipher where he may have went."

"Here are a couple of names you ought to look into," Tyrell began. "He has a lawyer down west by the name of

Ted Applegate from Applegate and Associates. Also, look for Archie Hauser, a banker from Coastline Bank and Trust, also from down west. I would bet that Gabe has gone to meet one or the other or both. There are also a couple of surveyors he knows, a Neil and Rodger Kormac. I ain't sure where they are from. Gabe said they were from around here, but that could be anywhere."

Bash wrote down the names. "Why weren't those names in the documents you sent back to the Fort?" Bash wanted to know.

"I really didn't see any point in that. I see now, though, that it would have helped you and Cannon out, my neglect, Bash. Sorry."

"That is all right, I have the names now, and we'll certainly be looking into this. Now, can you tell me the story about what all took place before Bob and I arrived?"

"Simple. Gabe sent men here to muscle Pete out of his land. On one occasion, I was with them. We was turned away though quickly by Alex and the others. Alex took my boots."

There was some chuckling around the table as Tyrell said that. He looked over to Alex and shook his head.

"Then he made me leave behind my horse, which was Colby's horse, and I walked back to the shack Gabe offered to me whilst I was shadowing him."

Bash cut him off there and questioned why he had Colby's horse.

Tyrell told the tale.

"Ahh, yeah, I remember Ed mentioning that. All right so now I know why you had Colby's horse, so, carry on with the rest."

"From there I learned that Crying Wolf was kicking it around here and that he was looking at putting Gabe in the ground for the atrocities he committed to both his niece and for killing his brother."

"We do have that accusation among the documents you sent."

"Right, I knew it was him simply because I had run into him on a couple of different occasions." Tyrell paused for a moment as he took another slurp from his coffee. "I tracked him down and tried to convince him to leave Gabe alone and to let the law deal with it. In the end, I thought Crying Wolf took my advice and I left him.

Next, Gabe had me accompany him to a meeting with a man by the name of Will Novall that owed Gabe a sum of money. The meeting was like all the others. When we left, we were heading back toward Gabe's place when Will started firing at him.

Once I knew Gabe hadn't been hit, I chased after Will, but lost him in the mountains. Ain't even sure now if the six man posse that followed behind me ever caught up to him," Tyrell shrugged.

"I really don't care. I made my way back to Gabe's place and told him Will got away. Next Gabe wanted me to assist in taking Pete's land by force. He said he could get a handful of men together to make it happen. Of course, I said 'No' and he fired me. The rest is history, Bash. The men came, the men died; nothing more to it than that," Tyrell finished.

"All right, well that coincides with everything you sent back to the Fort and what has all happened since then. We now have Gabe's banker and lawyer's names, which will also help us in finding him. I guess then, that is all we need to know. I'm sure everyone has the same opinion of events."

Bash looked at the others. "Is there anything any of you can add or want to add?" he questioned.

None did. Finishing his coffee, Bash stood up, and thanked Travis and the others for their time. Tyrell and Riley walked him to the door.

"If there is anything else you need, Bash, or you need help with one thing or the other, don't hesitate to ask. We're gonna be around for the next while leastwise." Tyrell said referring to himself and Riley as the three of them stepped out onto the front stoop.

"I don't suppose you can share with me why you came along with us, can you Riley? I mean up here to Willow Gate," Bash questioned.

"I told you and Cannon it was business, what more do you want to know Bash, and why the hell would ya?" Riley questioned back.

"Travis here just offered any help, and maybe we might need some, but if you two have business, then I guess it really doesn't matter."

"Hold on, what kind of help might you and Cannon be looking for?" Tyrell asked although he was sure he knew the answer.

"I'm not saying we do, but if we did, would the two of you consider working for the Provinces law enforcement as Private Investigators?"

"I reckon that'd be up to Ed. It is McCoy's that we work for Bash. You know that."

"All right, answer me this. Is the business the two of you have more pressing than running down Gabe Roy?"

"Damn it! I knew that is what you were getting at, and to answer, it might be."

"That isn't too definitive Travis."

"No it ain't, but unless the Province's law decides to hire McCoy's, that is the answer I'm givin'."

Special Constable Rick Bash looked toward Willow Gate as he contemplated. "I guess then we'll leave it at that for now," he said as he looked back at Tyrell and Riley.

Exchanging a few more words of pleasantries and casual conversation, Bash unhitched his horse from the

citizen's arrest on Gabe all you want." Tyrell looked around at all those sitting at the table.

There was a period of awkward silence, for two reasons. The first was that Tyrell had made it clear that he wasn't interested anymore in Gabe Roy. His job was done and he had done the job well. The second thing was the fact that in time, maybe only days, he and Riley would be riding away from Willow Gate, and chances were after that, the relationship that each had with the other that had built up over that, period of time whether good or bad, would likely fade into history.

It wasn't such a bothersome thought for the Brubakers and Alex, but for Colby it was. He had grown quite attached to both Riley and Tyrell. He respected both men, and in a sense, wished that he could ride alongside them. Alex and the others, he knew, would survive whatever life they decided to choose and so would he. The thing was he wasn't sure which life he wanted. He could stick it out at Cross's place and work alongside Alex and their cousins, but there was no adventure or sense of accomplishment he could see in being that grounded. There had to be more to life.

He liked what Tyrell and Riley did. They were always on the go, travelling this way and that. They were living life hard and fast, not knowing if the next cowboy they hunted down or job they took wouldn't find them dead. There was a type of nostalgia to that kind of life. It wasn't much different than when he was on the wrong side of the law running with the Rebel Rangers. Everyday something exciting happened that got one's blood pumping. That was the kind of life he wanted except this time, he wanted to do it right. The question was. Would the laws of Canada allow him to pursue such a dream?

The silence was finally broke by Renatta as she entered the dinning-room, arm in arm with Pete, who was a little weak but nonetheless walking. They were all surprised to see him up and about.

"Pete! Jesus you don't know how relieved we are to see you up and about," Tyrell said as he stood up and helped Renatta to get Pete seated.

"Thank you, Travis, Renatta. I was lying in bed and decided today would be the day, that, I get out of bed. Renatta was kind enough to allow me." Pete chuckled as he made himself comfortable, and acknowledge them all. He looked again at Riley.

"You must be Riley?"

"Yes, I am. It is nice to finally meet you, Pete."

"And you as well. I was a little under the weather when you and the others showed up."

Riley chuckled. "If you call almost being dead as a little under the weather, than yes you were."

"A little bullet here and there won't usually kill a man unless they die," Pete chuckled.

"I'd say it sure is good to see you is back to your usual self, Pete," Brett said with a smile.

"Men don't change after being shot. They just become more alert." Pete paused for a moment as he looked around the table, "Renatta, has informed me that we have another wounded man in our midst?"

"Yes sir, an Athabasca by the name of Crying Wolf, he was shot through the lung. He was here the day Gabe's men came storming down your road, unknown by any of us until it was over. He killed three men helping us defend your land," Tyrell responded.

"He is welcome here until he mends or decides to leave. I have nothing against the Athabasca or for that matter any of the indigenous peoples of these lands. After all, they were here first," Pete, pointed out. "I guess now you will soon be leaving us, Travis, now that Gabe has been sent running?"

Tyrell looked at Pete and nodded, "As soon as Crying Wolf can ride, the three of us will leave," he began referring to himself, Riley and Crying Wolf. "We will be leaving because my job is done, Pete."

"Yes, I suppose it is," Pete looked at the Brubakers and Colby, "And you fellows you will still be here, yes?" he asked with hope.

"As far as I know, yep, we is here for the long term, Pete, like we talked about," Alex replied.

"Good. I will need you all here when the work in spring begins."

"I ain't so sure I'll be here," Colby said.

"What the hell do you mean, where are you gonna go? And why the hell would you?" Martin questioned as the others waited for his reply.

They were all shocked to hear Colby say that.

"Shit, Martin, I ain't the type to keep still. I need to keep moving. It keeps me sane. I ain't sure where I'll go and I ain't sure I know what it is I'll do, but working cattle or digging dirt ain't something I want to spend the rest of my life at. There has to be more to it than that," Colby looked into his empty cup. "To be right honest," he looked over to Tyrell and Riley. "If you could still deputize me Travis, I'd like to tag along with you and Riley for a bit. I could be of use for what it is the two of you is heading for next."

"What the hell are you doing, Colby? Why the hell would you do that and why would you want to?" Alex asked as though it was the most undignified thing he had ever heard.

"I thought I already explained that. I ain't one to keep still. It ain't that I don't appreciate Cross's offer or either of you and your decisions to stay on. I'd simply rather do something else. That is all there is to it, nothing more-nothing less," Colby made clear.

"I guess all those months we talked about sticking together and such means nothing then," Alex voiced.

"During those months we never once talked about working cattle or digging dirt. We talked about bringing in bounties. We talked about adventure. It wasn't me that changed that plan it was the four of you, it just so happens that Martin likes the idea as much as you fellows do and since I don't, why would I stick around?"

The conversation just got deep, not only because Tyrell and Riley would be leaving soon, but apparently, it appeared that Colby would be too. It was a saddening situation, but one that couldn't be denied. The Brubakers knew Colby all too well and they knew there was nothing they could do to change his mind.

Colby looked again over to Tyrell and Riley still awaiting their response to his question. "So, what of it Travis, can you deputize me or not?" Colby pressed again.

Both Tyrell and Riley weren't sure how to answer. Tyrell knew he could certainly deputize Colby if Ed saw reason and if what he assumed Colby was getting at was helping them in tracking down both Atalmore and the Apache Kid, maybe it wasn't such a farfetched question to answer. After all Colby knew where the hideouts of the Rebel Rangers were, knew their tactics, knew where they might find the Apache Kid. Hell he was a shoe-in.

"I know you mean well, and all, Colby, but I could've only deputized you during this thing with Gabe. As for what it is you're asking now, to be honest I can't say for sure. I do know how you could be of help and trust me, I wouldn't mind one bit if you were to help us," Tyrell said as he contemplated.

"Then have me read that damn oath, you talked about. If you know that I can be of help and I'm willing to abide by the governing laws, what stops you from accepting my help?"

"Well," Tyrell began as he scratched his whiskered face, "there really isn't anything stopping me from accepting your help, Colby, but are you sure that is something you'd be up for?"

"Damn right it is. I know who it is your looking for and I can lead you to him and them," Colby said, referring to both the Apache Kid and the Rebel Rangers.

Tyrell looked over to Riley as though looking for another answer to Colby's question.

Riley shrugged, "I don't know of any reason why we couldn't deputize Colby. McCoy's would have to accept responsibility if he did anything wrong or something went awry. And of course he'd have to read the oath in front of Bash or Cannon, once Ed agreed," Riley stated.

"What the hell are the two of you trying to pull here? You both have said you'd not come between Colby or any of us, and here you are doing exactly that," Alex said with hostility.

"We're not trying to come between any of you, Alex. We're answering a fair question. It isn't up to us what it is that Colby wants to do. He asked a question and we answered. That is all. Would you have preferred if we told him a bunch of lies?" Tyrell questioned.

"Never mind what Alex is going on about. This is my decision not his or theirs," Colby pointed out referring to Alex and their cousin's.

"I don't think you're thinking this through Colby."

"The hell I ain't, Alex. I ain't so stupid to get involved in something I don't think I couldn't handle."

"Fine! Do whatever you want Colby! I'm done with it," Alex said in a huff as he stood up and slammed his chair as he walked away.

"Sheesh, I think you've upset Alex, Colby. He did make a good point, regarding you thinking this through," Martin interjected.

"I don't think he made any good points whatsoever. He's mad 'cause I don't want to be a cowhand and I don't see any reason why I'd stick around," Colby sighed. "My mind is made up. Either I help Travis and Riley, or I head back to where I came. I ain't sticking around here, Martin. Alex will have to get used to the idea that I've come to a crossroads of sort. Whether he, or any of you, like it or not, I'll be leaving here when the time comes."

"To be honest, Colby, I myself saw this coming a while back. I get it, but I do side with Alex. I ain't sure you thought this through. Hell, the five of us are damn fine together. We've taken down the Ridgeback Gang, have protected Pete's land, chased off Gabe Roy and put to rest a few more bad guys. Shit. When we're together there ain't much the five of us can't do. I ain't going to give you no speech. I only hope you know what it is you might be getting into. We'd all hate like hell to hear later on down the line that our cousin, Colby, has been killed," Brett added to the conversation.

"My chances of getting killed, Brett ain't any greater than what it is now that we do. The bullet wound I got is proof of that. I know we've often talked about blood being thicker than water and that is true, but I'm still young enough to do more with my life than I've done so far." Colby grew silent as he thought about what his cousin's meant to him, and even though they meant a lot, so did the life he wanted to live. Choosing between the two wasn't easy for him, and, in fact, he already missed his cousins. He was determined, however, to lead his life as he chose and he had chosen to leave them behind.

"If I can say a few words, Colby," Pete began.

Colby looked over to him and nodded. "What is it you have got to say, Pete? I'm listening."

"When I was a young man, I wanted adventure too. I joined the Cavalry and became a field surgeon. I saw a lot of men die and watched others kill. There wasn't a mile that went by as I travelled through life, that I didn't see death, or had an adventure, in time, I realised that all I really ever wanted was a home, a place I could call my own. When the Indian wars ended, I travelled without cause, ambling from town to town, province to province, always looking for that place where I wanted to be.

As I sit here today listening to you and the others, I can't help myself but to think, that you are going to do whatever it is you decide. No man here, sitting at this table can deny you that, and any that does is selfish. I want you to know that you'll always have a place here for as long as I live leastwise. That is all I wanted to say. Now, if you'll all excuse me, I need to rest."

Pete stood up and slowly made his way up the stairs to his room. Lying down on his bed, his mind drifted to his younger days and he smiled to himself. He had done well for himself and he knew, deep down, so would Colby.

"That kind of puts everything into a different perspective now, don't it?" Cape pointed out.

None at the table could disagree. Pete had pretty much summed up the entire argument. He was right that any man denying another man his wants in life and desires to be whatever it was he wanted to be, was a selfish man. Every man had the right to decide on what it was he wanted to do in life. Whether he chose right or wrong in the eyes of others, all mankind had free will.

"There ain't anything more I could add to what has already been said, but if you get yourself killed Colby I'm going to kick your ass at the Pearly Gates when I get there." Martin smirked. He understood Colby's reasons and he respected them.

"If you get there before me, Martin, I'll be doing the same to you. That goes for you too Brett and Cape. I'll even kick Alex's ass too. There ain't no reasons for us to lose touch with each other. I know how and where to find you and I reckon before I do decide to leave here, you'll know where to find me too."

Both Tyrell and Riley could hear the determination in Colby's voice as he spoke that morning. Both knew without a doubt that Colby Christian would be an asset to McCoy's. The only problem was, and it was one that could be sorted out was the fact that Colby once rode with an outlaw gang of sorts, the Rebel Rangers. Although the Rebel Rangers weren't your typical outlaw gang per se, they did break laws. Even if the laws they broke in Canada were minor down south the laws that they had allegedly broke were not minor by any sense of the word.

Colby would never be able to undertake any assignments in the USA, not much different than, the restrictions on Matt Crawford. Then again, it wasn't often that McCoy's were hired by USA. Residents, in all actuality it really didn't have much bearing on what Colby was asking. Being deputized wasn't meant to be a permanent assignment. It wasn't much different than hiring men for a posse. There were no reasons as far as Tyrell, or for that matter even Riley, could conjure on why they couldn't or shouldn't deputize Colby.

Tyrell looked over to him, "I'll tell you what, Colby. If this is something you want to do, I can deputise you right now, if Pete has a Bible. I can't guarantee pay; that is up to Ed, but you help us track down the Apache Kid. I'll offer you a percentage of my wage on a weekly basis." Tyrell paused for a moment as he thought about what a fare percentage would be.

"Say twenty percent of my weekly wage for the duration of time it takes to put cuffs on the Apache Kid. It ain't a lot of money Colby, but while you're under this agreement, we will pay your expenses such as food, bullets, gear, that type of thing. That way no matter what comes about McCoy's ain't held responsible in paying you a wage. Nor would they be responsible for any actions you take. That would also be on me and Riley," he looked over to Riley. "That is, of course, if Riley agrees."

"I would agree to that," Riley nodded, "I certainly would, yes sir."

Tyrell nodded and looked again to Colby, "In time when we finally make it back to the Fort, if Ed decides to keep you onboard it'll be up to him to start paying you. If he decides the other way, then once we get the Apache Kid put back where he belongs, and maybe even Atalmore, he is an escaped convict after all, our agreement then expires."

That was all Tyrell could offer for the time being. It was also a simple loophole in the system. Colby wouldn't be allowed to act alone and would always be expected to abide by the governing laws of Canada. Tyrell and Riley both would be his superiors and would share the responsibilities of any actions Colby took, while under the simple agreement.

"Sounds to me like Colby ain't guaranteed a permanent position, and don't sound like he'll make much money either," Martin brought up.

"You are right. It ain't much money and it ain't guaranteed employment afterwards either. That is all I can offer though," Tyrell said as he looked over to Colby. "It is up to you now, Colby. I laid out what I can offer without going through a bunch of red tape that I ain't got the time to cut."

"Basically, what he's saying Colby, is that he and Riley will hire you to guide them for the next while. After that, well, shit you're on your own, 'less McCoy's hires you."

Colby looked at Martin and shook his head, "Jesus, Martin, I know what was said. I understand it as well as you. Maybe you ought to think about hitting some law books. You'd make a fine law interpreter. I ain't got a problem with what's been offered and I'm fine with it. So,

Travis, how do we go about gettin' me deputised?" Colby was frank.

"Firstly, we need a Bible. Then you'll have to repeat a few words and agree to them in front of witnesses which we have a lot of here. Riley will write down all that I say and then the three of us will sign it at the end. It isn't so much a legal binding contract, but rather an oath and agreement, agreed upon by the three of us, you, me and Riley."

"Let's get to it then. Pete has a Bible I know of in the sitting room," Colby said as he stood up. Tyrell and Riley followed along with the others. Finding the Bible, Colby handed it over to Tyrell.

Taking it, he had Colby raise his right hand and put his left on the Bible. Then he had him repeat a few words.

"Repeat after me Colby; I, Colby Christian, am bound by this agreement between Travis Sweet and Riley Scott, to uphold the laws that govern the country of Canada, and to assert myself in a professional manner while bound by this agreement."

Colby repeated it word for word and Riley wrote it down.

Tyrell now carried on. "I, Colby Christian of sound, mind and body will as of this date December 14 the year 1891, agree to help pursue and apprehend the wanted felon known as the Apache Kid. If I am required to help with further apprehensions of any man or woman during the date of this oath and agreement and/or the apprehension of the Apache Kid, I shall be bound by the same oath."

Colby repeated it word for word and Riley wrote it down.

"There you have it Colby, now we'll each sign what Riley wrote down."

The three of them signed it.

"You are now deputised by McCoy's." Tyrell and Riley both shook his hand.

Cape was the first to speak up afterwards. "Who gets to keep that piece of paper you three signed?"

"Cannon or Bash will have to write it out in duplicate and we'll sign our names to that one as well. The Mounties get one and the original goes to Ed," Riley replied.

"Just like that and Colby is now a deputised member of McCoy's?"

Tyrell nodded. "Just like that Martin."

"Well, shit! How does it feel, Colby?" Martin smiled.

Colby chuckled. If he were honest, it felt damn good.

"Feels like I got purpose now, I suppose, almost like I'm a virgin all over again. It feels pretty good, Martin, it really does." Colby was glowing with pride.

"Don't let it get to your head none. You'll always be one of us Colby," Brett said as he too shook Colby's hand to show his cousin the due respect he deserved.

"Yeah, I'd say that was quite the inauguration," Alex said from the shadows.

He had watched the entire thing without anyone knowing. He stepped forward and made his way over to where Colby stood.

"I have to say, Colby, although I don't agree with this much, I'm damn proud of you."

"Thank you Alex. That means a lot more to me than you'll ever know, and like Brett suggests I won't let it go to my head. I'll always be one of you," he said with a glowing smile.

By four o'clock that day, Cannon and Bash had the duplicated oath and agreement. They never even batted an eye when Tyrell, Riley, and Colby showed up with the document. Nor did they question its validity. The three men signed it, Bash stamped it and so it would be. Things were settled and the Brubakers had accepted Colby's decision. It wasn't easy for any of them, but things in life were never meant to be easy, and especially not when family knew they would soon be parting ways.

Chapter 19

Three days later on the morning of December 17, Crying Wolf was finally able to talk and was well on the healing side of things. At first, he wasn't sure where he was, until Renatta told him.

"Travis, found you and brought you here. You were wounded gravely," Renatta explained.

"Travis?" Crying Wolf questioned.

"Yes, he and his friend Riley as well young Colby went looking for you after it was discovered that you had been wounded in the battle that took place here. You are at Pete Cross's placc."

"I must speak with Travis," Crying Wolf said with urgency as he tried to get up from the cot he was lying on.

"No, you must stay put," Renatta said, as she got him to lie back down. "I will fetch Travis for you."

"What day is it?" Crying Wolf asked as Renatta was about to leave.

"It is Thursday."

"How long have I been here?"

"One week and one day."

"Many days have come and gone, then?" Crying Wolf closed his eyes as he drifted in and out of consciousness. When he woke, Tyrell was sitting in the chair next to his cot.

"Hello, Crying Wolf. Renatta said you needed to speak to me. How are you feeling?"

"I am better knowing where I am, and that I was not dreaming when that Indian woman you call Renatta was here," Crying Wolf managed a meek smile. "Her beauty made me think she was an angel and I had gone to be with my forefathers. Seeing your ugly face though makes me realise I have not died. For things in heaven should not be so ugly."

Tyrell chuckled. "Nope, you ain't dead, Crying Wolf. That beautiful woman you saw sitting here saved your life, so in a sense she is an angel."

"Yes, I have come to that conclusion. I am glad to be alive." Crying Wolf once more faded into an unconscious state. Tyrell remained seated and he waited. It seemed like hours before Crying Wolf opened his eyes again and talked. "You, you are still here?"

"Of course I am. You wanted to speak to me."

"Has there been snow since you found me?" Crying Wolf asked in a weak soft voice that was barely audible.

"Yes, it has snowed. There was a winter storm the day we found you. It has snowed on and off since," Tyrell responded wondering why Crying Wolf cared.

"When you found me, did you find anything else?"

"What do you mean? We have your horse if that is what you are concerned about." Tyrell leaned forward so he could hear him better.

"Ah, yes my horse, I am glad you found him. But he is not what I question."

"What is it you question then?"

"You did not find the body of Gabe Roy?" Crying Wolf asked with trepidation.

"What?" Tyrell wasn't sure he heard what he thought he heard. "What, what do you mean, Crying Wolf?"

"Gabe Roy. He was running away from the justice he had coming while I headed for a place to die. I killed him."

Tyrell stood up. Shocked, surprised, and overwhelmed by what Crying Wolf said.

"What are you saying, Crying Wolf? That you killed Gabe Roy?"

"Yes, Gabe Roy, I slit his throat from ear to ear. He shot me twice..." Crying Wolf began as he passed out for the second time. Tyrell looked around in disbelief, trying to make sense out of what it was he was hearing. He didn't know how to feel. Hell, he wasn't even sure if Crying Wolf knew what it was he was saying about killing Gabe Roy. He looked at him and for a moment, his mind raced back to when he found him and the wounds he had. One bullet hole he remembered was smaller than the rest.

He knew Gabe always carried a pearl handled Remington .41 two shot derringer in his vest pocket, the same bore as the one that he had holstered under his left shoulder. The more he thought about that, the more it made sense that one of the wounds Crying Wolf suffered was likely that from a derringer. He kicked himself for not thinking about that when they raced Crying Wolf back to Pete's house. He knew damn well that one of the wounds was that of a smaller calibre.

Tyrell sat down again and brought his hand to his face in deep thought. *Stupid, stupid me, goddamn, I should've thought about that...* he retraced the events that led up to them finding Crying Wolf. There were two blood-trails that, he recalled. One was beneath the cedar tree, likely the first place Crying Wolf was hit. Then there was another more discernible blood splatter near where Crying Wolf mounted his horse.

The trail they followed had no more blood splatters that they could see due to the falling snow, which, could have covered up any blood afterward that spilled from Crying Wolf's body.

In his mind, he could account for only two shots hitting Crying Wolf in Pete's front yard when the gun battle was going on. Yet when they found him, he indeed did have four. There were no bullets pulled from his body that he knew of. They had all managed to exit and only the one to his lungs caused the most damage. From what he could remember, it was of the smaller calibre.

Finally, as he sat there running it all through his mind, Crying Wolf stirred. He looked at him and slid his chair in closer so that if he spoke again, he could hear him. It took only a few moments for Crying Wolf to open his eyes again. He looked at Tyrell, "Good to see your presence again. I will try not to drift this time."

"You were saying that you killed Gabe Roy."

Crying Wolf nodded, "If he has not been found yet, he will be nothing more than bones. He will have been chewed up and pushed through the bowels of animals," a smile crossed his face as he said that. "Will I hang, Travis?"

"Jesus Christ, Crying Wolf, I don't know. Can you tell me in more words what happened, were you the aggressor?" Tyrell wanted to know.

"No. I was not, but I was the one who killed him."

"We've already established that Crying Wolf. You need to tell me in more detail on what happened."

Crying Wolf inhaled deeply, sighed, and told the tale.

"He shot you once while you were on your horse, and again as you struggled with him, is that correct Crying Wolf?"

"That is what I have said, yes."

"Was your intent to kill him?" Tyrell hated having to ask that question, but he needed to know.

"Only after, he shot me the second time. I drew my blade across his throat after that. At first, all I wanted to do was beat him until he could no longer stand or I was killed."

"If things never turned out as they did what were you going to do with him after you beat him?" Another question Tyrell did not want to ask, but needed to know.

"I would have left him and carried on with my journey to die in the woods."

"Even after he shot you that first time, you would have beaten him and left him to make his own way back to safety or die trying?"

"Yes, he is a bad shot. Up close, though, he did not miss so well."

"You're lucky it was a small gun." Tyrell chuckled and shook his head, "From what I can gather from what you have said, it was self-defense, Crying Wolf. I don't think it will be punishable. Can you tell me where I might find him?"

"From memory, no, but I can take you there," Crying Wolf made clear.

"You ain't going to be able to ride for a couple more days, Crying Wolf. Can you give me a general idea on where it all happened?"

"Perhaps," Crying Wolf closed his eyes as he thought back. "It would not have been far from where you may have found me. I remember getting back on my horse, and we headed into the dawns sunrise, so east. That is all I remember. It was in a clearing in the forest. That is the only picture I can paint from memory."

"So then, it may have taken place west of where we found you in a forest clearing?"

"Forest, clearing, yes," Crying Wolf inhaled deeply then grew silent, again, overtaken by his need for rest.

Tyrell looked at his friend lying on the cot and tried to visualise where they had found him. If he could find that spot again, they could begin their search from there, but with all the snow and the time that had elapsed since then, he knew it would be tough. They were in too much of a hurry to get Crying Wolf to Pete's place to have paid much heed to where it was they found him or for that matter what may have been west.

The door to Crying Wolf's room opened and Renatta stuck her head in. She looked at Tyrell and gestured with her chin. "Is he resting now?"

Tyrell looked up at her and nodded. "Yep, he's out cold again."

Renatta stepped into the room and quietly walked over to the cot. She dabbed Crying Wolf's forehead with a damp cloth. "We must let him rest now. Were the two of you able to speak, it seemed quite urgent to him that he speak to you."

"Yes, we spoke. It wasn't anything I was expecting to hear, but if he is in a stable frame of mind, he claims to have killed Gabe Roy." Tyrell stood up.

There was a shocked look on Renatta's face as she turned and looked up to Tyrell. No words came from her mouth, but Tyrell knew exactly what she was thinking.

He simply nodded, "That is what he told me. I am as dumbfounded by it as you. If it is true, Gabe has been dead and lying in the woods somewhere for more than a week," he grew silent for a moment, "Not to worry, though. From how he explains it, it was self defense and I'll be certain to point that out if it is ever a need."

"That does make me feel somewhat better. I don't think Crying Wolf is a bad or dangerous man, but he is Indian and we have all had unfair judgements cast upon us. Does this mean he will not hang?"

"I wouldn't let that happen. The only thing he may have to do is give a statement to the Mounties, Bash, and Cannon. Can you tell me, Renatta, if you can recall, were there four wounds, and was one wound smaller than the others?"

Renatta didn't even hesitate and she nodded. "Yes, the one near his chest. I removed a small bullet fragment, but could not find the rest."

Tyrell's eyes got big, that was the best news he heard. "Did you keep it?"

"It was tossed out with the rags. The rags though have not yet, been cleaned, but sit in soak. Come let us go see if I can find that fragment." She stood up and with Tyrell, trailing close behind they headed to the cleaning room where laundry was done. In the corner was a large tin bucket and in that bucket soaking in a brine of soap and disinfectant, were the blood-soiled rags.

Renatta picked up the bucket and dumped the rags into the big cast iron washtub she used for such. She pulled out the spigot and waited for the liquid to drain off. Then, slipping on a pair of sloppy rubber gloves, she began removing each rag from the washtub and shook them out as she tossed them back into the bucket. Finally, the sound of something iron bounced into the washtub.

There it was, the bullet fragment, Tyrell picked it up, "This here," he began as he held the fragment between his finger and thumb, "is worth ten times its weight in gold."

"It is what will help Crying Wolf in the white man's courts if it shall ever come down to that, yes?" Renatta questioned with hope.

Tyrell nodded with a big grin, "That is exactly what it is. If it comes down to where Crying Wolf needs to prove he killed Gabe in self-defense, this lil' fragment right here between my thumb and finger is all the evidence he'll need. C'mon, let's go tell the others what it is that Crying Wolf says and the evidence we have found," he suggested so they could both share in the news.

"No, no, you go. It is your business. These rags have soaked long enough in disinfectant. They can be washed now we may need to use them again."

"All right, then," Tyrell said as he turned and made his way to the sitting room where he knew the others were lounging. He could hear their voices and chuckles as he made his way there. Stepping through the doorway, he could see that, they were all there, except for Pete, who he would talk to later. "Sure glad to see you're all here and that you're all sitting down," he looked around the room at each of them as he spoke, "We have a corpse to find," he started.

"What, what the hell do you mean?" Riley questioned with a frown.

"According to what Crying Wolf has told me, he killed Gabe Roy a week ago."

Alex began to laugh, "Jesus Christ, do tell, Travis."

"Yeah, do tell," Riley, said as the room grew silent as they waited for him to fill them in.

He took special care in telling it to them exactly as Crying Wolf had told it to him, and with a few deep breaths and pauses, the story was told.

"He slit the son-of-a-bitch's throat. Goddamn, ain't that something. I have a totally new respect for that redskin," Alex pointed out.

"How about showing him your new found respect by using his name," Tyrell suggested.

"Sure, all right then, I got a whole new respect for Crying Wolf," Alex corrected.

At that point, Tyrell didn't care whether Alex meant it or not. He had said Crying Wolf's name and for now that was all that mattered, "Back to the discussion at hand, we can bet that Gabe's corpse has been gnawed up and scattered by vermin and birds, the animals will have had their way with it. It ain't going to be a pretty sight," Tyrell pointed out.

"That is the bastard's fate, I guess. He lived by the sword and died by it. I hope his remains is scattered from here to Kingdom Come," Martin paused for a moment and nodded, "if that ain't *Willow Gate justice*, I don't know what would be."

Tyrell and Riley couldn't agree more, there could not have been a better ending to Gabe Roy's life, if not by the blade of an Athabasca brave. As the murmuring settled to a hush, Tyrell continued. "The amount of snow that has fallen since then and the time that has passed is certainly going to hamper our search."

"Hold on a second," Alex began, "our search? I don't think so. I couldn't care less if his remains were ever found. I won't be helping," Alex made clear as he finished.

"Lucky for you, Alex, you ain't required to help. Only Riley and I would be expected to do that."

"Shit, I'd help," Colby pointed out.

"I reckon I would too. What about you, Cape, Martin?" Brett questioned as he looked at the two of them.

"I kind of side with Alex's point of view," Cape replied.

Brett shook his head and rolled his eyes at his brother. "All right, what about you Martin?"

"I ain't ever saw a man tore up by animals before or for that matter a man as deserving as that piece of shit Gabe Roy, I'm in. Damn right."

"Okay, so we'll have five sets of eyes. That is better than two," Brett nodded, "I'm ready."

Riley looked over to Tyrell, "I don't reckon sitting here any longer is going to make Gabe any more visible."

"No it sure ain't, Riley. I'm ready to get too. C'mon, let's get to searching," Tyrell said as he and Riley stood up and the three volunteers followed close behind. They saddled up their horses and following Tyrell and Riley, they headed in the direction of where Crying Wolf had been found.

"Can you remember how long we travelled before, coming across Crying Wolf?" Riley asked Tyrell or Colby for that matter as they travelled. He himself couldn't remember.

"Nope, not me," Tyrell answered, "I do know though we travelled this way. We'll have to keep going until we see something familiar. I didn't pay no heed to any landmarks, was in too much of a damn rush. What about you Colby, you have any sense on how long we rode before finding him?"

"Hell no, not a clue Travis," Colby responded as they carried on.

"Shit. A learning experience for all of us I guess. We should've looked around a bit more closely. The damn snow is certainly hindering my memory of which way and where," Riley, pointed out.

An hour later, they slowed their horses to a halt.

"I'm most certain we didn't travel this damn long. Let's turn back. We must have passed the place back some," Tyrell said as they turned their horses and carried on back the way they came.

"Didn't we cut through some bramble, when we was looking for him?" Colby questioned. He seemed to remember going through some bramble.

"You know what, I think you're right. There is that bit of forest up ahead. Maybe we should cut that way and see if anything jars our memory?" Tyrell suggested.

"We've already be out here for more than an hour. You know what my thought is. We turn back and wait 'til that friend of yours and Riley's can ride. He did tell you he could find the place, didn't he?" Martin pointed out and questioned.

"He did. The thing is the longer Gabe's corpse lies out here, the harder any remains is going to be to find. I think we best keep looking for a while longer, Martin."

Martin shook his head. "All right, but unless something pops back into either of your memories soon, this is a goddamn wild goose chase. Any trail that was left behind a week ago ain't going to be found now."

"And say we do find his gnawed, possible limb-missing corpse, are we going to tie it to one of the horses and take it back to the Mounties?" Brett asked as they continued.

"If we find it, I got some rope and we'll tie off the area so it can be noticeable. Then we'll fill in Bash and Cannon and they can deal with his remains," Riley replied.

"Yep, that is how it'll be done. We don't find it then we'll wait for Crying Wolf to be well enough to ride and he can take us to it. We'll go through the same process then, too. Mark the spot and send the Mounties."

It was then that Black Dog stopped and started scenting something in the air. It was Colby, who noticed the dog acting peculiar.

"Hey, Travis, hold up a minute. Looks like your dog is scenting something and I do believe he's facing west."

The riders slowed their horses and looked in the direction Black Dog seemed to have taken an interest in.

"That is west all right. Let's head that way, could be Black Dog smells something." Tyrell looked down, "good boy, Black Dog, take us to what you're smelling, go on," he coaxed and Black Dog took off in the westerly direction. The riders followed him and as they drew closer to the forest, a flock of crows took to flight.

"That right there, I'd say is a telltale sign. Something is dead up yon," Riley pointed out. "Now why didn't that damn dog of yours scent whatever it is now that he's scenting when we passed here before?"

"He likely knew it was there. Jus' didn't care, he was happier going for a ride with us," Tyrell chuckled.

A few moments later, they could see the area where the crows had been through the bramble and beyond the bramble was indeed a clearing. Black Dog by now had already made the distance, and the riders followed his trail. They could see that the ground was crimson in color, and packed down. A few steps further and the smell came, halting their horses they all gagged.

"The bitter smell of death and rot," Colby said as they pushed their way through the last bit of undergrowth. There in the middle of a small clearing was a heap of meat and bone. Wolf and coyote tracks scattered the area. They stopped their horses a short distance away and covered their mouths. It was a grotesque site.

"Goddamn! Who is going to be the brave son-of-a-bitch to go over there and see if that is what is left of Gabe?" Tyrell teased. He knew damn well it would have to be either him or Riley. "What about you, Martin. You were the one so keen to see a dead man ripped up by animals. This here might be your chance."

"Nope, that is all right, I wouldn't want to take the glory away from you or Riley. I'm quite fine with what I can see now."

Swinging off their horses, Tyrell and Riley made their way closer. Pulling out bandannas from their pockets, they wrapped them around their faces. The stench was putrid the closer they got. Finally, they knelt down next to the heaping mess in front of them.

"Jesus Christ, Riley, that is Gabe all right. There ain't much left of him is there? I know that hat though and the clothes." Tyrell stood up, "I've seen enough."

Riley stood up next and nodded, "Me too. Let's get this area roped off or marked so the Mounties can find it." Turning, they made their way back to where the others remained on their horses.

"Is it Gabe or what?" Colby asked.

"What is left of him, yep, there ain't much I'll tell you that," Tyrell said as he waited for Riley to get the rope he brought with them.

"I'm curious now," Martin said as he swung off his horse. He walked over to where Gabe's remains were, then stepped back as quickly, and began to vomit. "Jesus, one of you should've stopped me," he said between gasping for air and puking as he hastily walked back.

"Not very pretty is it, Martin?" Tyrell questioned. "I think Brett and Colby ought to take a look too. That mess over there is what happens when you die in the woods and no one knows it. Go on, Brett, Colby, go have a look." Tyrell said daring them.

"To hell with that, I ain't interested in seeing anything that makes a man throw up his breakfast. I get it. It's a corpse and it's been gnawed up by crows and vermin," Brett made clear that, he was not interested.

"What about you Colby? You might see something like this in the next while," Riley said as he found the rope and he and Tyrell tied it around some trees to mark the spot.

Colby swung off his horse and made his way over. He knelt down and looked at the remains. "I'd say this is a damn mess for sure. Like Martin said if this ain't *'Willow Gate Justice'*, nothing is." Colby stood up and continued to gaze at the maimed corpse that was once Gabe Roy.

"That don't make you sick Colby?" Martin asked from a distance.

Colby shrugged, "It is just guts, meat, and bones, Martin, of what was once a man. The stench is more off putting than what is left of him." Colby made his way back to his horse and swung up on the saddle, as though it were nothing he hadn't already seen a time or two before.

Riley and Tyrell raised their eyebrows in surprise.

"That didn't get to you Colby?" Riley asked as he and Tyrell now made their way back to their own horses and swung up onto their saddles.

"Not so much, nope, were you expecting me to lose my breakfast, like Martin, Riley or piss myself?" Colby questioned with humor. "I once saw a man hang and his head came clean off. I think that was more of a breakfast loser and pants pisser than a body chewed up by critters. At least they was able to eat. And I bet you they kept it all down too."

Riley chuckled and shook his head, "Well, all right, let's get to Willow Gate and fill Bash and Cannon in and point them in the right direction," he responded as they turned their horses and headed back the way they came. They rode in silence most of the way and speaking only every now and again, their minds simmering over the fact, that Gabe Roy was dead, his remains were gathered up the next day, on December 18, 1891 by Bash and Cannon.

His weapons were found nearby and both his .45 Colt and, .41 pearl handled, Remington two shot derringer, were both missing bullets. The news of Gabe Roy's death, reached the residents of Willow Gate in newsprint the following day and for the first time in decades, the towns people would embrace a truly Merry Christmas for Justice had been served. This brought to end the suppression that Gabe Roy held above the heads of Willow Gate residents, and a new chapter in Tyrell's story began.

On December 20, 1891, Tyrell Sloan *aka* Travis Sweet, Riley Scott, and Colby Christian left behind those staying at Pete Cross's place and headed into uncharted Indian Territory in search of the Apache Kid. The Athabasca warrior known as Crying Wolf travelled with them for a distance, then wishing them luck he headed north. No charges were against him for killing Gabe Roy, and he was free to return to his people.

www.ingramcontent.com/pod-product-compliance
Lightning Source LLC
Chambersburg PA
CBHW061233210726
48293CB00003B/749